REFUGIUM

REIGN
OF
FREEDOM

USA TODAY BESTSELLING AUTHORS
C. HALLMAN
& J.L. BECK

TRIGGER WARNING

This is a dark romance containing various tiggers. We will not list triggers specifically due to spoilers, but if you have any concern about a certain trigger you can reach out to us any time at read@ bleedingheartromance.com

Thank you!

Josi & Cassy

1

LUCAS

Sitting in my brother's black SUV as it pulls up to the side of the road, the brewing anger in my gut reaches a new high. Looking out at the building in front of us, my whole body is tense, ready to kick down the door and drag Delilah out of this nasty place by her hair.

"This is it," the driver tells me. "I can wait here for you or come back later."

"You can go but stay close. I'll call when I'm done."

"Yes, sir."

Knowing Nic, he probably has a backup team posted a few blocks away. He offered to come with me, but I figured a quick in and out would be easier. At least, if everything goes as planned.

Stepping out onto the sidewalk, the only light source is the old neon sign on the front of the brick building. KISS is the name, but the I is burned out, making the sign read KSS instead. There are no working streetlights either, which is most likely by design, considering it's a brothel.

Letting my growing irritation get the best of me, I slam the car door shut harder than necessary before heading to the entrance. Lifting my arm, I bang against the heavy wood with my fist until the door finally opens.

The bouncer on the other side looks like an ogre dressed in a suit too small for him. He's a good bit taller than me, which is impressive since I'm six-two. The suit stretches off his muscular arm like it's about to burst, and I can't help but smirk. They put him here to fight people off. What a joke. I would take this guy out in less than twenty seconds.

"Can I help you?" ogre guy asks.

"Yes, I'm here to talk to your boss. I want to buy one of your girls."

"You can rent our girls. We don't sell them."

"How about you keep being a guard dog while the adults talk business?"

His nostrils flare, and his hands turn to melon-sized fists, but he doesn't make a move to attack me. *Good boy.*

After a moment, he pulls his phone from his pocket and punches in a number with his meaty fingers. "Boss, someone is here to see you about buying one of the girls." I can hear someone talking on the other side, but it's not clear enough to make out the words. "I see. I'll send him up." He ends the call and shoves his phone back into his pocket.

"Boss has been expecting you. But before you can go in, I need you to leave any weapons with me." He reaches for a metal detector hanging next to the door and starts running it over my chest, then down my side to where my gun is sitting in my holster.

The metal detector goes off, and ogre guy holds out his hand like he is waiting for me to give him some candy. Rolling my eyes, I reach for my gun and hand it to him. We go through the same spiel with the gun tucked in my waistband and again with the knife in my boot.

Once I'm completely unarmed, he steps to the side and points down the hallway. "Go to the end of this hall, up the stairs. First door on the right."

Not wanting to waste any time, I shove past him and follow his direction. As I move through the house. I notice armed guards in every hallway, cameras in every corner, and most of the doors are made of steel instead of wood. *Fuck.* This might be harder than I anticipated.

I don't bother knocking when I get to the door I was sent to. I pull the door open and step inside the lavish office that doesn't fit the rest of the building. The large space is sleek and stylish, while the rest of the place looks exactly like you'd imagine, run down and sleazy.

"Lucas, what a surprise to see you here." Nathaniel grins, sarcasm dripping from his voice.

"Cut the crap," I warn, stepping into his office and kicking the door shut behind me. "Where is she?"

"Please, come in, make yourself comfortable."

"Where. Is. She?" I grind my teeth together so hard that my ears hurt.

"Delilah is in her room, getting ready for her next customer."

"I'm taking her back to Corium. She needs to face her punishment for trying to kill another student."

"That's odd. She told me it was your daughter who let her go. Is Aspen being punished as well?"

"She is being dealt with accordingly, inside school walls. It's Delilah who needs to return."

"Actually, she does not. You let her go, and she is working here now. I must say, I was surprised to find out about your attachment to her. According to rumors, she was staying in your apartment at Corium. Did you not have enough fun with her?"

It takes every ounce of restraint I have not to slam my fist into his smug face. The only thing keeping me from doing it is knowing Delilah is in his clutches.

"That's none of your business."

"You are in my establishment, wanting to take one of my employees. Sounds like it's my business now."

"How much do you want? Name your price."

"Delilah is not for sale."

"Just tell me what you want."

"What I want is for my son to be alive, but that is not possible, no thanks to you."

"Nash brought it on himself. They took it too far, and you know it."

"Nothing you say is going to change my mind. I want Delilah to work here for me like she is contracted to do."

"What the fuck are you talking about?"

His grin widens as he pulls a stack of papers from his desk drawer. "Her father sold her to me, and Delilah signed. It's a done deal. She is working here until I don't see her value anymore."

Without a word, I grab the papers from the desk and read over the contract, which I'm hoping is fake. My stomach sinks further with each paragraph I read. To my disappointment, it seems to be real. In our world, at least. Obviously, something like this won't ever be legal in mainstream society, but it is very much binding in the world we live in.

"You know I'll find a way to get her out of here."

"And until you do, I'll enjoy every second knowing that I have something you want."

I slam my fist into his desk with such force that Nathaniel jumps off his chair and steps back. The lamp sitting on the table still shakes when the door bursts open and two guards storm in.

"Everything okay, boss?" one of the goons asks.

"Yes, yes. Mr. Diavolo was just leaving."

"No. I want to see her. I'm not leaving without seeing her."

"I'm afraid Delilah is busy working tonight." Nathaniel can barely contain his joy about rubbing this in my face.

My anger is also barely controlled. My patience dangling on a tiny string, about to rip and unleash the monster hiding beneath my skin. "Listen, fuckface. You might have the upper hand here, but we both know what would happen if I don't return to my brother in one piece. So sit your fat ass down, tell your meathead goons to get lost, and bring me Delilah. Now."

That finally has Nathaniel's smug face falling. The corners of his mouth turn down, and a vein on his forehead begins to pulse angrily.

"I'll tell you what. If you want to see her so badly, be my guest, but you'll have to pay her hourly rate. It's one fifty for an hour."

"I'll pay for the whole night." Pulling my wallet out, I pull a wad of hundred-dollar bills from it and throw them on Nathaniel's desk.

"Thanks. I gave you a special rate, of course. Normally, I only charge fifty an hour."

"I don't give a fuck what you normally do. If you let anyone else touch her, I will do to you what Quinton did to Matteo." There is no way he knows the details, but he knows enough to be threatened.

Nathaniel forces a smile, the vein on his forehead still looking like it's about to burst. "Tommy, will you show Mr. Diavolo to Delilah's room."

"Sure, boss."

"I will be seeing you soon, Nathaniel. Very soon," I promise before spinning around and following Tommy down the hall.

I don't know how this night will end, but I know one thing for sure. Nathaniel Brookshire is living on borrowed time.

2

DELILAH

I pull myself off the floor after what seems like an eternity. It doesn't matter where I fall asleep, or if I do at all...nothing matters. Turns out, everything was a lie. Nash was never going to save me. He was going to whore me out to any person who offered him a dollar.

How could I have been so stupid? So naïve? All I can do is shake my head in defeat, swiping away the tears that slip down my cheeks. The last thing I should be doing is crying, especially over him, but I can't help it. I loved him, and this is what it got me. They say love is blind, and I believe it.

I balance on a blade's edge of anger and defeat. I expected something that was never going to be, and now I have to find myself out of yet another shitty situation. I slam my fist against the mattress. I've escaped one cage, only to become trapped in another.

Stupid, so stupid. I squeeze my eyes closed in an ill attempt to escape what is now my reality, but my tiny sliver of escapism pops like a bubble when a knock resonates through the room and right into me.

My eyes pop open just as the door comes swinging open. I fly off the bed, my heart thundering, and my fists clenched. I'm ready for a fight, except it's not a fight I'll be getting, at least not yet.

"Get ready!" Grace orders, and her voice stuns me.

"Ready?" I ask, confused. "For what?"

"A man is coming to see you. He paid for an entire night with you, and the boss has asked me to get you ready."

It takes me a moment to digest what she's just said, so all I can do is stand there staring at her. Crossing the room, she snaps her fingers in my face.

"You should put something else on besides this." She points at my jeans and shirt I found in the corner of the closet. "Did you hear me?" She does it again, and this time, I shake myself out of the stupor.

"I heard you." My voice cracks. "But I never agreed to have sex with anyone. I never even agreed to stay here."

Grace shakes her head. "None of us really want to be here, and your first client is always the hardest, but I promise you, it gets easier. Why don't you put on a dress? Maybe the short white one; men love the innocent look."

"No, no! I don't think you understand me. I need to leave." Panic clings to each syllable I speak.

"You can try to leave, but they'll just drag you back here kicking and screaming. It's easier if you just follow the rules. This place isn't half as bad as you think it is," Grace assures. "Now, feel free to freshen up with some makeup if you'd like. There should be some in the bathroom."

"I'm not putting makeup on. In fact, I'm not doing anything."

Grace shrugs her shoulders. "Whatever you say. It's your tip that's on the line. In the end, they always get what they want even if you fight them."

They're in for much more than a fight, but I don't tell Grace that. She'll find that out later once I've escaped this place.

"Fine. I'll get ready," I say through my teeth.

I let the rage and frustration fester. I'll need those emotions to fuel me in my attack on whoever the man is who bought me for the night. I never considered myself a killer, but I'm at a point where I'll kill to protect myself.

I sit back on the bed, and Grace turns to walk out of the room but pauses before she reaches the door. Looking over her shoulder, she says, "Look. I like you and don't want anything to happen to you. This place is a sanctuary for most, and it can be that place for you too if you let it."

"I don't want to stay here, and if I knew what this place was when I walked in, I would've turned around and gone back where I came." The end is a lie. There was no way I was ever going back to that hell, but at least there, I was safe and protected. Here I'm vulnerable and at the mercy of any man who pays for an hour with me.

Grace frowns. "I'm sorry you feel that way. They'll send your client up in just a few minutes."

I cross my arms over my chest and stare defiantly ahead. I'm trying my best to appear strong, while inside, I'm crumbling. I want to cry, surrender to the chaos, and let what has happened happen, but I can't. I've been through too much in my life to let this be the thing that takes me out.

The room's silence is drowning, and anxiety rises with every passing second as I wait for this man to show up so I can attack him and escape.

Nothing in the room could be used as a weapon that will inflict permanent damage. A lamp sits on the bedside table, and I eye it warily, wondering if it will do the job I need it to do. I don't have much strength behind me, but if I put my all into hitting someone with it, I could knock them out, and that might buy me enough time to escape.

I don't get much time to contemplate it because the door to my room comes flying open, causing me to react without thought. With the lamp in my hand, I rush the doorway, hoping to catch the man off guard. I raise the lamp just as he steps into the room, putting all my strength into hitting him. I don't look up, refusing to see him. What I need to do is knock him out so I can get out of here.

The lamp slips in my clammy grip, and all I can hear is the racing of my heartbeat. *Thump. Thump. Thump.* My eyes catch a glimpse of the sharp edge of the man's chin right as I bring the lamp in a downward motion, but that's as far as it goes. A hand comes out of nowhere and clamps around my wrist, stopping my assault. *Oh, god.*

"What the fuck, Delilah?"

That voice. I know that voice. It's deep and rich like sin dipped in honey. I look up at the man standing in front of me. *Lucas.* A shiver ripples down my spine. He's here. He came for me, but my next question is why?

"What the hell are you doing?" he growls, his voice deeper with each word he speaks.

My carefully constructed facade of strength dissolves into thin air. "I-I... I can't believe you're here." I try to hide the wobble in my voice, but it's no good. Lucas can see right through me, see all the broken, jagged pieces.

"Who else would be here?" he questions, almost jealously, as he uses his foot to kick the door closed. He releases my wrist, takes the lamp from my grasp, and walks across the room, returning it to the nightstand. I'm still standing there, flabbergasted by his presence.

"How? How did you find me?" I shake my head in disbelief, waiting to be woken from a dream.

"It wasn't hard, and it doesn't matter. Not really. What matters is getting you out of here."

I perk up immediately. "Out of here? What do you mean?"

"I mean, you're leaving this place."

My mouth pops open, and now I'm not only shocked he's here, but I'm shocked that he came for me. Everything that happened between us, what he did. I should hate him, and a little part of me does, but the other parts of me, the ones that know he cares—because why else would he be here?—don't. "Right now?"

Lucas shakes his head. "No, not yet. I'm going to devise a plan to get you out of here, and then I'll come back for you. I'll do my best to work quickly, but I don't know how long it'll take."

I frown, though thankful he even came. Still, I'm terrified of what will happen when he walks out that door. This is a whorehouse, and I'm trapped here, forced to work or endure god knows what.

"Lucas..." My lip trembles, and I've never felt so weak before. I don't want him to see me like this. I need to be strong, but even the strong can only be that way for so long. "They want me to sleep with other men. I don't think I can do it." I'm on the verge of tears all over again.

In a flash, he's on me, his fingers thread through my hair, and he pulls my head back, aligning our faces. His blue eyes are icy, and the fury in their depths makes it hard for me to breathe. I've never seen him like this, so... jealous.

"No one will touch you. I'll make certain of it." He hisses through his teeth moments before he crashes his lips to mine. His mouth is hot against mine, and his tongue exploring mine is even hotter. The kiss isn't sweet or gentle. No, there is none of that. It's passion and fire; it's him saying he owns me without saying it.

He walks me backward until my legs bump into the bed, and I'm pushed onto the mattress.

"Why don't we take your mind off things? I paid to have you all night," he teases, unbuttoning his shirt slowly. "Am I going to get my money's worth?"

My mouth is so dry that all I can do is nod as I unbutton my jeans with trembling fingers. Now I do wish I had worn the dress. Lucas helps me out of my pants before pulling the rest of his clothes off.

I watch in awe as his muscular, tattooed body comes into view. He might be twice my age, but he's in better shape than most men I know. His fingers wrap around my ankles, and with one harsh tug, he pulls me to the edge of the bed, forcing my legs apart.

His display of strength is a sudden reminder of how much stronger he is and that he has used that strength against me. A memory of being locked in the cell flashes over my eyes. The way he held me down, forcing himself inside my ass. The pain. The loneliness after.

"What's wrong?" His concerned tone brings me back to the present, but the icky feeling of what he did to me remains.

"I-I…" I don't want to ruin the moment, but I can't just forget what he did to me either. "I just remembered the last time we…" I trail off. The last time we had sex doesn't seem like the right phrase to use.

Lucas's face falls, and his eyes turn rueful, but I doubt there will be an apology. Not that a sorry would make things better.

"That won't happen again. Right now, I want to make you feel good and take your mind off this mess. You'll just have to trust me. Close your eyes and let me make you come so hard you'll forget where you are for the rest of the night."

"I wish I could."

"You can. Let me take care of you. Let me take care of this pussy— my pussy!" He spreads my legs a little wider, and before I can get another word in, his mouth is on me, on my clit, his tongue caressing it like it's the most precious thing in the world.

It doesn't take me long to forget what I was thinking about five minutes ago. He sucks, nibbles, and licks the small bundle of nerves until my toes curl up and my back arches off the mattress. I need more. I need him deep inside me.

My first orgasm still lingers in my bones when Lucas crawls up over my body and aligns himself with my pussy. He peppers kisses over my chest until his lips find mine. I can taste myself on his tongue as he kisses me, his mouth like a branding iron on my soul. I want to shatter in his arms because I know only he has the power to bring all my tiny shards back together.

His kiss is so slow and intimate that I don't expect him to slam his cock into me the way he does, burying himself into my tight channel with one thrust. He swallows my pained moan and pulls out all the way, just to thrust back into me with equal force.

This would probably hurt a lot more if I hadn't already come. Luckily, I'm so wet, I can feel my arousal dripping down my ass cheeks, giving him no trouble fucking me with hard thrusts. My clit is still swollen and sensitive, driving me closer to a second orgasm with each brutal thrust.

"No one touches this cunt except me," Lucas grunts between pounding into me violently. "Do you hear me? This is my pussy, and you don't let anyone else near it." His hand circles my throat, and he squeezes, causing dots of black to form over my vision. It's the most terrifying and exhilarating thing ever.

"It's yours," I manage to wheeze out through his grasp as I hover over the edge of a cliff. He fucks me like he hates me and cuts off my air supply like he wants to strangle me, and I let him because I know deep down that hurting me is the last thing he wants to do right now. It doesn't take much longer until I fall off, giving myself over to the place he takes me. He fucks me through my release until my brain is swimming in endorphins, and my body feels like it's about to float off the bed.

The only thing keeping me from floating away is Lucas's heavy body on me and his cock impaling me. I don't know how long he continues fucking me, but I want it to be forever. I'm barely awake, exhausted, and high on my own body's hormones, but I know I'm safe, at least for now.

I didn't think I could possibly come a third time, but when Lucas grunts into my ear like a lover's chant, and his cock swells inside me with his own release, a final orgasm wrecks through my body. I clench around him, squeezing him so tightly I think we both might die.

All I want to do is go to sleep. My mind and body are sated. Lucas is here protecting me from everyone and everything. For a few hours, everything is okay.

My mind is hazy when Lucas slips out of me and repositions us on the bed, so I'm lying on top of him.

I rest against Lucas's chest, letting the aftershocks of pleasure ripple through me. Maybe I shouldn't have let it happen after how everything ended back at Corium, but he came for me. He came to save me, and that has to mean something.

After a moment, Lucas pulls away, and I'm reminded that I'll have to remain here while he leaves to figure out how to get me out of this mess.

He pulls on his slacks and buttons them. My eyes linger on his chiseled chest and abs that are perfectly indented into his skin. I drag my gaze away from his half-naked body to see him pulling out a phone from his pocket.

"I'm going to leave you my phone. Keep it hidden. I'll message you from another number so you have it and can call me."

Relief pools in my belly. I can call him at the very least so I won't be completely alone.

"Okay, thank you," I whisper.

I take the phone from his hand and slide it under the pillow, then I crawl off the bed and slip back into my clothes. By the time I'm dressed, he is buttoning the last button on his shirt. I look up at him and wonder if I can really trust him.

Everyone I've ever trusted has let me down or led me astray. Putting my trust in Lucas is giving him the bullet to kill me, but what other choice do I have?

"Call me if anything happens." I nod, and my lips turn down at the sides. "I promise, Delilah. I'll come back to you, and I'll kill anyone who touches you. Do you understand me?"

My heart tightens in my chest at the notion.

"Yes, I understand."

"Good, now be good and don't cause any trouble."

I nod and watch as he leaves the room. As soon as he steps out the door and it closes, I hear a lock engage. I fall back against the bed and stare at the ceiling. He's going to come back for me—he promised, and all I can do is hope he keeps his word.

3

LUCAS

"You know, I did tell you—"

"I don't want to fucking hear it, Nic. Yes, you told me, but how could I have known he has a goddamn contract."

Nic leans back in his chair with a deep sigh while I continue pacing in front of his desk. I haven't sat still since I left that place a few hours ago, and I don't think I will until I have her with me again.

"Lucas." Celia's concerned voice meets my ear. "Why don't you sit and let me get you a drink?"

A part of me knows she's only trying to help, but the bigger part of me is irritated that she can't actually help, so I snap at her. "I don't need a drink. I need to get her out of there."

"We're almost ready to go. My men are loading up as we speak," Nic tells me for the third time in the past thirty minutes.

What the fuck is taking so long?

Just as I'm about to demand to leave and not waste any more time, a voice booms through the intercom. "Sir, we are ready to go."

"Finally!" I throw up my arms. My legs are already carrying me out. I don't even wait for Nic to get up. "Let's go, or I'm leaving you behind."

"So you can get in more trouble," my brother fires back. He is a few years older than me but still in better shape than most men half his age, so it's not surprising that he has no problem keeping up with my fast pace down the stairs.

"Be careful!" Celia yells before the door closes behind us, and we're speed walking outside to where four SUVs are waiting for us.

Nic and I slide into the back seat of the second SUV, which is the only one that doesn't have at least five people inside already. All my brother's men are dressed in black from head to toe and armed to the teeth.

Brookshire's goons won't stand a chance. Nathaniel is stupid enough to hire the biggest and most scary-looking guys he can find to guard his place. Ten of his men would not stand a chance against five of these guys. My brother makes a point of hiring the best of the best. He has three Navy SEALs on his team, two Special Ops Marines, along with CIA-trained snipers and a few former FBI agents.

It turns out that when you offer people double what they are making, without the political bullshit attached to their job, they are very eager to switch to the other side of the law.

"Do me a favor."

Nic's voice shakes me out of my dark, troubled thoughts. I can't help but imagine smashing Nathaniel's face into his desk, balling up that contract, and shoving it down his throat. The thought of watching his eyes go glassy the longer he chokes is almost as satisfying as the most erotic fantasy I've ever had.

I look at Nic. "What's that?"

"Don't take any unnecessary risks in there."

"What? You're going to parent me all of a sudden? Where is this coming from?"

"We both know I understand how you're feeling right now."

"You don't have the first fucking idea."

"In general, yes, I do. Let's not pretend this is anything it isn't. Kid yourself all you want, but don't kid me. This is personal for you."

"Of course it is. Why wouldn't it be? I told him I wanted her, and he refused me. Didn't give me the chance to negotiate."

"Right." He shakes his head, snickering softly while tucking a Glock into his ankle holster. "That's all it's about."

"She's mine to punish, Nic. Only mine."

"I understand that." He adjusts his earpiece, and I do the same with mine. "So long as it stays there, and you don't let your personal feelings about her get in the way."

He's not going to let it go until I admit I care about her. It's not going to happen. "What's your point?"

"The point is, I understand the temptation to say fuck it and be reckless. But we both know we can't forget who we're dealing with here. I want to cut that piece of shit's dick off and dangle it in front of his face, but we can't always do what we want in these situations."

Suddenly, he wants to talk about diplomacy. "I know what I'm doing."

"You sure about that?"

"You just worry about your guys. I'll worry about myself."

He growls something unintelligible but is smart enough to let the matter drop.

Every mile brings me a mile closer to her. Has anyone else had enough time to put their hands on her? To sink their cocks inside her? Burning heat spreads through my chest like I swallowed a lump of blazing coal, and it's eating me up inside. Is she hurting? Is she afraid? That much, I can assume. She's terrified right now. And she's counting on me. Hold on a little while longer. I'm coming for you.

The unlit sign is the first thing to catch my attention as we roll up on the building. "Closed for the evening?" I mutter, exchanging a glance with my brother.

"Either that or he knows this is coming." Of course he would. He had to know this was coming next. We're counting on it.

"I assumed he'd use the other girls and his clientele to shield himself, then make his escape in the middle of all the chaos." That's still a possibility, though, whether or not the place is crawling with men ready to pay for sex.

The SUVs pull to a stop, chatter overlapping in my ear thanks to the earpiece tucked firmly inside. "Testing the door," one of the guys reports while another three men take the alley running alongside the building to survey the rear.

"All clear," one of them announces. "Eyes on the exit." In case Nathaniel decides to sneak her out the back.

I join the men at the front door and pound my fist against the wood like I did before. This time, there's no answer. No goon in a suit that's too tight for him. Nothing at all.

I fall back to let the experts do their work. She's in there, locked up, probably wondering if I'll ever fulfill my promise of getting her out. I'm practically bouncing up and down on the balls of my feet as I wait for the C4 to be packed around the lock. Like everyone else, I retreat behind one of the SUVs in preparation for the explosion.

"Three... two... one." With that, a blast tears through the otherwise peaceful night and blows the door open. We're moving before the smoke clears, pouring into the building and fanning out, weapons drawn, heads on swivels.

"Deserted?" Nic asks as we move farther into the darkened building. No customers wander the halls, no chatter or laughter. Not even the laugh track from a TV show playing somewhere. Not a sound.

The rapid patter of gunfire answers Nic's question. We plaster ourselves to the walls, the lead man rounding a corner and returning fire. There's a strained grunt quickly followed by a heavy thud as the gunman falls.

In my earpiece, I hear the firefight taking place in the rear of the building. "Two of them trying to get out!" one of our guys shouts, the rest of it drowned out by more fire.

"Is she one of them?" I shout, pressing my hand to my ear to hear better. "Is it her?"

Waiting for the noise to die down is torture, every passing second aging me a year. Finally, I hear, "Negative. Two guys. Both down."

"Is Brookshire one of them?" Nic asks.

"Negative."

I round the corner and find the bouncer I met on my first visit now slumped against the wall, legs splayed at awkward angles. He's gasping for air, bleeding freely from a wound in the stomach and another in his shoulder.

Crouching, I lean down so my face fills his field of vision. "Where's your boss? Where is Delilah?"

He looks up at me, eyes unfocused at first. Once he recognizes me, it sounds like he's trying to laugh, but all he manages is a wet gurgle. "Go fuck yourself," he grunts, blood dripping down his chin from the effort.

I slam my fist against his wounded shoulder, and he howls before spitting out a mouthful of blood. "You think he'd tell me?" he bawls, raising a hand to his wound like that's going to help anything. He looks down at the mess his gut has become. "Aw, shit."

"You're dead within fifteen minutes," I remind him. "If that. You wanna die with that girl on your conscience? Where is he? Was he waiting for this to happen?"

He lifts his head, blinking slowly. "I thought I told you to fuck yourself." I almost have to give him credit for holding out until the end, even if he sucks at choosing sides.

"You backed the wrong horse." He doesn't have the chance to draw another labored breath before I blow his brains out.

Then I stand, my mind made up. "He was ready for this." Let the others search the rest of the place. I know exactly where I need to go.

"Wait!" I ignore Nic's plea in favor of taking the stairs two at a time and going to the room where I first found Delilah. There are so many doors, all of them closed, and from behind more than one of them, I hear weeping. I ignore it in favor of going to Delilah's door and testing the knob. No surprise, it's locked and unmoving.

"Delilah!" Silence. "I'm coming in. Stay away from the door!" I take a step back and deliver a solid kick that sends the door flying open hard enough to bounce off the wall beside it.

The room is empty, the lights off. I flip the switch on the wall, and the overhead bulb reveals nothing to give me a clue about what happened. No blood, nothing broken. The bed is neatly made.

Not once I strip the thin blankets from it and throw them across the room. "Goddamnit!" The pitiful excuse for an adjoining bathroom is also empty—and grimy. The man couldn't be bothered to keep the place livable for the girls he sells.

I return to the hall, colliding with my brother. "She's gone." Without giving him a chance to respond, I begin with the door directly opposite Delilah's and repeat the effort of kicking it open. A girl with dark skin and wide, tear-filled eyes cowers on the corner of the bed, holding a pillow in front of her like a shield.

"Nobody is here to hurt you," I grunt, approaching the bed. "Where's your boss? What happened here?"

"I-I don't know!"

"Is your door always locked?" Nic asks, standing in the doorway.

Her head bobs up and down. "Always. We're never allowed to leave our rooms." I figured as much from the time I spent with Delilah, but now I know she wasn't a special case.

I leave her and go to the next room and the next. The girls are too thin, dressed in cheap, skimpy lingerie meant to excite their customers. The rooms are like closets, bleak and depressing.

"Do you know where your boss is?" I ask a redhead at the end of the hall as she wipes tears from her freckled cheeks. She can't be older than Aspen or Delilah. None of them can.

"I never see him unless he wants to feed." When all I can do is stare at her in confusion, she gestures toward her swollen tits. "Some customers like to feed. I have to make sure my milk stays in so they can get some. He likes to do it sometimes."

Holy fuck. And I thought I was sick. "Did anyone say anything about closing for the night?"

She shakes her head. "They don't tell us anything. All of a sudden, there were gunshots, and you came in." I guess they have to keep the girls disconnected from the rest of the world as much as possible.

In my earpiece, one of the men downstairs reports, "No sign of him. The entire first floor is clear."

"No sign on the second floor, either," Nic responds. "One more sweep of the place. Include the roof."

"I'm going to his office." I storm down the hall, past doors I kicked open and girls I might have inadvertently freed. Their problems aren't my problem right now. Where would he have taken her?

Would he kill her to keep her away from me? No matter how I try to push the idea away, it bounces back to me like a rubber ball. I would put nothing past that bastard.

One thing is for sure: his office leaves the impression of someone who left in a hurry. Papers are strewn over the desk, and half a fast food meal sits uneaten. The food is cold. So is the chair. Where the fuck is he?

I sink into the chair and begin searching the desk. "What are you looking for?" Nic asks from the doorway.

"I'll know it when I see it." I glance up at him in time to notice his scowl. "What?"

He shakes his head. "We already have a list of his other properties. He could've taken her to one of them—but there are over a dozen in all. It'll take time."

Time is something I don't think Delilah has on her side.

4

DELILAH

*M*y eyes feel heavy, like concrete blocks are sitting on top of them. I force myself to open them and mutter a hoarse, *"What the fuck?"* the moment they're open. This has to be a dream. Actually, scratch that. This has to be a nightmare. Where the hell am I?

I sit up slowly, my brain swimming in my head like that of a fish in a bowl. The room I'm in looks like a unicorn puked cotton candy everywhere. The walls are two shades of pink, with random princess décor on the walls and a dresser. The bed is white, with a dusty pink accent, and the whole thing reminds me of a little girl's room. A bookcase and vanity sit off to the far left of the room.

My stomach churns, and I move off the bed. My hands tighten into fists, and I continue to look around the room, hoping I'll wake up at any moment and realize this is a dream. It never happens, and the dread inside me mounts with each second that ticks by. Something bad is going to happen.

The door handle on the door jiggles, and my entire body tenses up. There's no weapon for me to use. I have no way to protect myself. The door comes flying open, and I'm caught like a deer in headlights. Every hair on my body stands on end, and the sudden need to vomit almost overcomes me when Nathaniel walks into the room.

As always, he's wearing a suit fitted to his round body. The white-colored shirt beneath his jacket has the top three buttons undone, and his thick dark curly chest hair peeks out.

The sick glint in his eyes makes me shiver. He's looking at me like I'm a toy he can play with, a toy he can break and toss in the trash.

"What do you want?" I growl, keeping as much space between myself and this disgusting human.

"That's no way to talk to the man providing you with a warm meal, bed, and roof over your head, now is it?"

I scoff. "I've asked numerous times to leave! I don't want your help, in case that wasn't obvious, to begin with."

Nathaniel tilts his head back and lets out a bellow of laughter. "Your father owed me. A deal was made, and now you belong to me. That was the plan all along."

"I belong to no one," I say vengefully. "Whatever deal my father made is void. I want out of this house of horrors."

His features turn murderous, and he takes a step toward me but pauses, almost like he's rethinking his actions. My heart hammers so hard in my chest that I wonder if he can see how terrified I am. To others, he would come across as the rich grandparent who lets you do whatever you want, but I know he is much worse.

Like a light being turned off and on, his face changes. The murderous rage dissipates into thin air, and suddenly, he's smiling.

What the hell is wrong with this guy?

"I look forward to breaking you of that fickle thought. A deal is a deal, sweetheart, and I'll make sure it's followed through with."

His mood swings are giving me whiplash.

"I don't care what deal you made," I repeat. "This is kidnapping and against the law."

"No one is going to save you, Delilah. No one cares about you. No one wants you. You're mine, and you'll do as you're told, or there will be grave consequences."

Each word he speaks feels like a sword being plunged deep into my stomach. They're words I've heard my entire life, words I've lived by and come to see myself as.

I don't respond to him. There's nothing I can say to him that will alter his thinking. He made up his mind long ago on who I was and what I meant to him and his son.

"Now that we've got that out of the way, I wanted to take a stroll down memory lane." Acid burns up my throat, and I'm close to vomiting. "Remember our little game... the one Nash ruined before we could finish it?"

The memories of that night come rushing back to the surface. *"There you go. Now, be a good girl, get on your knees, and suck me off for a little before I shove my cock into your cunt... I'll fuck your tight little pussy while you call me daddy."*

It all makes sense now. This is supposed to be a little girl's room, and he wants to play out his sick fantasies of being my *daddy*.

"You can go to hell, Nathaniel!" I snarl my lip, letting my rage out. I know it won't change what's coming, but it makes me feel better.

"Charming, you always did need an attitude adjustment." He shakes his head. "Over on the vanity is an outfit I want you to wear. I'm going to step out, and when I return, I hope you have that on as well as a better attitude to match it. If not, I'll certainly enjoy beating the disrespect out of you."

My eyes gravitate to the small vanity tucked in the corner of the room. On the bench seat sits a little schoolgirl uniform. I want to spit at him, scream and tell him there is no way in hell I'm doing what he's asked, but I simmer the rage down, reminding myself that I will get out of this.

"If that's what you want." I give him a smile that's so fake it hurts to force my lips into the movement.

"See, you'll come around. All you need is a little persuasion. I'll be right back." I don't miss the way his eyes drag across my body like he's already picturing me in his fucked-up costume. My skin crawls, and I hold my breath, watching as he wobbles out of the bedroom, the door closing behind him softly.

Once he's gone, the panic of what is going to happen finally sinks in. I place a hand against my chest, willing myself to calm down, and that's when I feel it. *The phone.* I'd been alternating between hiding it under my pillow and in my bra for safekeeping.

I yank it out and almost drop it as my hands are trembling so badly. Pressing the side button, I wait for the phone to turn on. It takes forever, and I worry I won't have enough time to make the call. "*Hurry. Hurry,*" I say to myself. Finally, the display screen appears, and I feel a sniggle of relief.

Lucas texted me from the number I'm supposed to call, so I navigate to the text messages, my eyes darting between the phone screen and the door over and over again. My stomach tightens with fear. He's going to return at any minute, and the nightmare of that night is going to be relived all over again.

My fingers slide across the screen, but somehow, I manage to hit the green call button. I bring the phone to my ear, hoping and praying that he answers, but after a second, I don't hear anything, not even the ringing of the line.

Pulling the phone away from my ear, I stare at the screen, watching as it says calling... *No!* Tears prick at my eyes. I'm on the verge of crying. At the top of the screen, I see the signal button. No signal. I have no fucking signal.

I squeeze the phone in one hand. I'm tempted to throw it but restrain myself. There's nothing I can do. Nathaniel's going to come back at any second, and then it's going to be too late for Lucas to save me.

Defeat threatens to consume me, but this small voice in the back of my mind starts to repeat itself. The sentence grows louder and louder... until it's the only thing I can hear. The only thing I can feel.

You don't need anyone to save you. You can save yourself.

5

LUCAS

Not knowing where she is and if she is okay drives me insane. I can't think straight; I can't sleep, eat, or talk to anyone without screaming. After I yelled at Celia for offering me a drink, Nic made me go to one of the guest rooms to cool off like I'm a fucking teenager.

So now I'm pacing through this room instead of his office. Sitting still is out of the question.

I have no idea how going after her was ever a question. If someone would ask me to let her go now, I would probably rip his face off for making such a suggestion.

A part of me wonders if the only reason I'm so obsessed with getting her back now is that Brookshire is the one who took her. Do I only want her back because he has her? Is there really something between us, or is this my subconscious's way of making up for letting Aspen down?

Where is Lauren when I fucking need her to make sense of this mess?

My burner phone rings, and for a second, I wonder if it's Lauren. Did she hear me thinking about her? Glancing at the screen, I find it's Xander calling. Not sure how he got this number but considering my current mental state, I think about not answering. Then I remember who we are talking about here. Xander is not someone who calls back later or leaves a message. He would find another way to get to me right now.

Swiping to unlock, I lift the phone to my ear. "Hello, Xander."

"Lucas, I hear you left Corium in a hurry. Everything okay?"

"Yes, just grabbing Delilah. Then I'll take her somewhere I can keep my eye on her and head back to Alaska."

"I see. Wouldn't it be easier to simply dispose of the issue?"

"No," I growl, tightening the grip on my phone. I'm not surprised he wants me to kill Delilah, but I am surprised by how angry the thought makes me.

"No? Why not?"

"I..." Shit. What am I going to tell him? Fuck it, I'm going with the truth. "I want her." It's the most honest answer, one I hope he can live with.

"Lucas..." Xander sighs into the receiver. "I don't like loose ends, and that girl is one. I took out her entire family, and Quinton kidnapped and held her prisoner for weeks. This girl can't be trusted. She is a danger to my family, and I can't let that go, no matter your infatuation with her."

"That's why I'm getting her from Brookshire and taking her somewhere far away."

"How is that going to help? Who's to say she won't come back for revenge?"

"She won't. You have my word." The words come out of my mouth before I can even comprehend what they mean.

A moment of silence hangs between us before Xander breaks it. "Is there something you're not telling me?"

"Like I said, I just want her."

"Want or need?"

"Maybe both." Jesus, this is more uncomfortable than talking to Lauren. "Look, I'll keep an eye on her. I will make sure she doesn't do anything stupid again. I was too lenient while she was at Corium. I won't make that mistake again."

"I don't know if that's enough."

"It has to be."

"You do realize you are putting both of our children in danger, right?"

"There isn't any danger."

"So Delilah didn't try to kill Aspen?"

I finally stop pacing, feeling the need to sit down for a moment. I take a seat at the end of the mattress. "Marcel was the one who tried to hurt her, and I dealt with him."

"You sent him away. That's not the same as dealing with him." Any other day, I would tell him that Marcel will soon have an unfortunate car accident. Today, I don't have the patience to explain my plan.

"You're just going to have to trust me on this." Xander has been my friend for years, so I hate leaving this tension between us, but my mind is reeling, and I can't deal with him right now. "I'll call you back once I have her. I have to go now."

"This conversation is not over."

"Goodbye, Xander." I pull the phone away from my ear and hit the red button. I already know this is going to bite me in the ass later.

Xander Rossi is used to getting his way, and not even years of friendship will get in the way of that.

Before I put my phone away, I dial my own number and hit the green button. Just like every other time I try to call, it goes straight to voicemail, which means Delilah turned the phone off or someone found it on her. Neither option is good.

I can't track the phone if it's off or out of range. My only hope is that she turned it off on purpose. I typed out a quick message earlier telling her it's me and to call when she gets it, just in case she turns it back on. Though my gut tells me she doesn't have the phone anymore.

If they hurt her, I'll kill their entire family.

A knock on the door pulls me out of the murder scene already playing out in my head.

"Yeah, come in." I stand from the bed just as the door opens, and Celia's head pops into the room.

"You okay?" The way she's looking at me like I'm a lost puppy annoys me to no end.

"No, but that's nothing new."

She frowns. "We'll find her. Why don't you come downstairs and eat something?"

I shake my head. "I'm not hungry."

"I know, but you have to eat. How about a protein smoothie? You want to be ready to go as soon as we find her, don't you?"

I let out a sigh. "God, you know you're not my mom, right?"

"I can be concerned as your sister. That's how family works. Now, let's go. I'm feeding you whether you want to eat or not."

"So bossy."

Celia rolls her eyes at me. "It's not like you and your brother respond to anything else."

"Actually—" My phone buzzes in my pocket. "Dammit, Xander," I mumble while fishing it out of my pocket. I glance at the screen, and my heart squeezes in my chest when I see my own number flashing at me.

Holding my breath, I answer the call and put it on speakerphone.

"Hello?" My voice cracks.

Silence.

Seconds go by, and there is still nothing on the other line.

"Delilah?" A quiet sob comes through the phone. The sound only worries me more. "Delilah, talk to me. Where are you? Tell me what happened, and I'll come and get you."

Another sniffle before her shaking voice finally comes through. "I-I don't know."

"You don't know what?"

"I... I don't know where I am."

"That's okay. Just keep the phone on, and I'll find you. I'm on my way."

I grab Celia by the arm and pull her downstairs with me. Nic meets us at the bottom of the stairs, glaring at my fingers wrapped around Celia's wrist. He's looking at me like he's about to chop my hand off. I let go of her and ignore his death stare.

"Are you still there?" I ask.

"Yes... I'm here," Delilah whispers, her voice sounding shaky and monotone as if her mind is elsewhere.

"Is anyone with you?" I point at the door, wanting to leave right away. Luckily, Nic understands and calls for a car.

"Nathaniel is here. I mean... his body."

"His body?" *Fuck.* As I speak, I run a hand through my hair. "Is he dead?"

"Yes." She says the word without a lick of remorse in her voice. Dammit, I wanted to kill him myself. I don't have the patience to ask her how it happened. That's something I can figure out later.

"Okay, hold on."

Celia gives Nic a kiss and waves goodbye to me as we rush out the front door and into the waiting car. Nic slides into the back seat after me and flips open his laptop. The car takes off while Nic pulls up the map and pings my phone.

"Are you hurt?" I don't really want to know because if she says yes, I'll drive myself insane until I get there, but I need to keep her talking. Plus, I need to know if she is seriously injured, whether I want to know or not.

"No... I don't think so." Her voice trembles a little less now.

"That's good."

A red icon starts blinking on the map. *Finally.*

"There she is," Nic mumbles before telling the driver where to go.

"We're about forty-five minutes away."

"Forty-five," she repeats. "I don't know if someone else is here. What if someone finds me before you do?"

"Delilah, listen. Find someplace to hide. And if you have a weapon, bring that too. No matter what happens, know I am on my way, and everything will be okay. I promise."

"If I hide, I can't stay on the phone. The signal is bad. The only place I could call is at the top of the staircase."

"You have to hide. Just leave the phone where you are and go hide somewhere. Don't come out until you hear me."

"Okay... I-I'll go hide."

"I'll be there soon."

I can hear her putting down the phone, followed by the fading of her footsteps.

"You are more attached than I thought," my brother points out after a moment of silence. "I hope that doesn't come to bite you in the ass later on."

I scoff. "You and me, both."

6

DELILAH

*W*here is Lucas, and what's taking him so long?

I don't even know how long it's been. He said he'd be here in forty-five minutes, but I left my phone out in the hall like he told me to. I have no way of knowing what time it is, but it feels like hours have passed.

It doesn't help that it's so dark in here. It's like a cave—the only light leaking in through the tiny gap under the closet door. The darkness is nice. Almost comforting.

I've been straining my ears, listening for any sounds coming from the rest of the house. It's as quiet as a graveyard at midnight.

A tiny giggle of nervous energy bubbles up from my chest, and I press my mouth against my knee. A graveyard? Like the one Nathaniel will be in because I killed him.

My fingers are still a little stiff and sore from how tightly I was gripping the bookend when I hit him. It wasn't until I dropped it on the floor that I even knew I grabbed it from the shelf when he came in.

And then I... what? I blacked out. Snapped. There was nothing to hold me back. Nothing to tell me I shouldn't kill him. And the proof of that was—is—the dead man on the floor.

I remember staring down at the bookend, confused. Why was it covered in blood? There's a hair on it, too, stuck in clumps. But why?

It's his hair.

I hit him in the head with it.

I did this.

Blood dripped from the wound and rolled down the side of his face, soaking into his shirt. The dripping held my attention the longest, and suddenly, everything started to make sense.

Every droplet shone like rubies before plinking onto the floor. There was an entire puddle by the time my phone buzzed, thanks to Lucas's call. The thought drags me back to the present.

Why isn't he here yet? What if something bad happens, and he can't make it? What if there's an accident and nobody else in the world knows where I am? I could die in this closet, breathing in mothballs.

Or I could die outside the closet when somebody shows up and drags me out and does the same thing to me that I did to Nathaniel. Only I doubt they would make it quick. If anyone finds out what I did before Lucas arrives, I'm as good as dead. What's taking Lucas so long? I need him. He's the only person who can help me now. The only person who'd want to.

I killed a man. He's lying down the hall not far away from where I'm hiding, in front of the vanity and that disgusting outfit he thought I would wear. The thought scares me—and thrills me. Something roars inside my head, something grim and satisfied.

I saved myself.

I doomed myself.

Icy realization skitters its way down my spine. I'm nobody. I'm not going to get away with killing a man like Nathaniel. My chest is too tight, my heart's racing much too fast, and I think I'm going to faint if this doesn't stop.

I'm a murderer. Nobody's going to care that I only did it to protect myself. They'll all say I had it coming or something like that. It's how people in this world think. I'm a nobody who murdered a powerful man when I should've given him what he wanted. That's how they'll see it.

Lucas! I need him. I'm rocking back and forth with my teeth chattering. I can smell Nathaniel's blood on me, the metallic odor running alongside the mothballs. I gag a little but hold back the bile before it can spill out.

Blood rushes in my ears, and that, mixed with the heavy thumping from my heart, drowns out everything else.

I'm going to hell for what I did, aren't I?

The closet door flies open like some unseen force is answering my question. The light from the hall is bleeding through. I turn my face away and cross my arms over the top of my head.

"No, no! I didn't mean to do it. It was an accident!"

"Delilah!"

Lucas's shout cuts through my panic and sinks into my brain.

I blink away the spots in my vision, and his body comes into focus. He's on one knee in front of me, half inside the closet. He pushes the hair away from my face with both hands and looks deep into my eyes.

His blue eyes shine like the sun glistening off the waves in the ocean.

"I'm here. You're safe now," he whispers softly, like speaking to a wounded animal.

Safe? I'll never be safe after what I did, but just having him here is enough for now. I bury my face against his neck and let out a long, almost painful wail. Why is this happening? Why is it happening to me? What did I ever do to deserve any of this?

Another man's voice meets my ears. "He's in here. She really did a number on him."

"Would you think before you speak?" Lucas sneers at the guy before he gathers me up in his arms. He stands up while holding me against his chest, and all I can do is lean into him.

I drape my arms around his neck and close my eyes, finally resting for the first time since I woke up in this terrible place. I don't even know for sure where I am. I only know I never want to return here.

"What's going to happen?" My question is muffled against his shoulder, but he understands me.

"Right now, we're going to my brother's. We'll get you taken care of there. Don't worry about anything."

"But Nathaniel—"

"He'll be taken care of." He leaves it at that, and honestly, I don't want to know anything else.

I only hope he means it when he says I have nothing to worry about. That he'll take care of me because I want to believe him more than anything.

I don't know how long we wait in the car before leaving, nor how long it takes to get to Lucas's brother's house. I only know Lucas clutches me to him all through the ride. I'm safe now. I'm with him, and nothing will hurt me. I don't even know how he tracked me or found me. I only know he did.

And somewhere in the back of my mind, I hope he's not going to end up paying for what I did—or rather, for helping me get out of there and away with it.

I must doze off because all of a sudden, Lucas gently shakes me awake. "We're here. I'm going to take you up to my room and get you washed up, all right? Do you want anything to eat?"

I only shake my head. My stomach couldn't handle anything right now.

My thoughts are a never-ending fishbowl. That monster was going to rape me, and if I fought back, he would've beaten me before raping me even worse. I might not have lived through it.

All I can do is remind myself that I had to protect myself. It was the only thing I could do, even if it still feels like somebody else did it. Like I stepped into somebody else's life, and Lucas is carrying someone else into what I can only tell is a very big house. I'm not interested in what it looks like or anything like that. I only want to hide and never show my face again.

A woman's voice is somewhere nearby, murmuring questions at a low volume. She sounds relieved, whoever she is. My face is still pressed against Lucas, so I don't get a good look at her. He carries me up a long flight of stairs and down a long hallway before we come to a stop.

I open one eye, peering over his shoulder at the inside of a very big, luxurious bathroom. "I'll run you a bath," he explains before setting me down on the edge of the tub. "Get undressed." I do it mechanically, and I'm glad to. Now that I'm looking at myself in full light, and my brain isn't frozen in shock, I notice the blood splatters across my chest.

He didn't drop right away. The memory is still fresh in my mind.

He staggered a little, and I backed away in horror when his arms lifted. His hands were curled into claws like he wanted to wrap them around my throat and squeeze the life out of me. He fell before he got the chance.

The memory evaporates into the air, and I notice steam rising from the surface of the water and bubbles floating on top in the bathtub. I get in without hardly feeling the temperature and only shrug when Lucas asks if it's comfortable. I must still be in shock, or at least numb. If this is how bad I feel when I'm numb, how much worse is it going to get when the feeling wears off?

"Just sit back and let me take care of you."

I hardly recognize him, kneeling beside the tub, dipping a washcloth into the water before dragging it over my shoulder. There's nothing sexual about the way he touches me, but he's not rough about it either. He takes his time, and my muscles eventually start to relax between his gentle touches and the heat of the water.

"I really didn't mean to do it." I wait until he looks at me. His blue eyes pierce the deepest depths of my soul. I couldn't lie to him at this moment, even if I wanted to. "I didn't. It just happened. He was going to—"

"I know what he was going to do. Remember, I visited that brothel. I spoke to him. I have a very good idea of what he had in mind." He dips the cloth into the water before easing me forward to wash my back.

"You don't blame me?" It matters so much. He can't blame me. I don't think I could handle it if he did.

"Not in the slightest." His voice is tight, flat, and serious. "So get that idea out of your head."

It's like magic, the way his words unlock the tightness in my chest. I let out a long sigh that ends in a strangled sob. It feels good. Cleansing. Like I'm letting go of all the pain held inside.

The water's a little cooler by the time he decides I'm clean. I stand, and he wraps me in a towel before helping me out of the tub. I don't even have to dry myself off. He takes care of it for me, rubbing me down in long, gentle strokes without saying a word or looking me in the eye.

His expression is of a man focused on his task. I don't know what he's thinking, but at least I know he's not blaming me for killing an important man.

The weight of what happened hits me hard, and all of a sudden, I'm tired. I guess now that the adrenaline has stopped pumping, my body's decided it's had enough. Like he can read my mind, Lucas leads me through a door into an adjoining bedroom. It's big and nicely furnished with a king-sized bed. The bed looks like the answer to a prayer, the sheets softer than anything I've ever felt though I haven't touched them yet.

"I don't know if I'll be able to get any sleep," I fret, eyeing the pajamas at the foot of the bed.

"Celia must've left them here for you while you were in the bath," he explains. "My sister."

"That's nice of her. I didn't know you had a sister."

"She's my brother's wife."

"Oh. Okay." At least now I know who I heard downstairs.

I slip into the nightshirt and shorts she left for me. They're comfortable and the right size, or close enough. The sheets are cool and soft, just as I suspected, and they smell of lilacs. I suck in a deep breath and soak in as much of it as I can before touching my head to the pillow. Lucas brings the covers up to my chest before stepping away from the bed. Panic clings to me at the thought of him leaving.

"Wait." I lift my head and reach for him. "You're not leaving me, are you?"

"Of course I'm not." He pulls his shirt over his head, and my pulse slows again. "I'm getting undressed and crawling into bed with you."

It's not ten seconds before he's sliding in beside me, one arm under my shoulders so he can turn my body toward his, and I'm so glad. He's my life raft in the middle of an endless, stormy ocean. He's all I have to hold, the only way I can keep my head above water.

"Thank you," I whisper into the darkness, my cheek against his bare chest.

He holds me close, stroking my hair, and his heart's steady beating begins to lull me to sleep before he murmurs his answer. "I didn't do anything but bring you here. You saved yourself."

I guess I did. But who's going to save me from what comes next?

7

LUCAS

The first thing I do upon waking is feel around on the bed to make sure Delilah is with me. That I didn't dream what happened. I need to know she's still safe with me, where no one can hurt her.

Her warm, sleep-limp body lies next to mine. I release a quiet sigh of relief, careful not to wake her when I do. She has enough on her mind. I doubt she needs my concerns on top of it.

Opening my eyes, I find her curled up beside me, fists tucked under her chin, and her knees pulled up. She looks so young right now, a fact that I seem to forget frequently. Not that me being more than twice her age is the biggest roadblock in our relationship. Compared to the odds stacked against us, our age gap seems insignificant.

One thing we do have in common is the nightmares haunting us day and night.

If the word haunted had a physical example, it would be an image of Delilah at this moment. Even in sleep, ghosts are chasing her.

Threats loom over her shoulder, and though she eliminated one of them, there will be others close behind as a result. They'll want revenge. It's only a matter of time.

The thought alone leaves me wanting to pull her into my arms again. Like as long as I'm holding her, she'll be safe. Nothing will touch her. I want that to be true—it's unbelievable how much I want it. The way something stirs in my chest when she lets out a shuddery breath that reverberates through her body. Dear God, how I want to wipe away whatever it was that made her do it.

This is a new feeling for me. I never wanted to protect anyone like I want to do with Delilah. Even with Aspen, the urge to keep her safe is not this overwhelming. That thought alone is more terrifying than anything I've ever faced.

I've never been one to turn away from facts, and the one looming largest is this: the woman beside me tried to kill my daughter. The fact that I haven't known for long about her being my daughter doesn't matter. I know it now. I know what's mine. How can I betray Aspen by protecting someone who pretended to be her friend, then lured her to what would surely have meant her death?

I shake my head. Even now, the thought of Delilah's betrayal doesn't stir the same outrage it once did. The last thing I need is to empathize with Delilah, but that's exactly what I've come to do. She never had a chance. Her father's interest in her only extended as far as her benefit to him. He sold her. The son of a bitch sold her, and I held the contract in my hands.

When I think about that, her actions come into focus. All she wanted was a way to belong. She's needed a refuge for so long. She was desperate to find it. So desperate, she walked straight into a brothel without the first clue.

Everything she's done has been a result of that endless longing to belong somewhere. The reality of it all hits me like a brick house. Still, that doesn't mean she has any business staying with me. A vast cavern of space lies between my sympathy for her and my being with her.

By the time she starts to stir, fully waking up, I've made up my mind. I'm going to do the only thing that makes sense. For the first time since setting eyes on her, I'll make the right choice. I won't be selfish to my needs or even hers.

She's ignorant to all of this, waking with a start before settling down once she remembers where she is. It takes a moment, and I wait for her to adjust before speaking.

"How did you sleep?"

She blinks rapidly, still clearly adjusting. Her big brown eyes still linger with remnants of sleep. "I didn't know I slept at all."

A smile tugs at the corner of my mouth, and I let it perk up. "That's the best kind of sleep. When you're in so deep, you can't even dream."

She snorts softly. "I didn't say that. Now that I think about it, I do remember a couple of nightmares."

Anger sizzles in my veins. "Then stop thinking about it. Let them fade away. Nightmares always do."

It's amazing, really. Back at Corium, she was already jaded. Wounded. It was almost entertaining, watching the wheels turn as she tried to come up with yet another way to get around me and escape.

She's only sunk deeper into that wounded, guarded place. There's a hardness in her eyes when they meet mine that wasn't there before, and I hate the sight of it. "What about the real-life night-mares? When do they start to fade away?"

She doesn't flinch from my touch, something I'm grateful for as I brush long strands of her dark hair away from her forehead. "They're called memories, and memories fade, as well. Once you've put enough time between them and the present day, you'll imagine they happened to somebody else instead of you. You'll find they have no power over you."

"How much time?" Before I can answer, she adds, "I don't know if there are enough years left in my life for that to be true."

"Don't say that." Who am I? I hardly recognize this version of me. I'm nobody's guru and certainly not a positive thinker. Yet there's nothing I want more at this moment than to provide a measure of comfort. She's too young to feel this way—hopeless and defeated.

Maybe my decision will spark a little hope for the future. I want it to. It might be the only thing that can save her now. "I've decided something. I'm not going to force you to return to Corium."

There's a light in her eyes for the first time since she woke up. "No? Not ever?"

"Not ever. I'm going to set you up someplace new. You'll have an entirely new life. You can decide for yourself what you want to do and who you want to be. You'll finally have freedom."

To my surprise and disappointment, the light fades away, leaving me with the same haunted girl who woke up beside me.

"I don't understand. You're getting rid of me?"

I should have known she would take it this way. She's only known rejection all her life after being passed from one bad-faith actor to another. Now it looks like I'm passing her off, too. "No, not getting rid of you. Setting you free. Isn't that what you wanted all along? To be free? You have it. You'll want for nothing. You'll never have to rely on anyone else again."

"Except for you."

"Of course, I misspoke. What I meant was I'll be hands-off—"

"I think I understood what you meant." Obviously not, or else there wouldn't be so much resentment in her voice. I'm doing this wrong, fumbling left and right. One skill I was never able to master was how to navigate touchy situations like this one.

"I thought this would make you happy."

"So did I." She sits up and swings her legs over the side of the bed like she's suddenly in a hurry to get away from me. "For my whole life, I've never been given a choice. I could never make my own decisions. Rather it was my father, my aunt, Nash, or you. Someone always took my choice away. First, I was trapped in a trailer, then I was bound to Nash. After that, Quinton kidnapped me, then I came to Corium, and even when I left there, I got myself captured again."

"Maybe it's time to break the cycle."

She shrugs. "I always hated being trapped and always yearned for freedom, but now that I am faced with the possibility of that all, all I feel is fear. I thought I would be relieved and happy to be on my own, but the truth is, I have no idea how to take care of myself. I don't even have a fucking driver's license. I don't have an education or any special skills. What the hell am I going to do?"

"You'll be fine. This is a good thing. You'll be safe and protected. I promise."

"So you say." The disappointment in her voice cuts me to my core. What does she want from me? She doesn't want to go back to Corium. Have I not offered enough? I can't help but have a slight twinge of resentment at the idea. How much more can I give her?

As it turns out, she has an idea. "I need you to do something for me."

"And what would that be?" I ask, guarded.

"I need you to take me back to the trailer where I used to live with my aunt."

"Why would you want to do that?"

"I still have things there I would like to take with me wherever I go. Can't I at least do that?" She pauses. "Remember, I didn't exactly expect to never go back, and I could only take as much as I could carry in a single bag. I still have clothes there, books, stuff like that."

"I can get you more clothes and books. You can leave all of that behind."

"Maybe I don't want to." The ferocity of her response takes me by surprise. Who would want to return to a place as bleak and depressing as she described? That's her past; what is the point of returning to somewhere you never belonged?

"Don't you want to start fresh? Why would you want to be reminded of a place where you felt isolated and ignored?"

She snorts as she stands. "Call it closure, I guess. Whatever you call it, I don't care. I want to go. I need to." Our eyes meet, and she holds my gaze. "Please."

How am I supposed to refuse that? The pleading in her gaze and her words. I can tell she needs this, even if I don't want her to return to that place.

"Fine. First, we get some decent food in you." As it is, I smell coffee wafting up from downstairs, and all it's done is wake up my appetite. I can only imagine she's hungry. What she needs now is to rest and get her strength back. Instead, she would rather walk down memory lane and reopen old wounds. I don't understand it.

What's worse, I don't know why I want to.

Celia and Nic are deep in discussion when we enter the dining room, so deep they don't notice our arrival until I clear my throat. Celia immediately sits up straight and smiles, her gaze focused on Delilah. "There you are. I thought we might have to send out a search party."

She's every bit the gracious hostess, rising from her chair and rounding the table with an outstretched hand. "Hi, Delilah. I'm Celia. I'm so glad you're safe. How are you feeling?" Things haven't always been warm or friendly between us—she didn't come to the family under normal circumstances—but she's proven to be an excellent partner for my brother. Raised in our world, she knows the ropes and can roll with the punches.

And right now, I couldn't be more grateful. Delilah's shoulders loosen and sink to their normal level instead of being up around her ears. "I'm doing... okay. Thanks for lending me some clothes."

"Of course. You wouldn't want to be in anything that reminds you of that place." Celia gives her a knowing nod. "I understand."

Yes, she would. I wonder whether Nic shared any of Delilah's background with his wife. Of all people, Celia would relate to being treated like nothing but a pawn by her bastard of a father.

She was a day shy of being sold into marriage when my brother's men kidnapped her and set her on the path she now walks alongside Nic.

She shows Delilah to a chair, and I follow close, holding Nic's gaze all the while. Let him give me shit about Delilah in Celia's presence, and I'll throw it straight back in his face. I wonder if he's thinking about that as Delilah takes a seat, with me taking the chair closer to him. The way she shrinks back in his presence, it's obvious she's uncomfortable. Why do I fucking care so much?

Because I can't forget how she threw her arms over her head and begged for mercy when I found her in that closet. She was a screaming, shrieking animal practically devoid of sense or logic. I don't know what it is about her, but she brings out every protective instinct I possess—for better or worse.

"Eat up," Celia encourages. "Take as much as you want. Unless there's something else you'd like, instead."

Delilah wears a disbelieving sort of smile as she takes a couple of pancakes and a pair of sausage links. "This looks and smells amazing. Thank you. I'm fine." I pour myself a cup of coffee and exchange a look with Celia, who only offers a shy little smile before taking the carafe so she can freshen her own cup.

Nic clears his throat. He was never good at subtlety. "So what's the plan now? You're going to need one, and fast. It's only a matter of time before everybody knows what happened." I can practically hear Delilah deflating like a balloon.

"I'm working on it." When he shoots me a dark look, I grit my teeth for the sake of the women at the table. "Unless you have ideas. Please, impress me."

"We're going back to my trailer today," Delilah says without lifting her gaze from the plate. Now she eats mechanically like it's a task she's determined to complete before moving on to the next thing on her list. "Not my trailer. My aunt's trailer. I want to get my things since I'm never going back there to live."

"That's good. I'm sure you'll feel more like yourself when you have your own things with you." Celia is trying. I'll give her that much credit. She glances at her husband, and a second later, he jumps slightly like she nudged him under the table. It's almost enough to make me laugh. Watching her get her way, knowing there's nothing he wouldn't do for her. She'd never take advantage—that's not the sort of woman she is—but she knows when to pull his strings.

So he grits his teeth and plays nice when he's entirely against the idea of us being connected in any way. "Yes, I'm sure that will do you some good."

The firm set of Celia's mouth tells me she isn't exactly impressed, but I know my brother. That's as good as it's going to get right now.

I'm not exactly looking forward to paying a visit to some shitty trailer park, but if it makes getting her off my hands easier, so be it. I can't have her in my world. She's a type of danger I've never faced.

The kind of danger that makes me want to forget everything I know in favor of making her the center of my existence.

8

DELILAH

We've barely entered the trailer court, and already I know this was a bad idea. Why did I do this to myself? It's so much worse than I remembered.

Time spent away gives me a clearer look at the things I learned to look past over the years. Plus, having a person with me makes me hyper-focus on all the bad. Just like when your room is messy, but you don't think it's that bad until someone else walks in and you see the look on their face.

A rusted bicycle sitting in a patch of dead grass. A little kid's plastic slide, cracked and broken and faded from too many days spent sitting in the sun.

There's a small dog on a chain attached to a stake in the narrow patch of dirt in front of one of the rusted trailers, lying with its chin on its paws, looking like it hasn't eaten in far too long. This is it. Home sweet home.

I used to see these things every day, but I guess I learned to ignore them. Along with the sad people in these worn down, neglected trailers.

Lucas hasn't said a word, and I steal a look at him from the corner of my eye, expecting to find him sneering or cringing.

He's unreadable, though. I almost wish he would say something about how depressing this place is just so I could hear his thoughts. Instead, all I can do is imagine and assume. As dark as I'm sure his life has been, it's nothing compared to the downright bleak atmosphere around here.

We pull up alongside my old home, opposite the courtyard running between the two rows of trailers. I can't figure out the feeling stirring up deep inside as I sit here, looking out the window toward the only actual home I've ever known. How sad is that? This was supposed to be my solace? Somewhere to escape to after a long day? What a joke.

"Are you sure about this?" Lucas's question stirs me into action. I open the passenger door without responding and step out. Right away, the sight of a used condom lying in the grass gags me a little. The sooner I get this done, the better. I don't ever want to set eyes on this place again.

"And your aunt isn't going to think the two of us showing up like this is strange?"

"She probably won't even care. It's time for her favorite soap opera, anyway." I walk up the wooden steps, the slats of wood broken in places, forcing me to pay extra attention to where I step. The closer I get to the front door, the more I notice how silent the place is. No TV blaring, nothing. Right away, I'm suspicious, but Lucas's presence behind me is all it takes for me to reach for the handle and open the door. My aunt never locked the trailer; what was the point with such a flimsy door?

"Hello?" I don't have to say it very loudly since there's not much space for my voice to travel through. The windows are closed, as usual, and of course, the aroma of stale cigarette smoke permeates the interior the way it always has.

"Something's wrong." I sniff the air, still standing just inside the door, my eyes analyzing the space.

"What is it?" Lucas nearly growls, his voice making me shiver. He's right on my heels, the energy rolling off him tells me he's ready for a fight at any given second.

I shake my head before it hits me. "There's no fresh smoke. It's usually like a fog in here." I walk over to one of the ashtrays and find it almost empty. The trash can is empty, too, without a fresh bag in it. "She hasn't been here in a while."

"You can't know that for sure. Maybe she went to visit someone."

It's almost cute how positive he thinks. Does he think it's going to make me feel better? "You mean walk three trailers down to see her friends? Because those are the only people she has in her life." Besides me. And I up and vanished.

"Hey! What the hell do you think you're doing over there?"

We both spin around, and I recognize Mrs. Porter from down the way. I step around Lucas and outside so she can get a better look at me. She stops short, her mouth falling open. "Delilah? Is that you? Where have you been? Nobody knew where to look for you. You just got up and ran off."

Charming as always. "It's a long story," I offer. "Believe me. I didn't want to disappear and not come back all this time."

"She was worried sick about you."

Somehow, I don't think that's quite true. Annoyed, I can believe. Irritated that I was making life complicated for her, yes. But worried? That, I doubt. "Where is she? It doesn't look like she's been here in days, at least."

Just when I thought her mouth couldn't drop open any farther. "Oh. You don't know."

I barely register Lucas's hand on my shoulder. "What don't I know?" I ask.

She comes closer, her mouth pulled down in an expression of sadness. "I'm sorry to be the one to tell you this, but she's not with us anymore. She died a couple of weeks back."

Lucas's hand tightens while I struggle to make words come out of my mouth. When all I can manage is a choking sound, he speaks up. "What happened?"

She's clearly overwhelmed by him for a few seconds but pulls it together. "I can't say for sure. I heard it was pills. She took a bunch of them and never woke up. They found her in bed after a couple of days. We all figured she was sick, but eventually, we had the owner go in and check the place out."

It isn't like we had a close relationship. In fact, seeing her today was what I dreaded most about this.

But I expected her to be here. Alive. It doesn't seem right, thinking about her not being alive and in front of her TV.

"We left everything the way it was," she tells me. "And we've kind of been keeping an eye on the place to make sure nobody gets it in their head to break in. She's paid up through the end of the month, you see. So it didn't seem right to clean the place out yet. I guess you came along at the right time."

"I guess so," I whisper. I'm numb. I'm completely numb. I don't even feel Lucas's hand anymore, though I know it's there. "Thanks for telling me."

"We're all real sorry, hon." She shoots one final, curious look toward Lucas, and even now, in the middle of yet another shock, I can imagine how the trailer court will be talking about nothing but him for the rest of the day, if not into tomorrow. There's nothing they love more than gossip.

I barely know what I'm doing as I turn back around and re-enter the trailer.

Lucas follows silently, only speaking once the door is closed. "Is there anything I can help you with? Do you want to get some boxes to pack up your belongings?"

"It's funny. I barely remember why I wanted to come so badly." It's like I'm seeing everything through new eyes. The grimy windows, the chipped refrigerator, the broken cabinet doors. The sofa that sags in the middle thanks to the frame being broken forever ago. I don't even remember it ever being intact.

I wonder how many surprises a person can take before they finally break.

"Delilah?" Lucas steps closer to me, and I can't decide if I want to tell him to back off or beg him to hold me. I feel like I'm being pushed around by too many emotions. Grief. Shock. Regret. Confusion. I don't know what to think or how to feel, or even how to take the next step.

I'm not even sure what the next step is.

"She said they left everything the way it was, right?" When Lucas only lets out a soft grunt, I go straight for the sofa.

"What are you doing?" he asks when I flip over the middle cushion.

"This was her favorite hiding spot," I explain, pulling back the strip of duct tape positioned over a slit in the upholstery. "It tore by itself, but she used it to stash things. Money, usually." I dip my hand inside, my fingers moving through the stuffing until they land on paper.

Only it's not money. It's an envelope with my name on it. I recognize her handwriting immediately, and a lump forms in my throat.

My fingers tremble as I open the envelope and pull out two pieces of paper with her familiar scrawl covering both sides. "Delilah," I whisper, my eyes moving over the page. "You've been gone for weeks. No one will tell me where you are or what might have happened to you. I even went to your father's house and heard what happened to the family."

I gasp. "She went to him?" She must really have been desperate.

I keep reading, hungry for more. "Of course, I worried what happened to them would happen to you, too. Nobody could give me any answers, or they refused to. Either way, it's had me worried about you—and me, too, since I've seen a couple of strangers wandering around where they shouldn't be. Maybe I'm paranoid, I don't know. That's why I'm writing this letter and hiding it where I know you'll find it if anything happens. I only hope you do before somebody tosses this piece of shit couch." Funny, but I can almost hear her voice describing the beat-up old thing the way she always did.

I look up at Lucas, who doesn't bother pretending he isn't reading over my shoulder. "She thought the family was after her?" I whisper.

"I'm sure they don't like people asking too many questions." Yes, I can see that.

"You deserve to know the truth," she wrote. "He always threatened me. Said he'd kill you if I didn't go along with his lies. But now he's gone, so I can tell you what's been in my heart since the day you were born: I am your mother."

I don't realize my body is folding up on itself until I end up plopping onto the sofa. The letter falls from my shaking hands. I'm barely aware of Lucas picking it up off the floor. "I'm sorry I never told you," he continues, "but it was my way of keeping you safe. I never knew for sure whether he would actually hurt you, but I didn't want to take the chance. I'm sorry I'm not able to tell you this in person, but I hope I'll be able to. I hope you come home, and I'm here when you do. But if something happens, I want you to know there was never a day I didn't love you, and never a day it didn't break my heart that I couldn't tell you the truth. Just know I always loved you, and I always will. Your mom." His voice trails off before he sighs, lowering his arm so the letter dangles in front of my face.

"My mom." It isn't real. It can't be real. But that's her handwriting. I touched those pages, felt them, and even felt the indentation from the pen like she was pressing hard on the paper. It's real. I can't deny it.

"Are you all right?" Lucas crouches in front of me. "Delilah. Talk to me."

"Lies. So many lies. My whole life, nobody was ever honest with me." I look around, a bitter laugh tearing itself from my chest. "And this is where he made us live. Where he hid us. He took advantage of her love for me by threatening to kill me if his dirty secret ever got out."

"I think we should leave."

I barely remember why I wanted to come anymore. It seemed important, didn't it? I was ready to stomp my feet and hold my breath until my face turned blue. Now I wish I had never thought of it.

Then again, I wouldn't have known the truth. I might have come back here one day and found an entirely different family living here. And that would have been it.

"But what's the point of knowing the truth if there's nothing I can do about it now?" I didn't mean to say it out loud, but now that I have, Lucas begins rubbing my back. I wish it didn't feel so good. I want to brush him off and tell him to spend his sympathy elsewhere. That I don't need it.

"I will say one thing." He stands, taking his comfort away. "This all seems a little too convenient. She suddenly takes too many pills? Did you ever know her to take pills?"

"No. She wasn't on anything I was aware of. But then, who knows, she could have been taking something." I look up at him, confused. "What are you trying to say?"

"I'm saying there was a reason she felt like she had to hide this letter—and a reason she felt like she had to write it in the first place. Which tells me we'd better get out of here sooner rather than later, just in case."

I pop up with a gasp. "You think somebody murdered her?"

"I don't know, but the possibility is there. I don't like taking chances." He points me toward the bedrooms. "You better grab anything you hope to see again because we're leaving right now."

I don't care anymore. But I do need clothes, so I go to the bedroom and shove as much as I can fit into the bag Celia lent me for this trip. I add as many books as I can fit before zipping it up. Anything else, maybe somebody around here can give to their kid or use for themselves. I know my mother didn't have any valuables, or she would've sold them before now anyway.

"At least now I know you weren't lying about this place." It's obvious Lucas is trying to break the tension, but I'm not in the mood.

"Do you know how many times I told her she couldn't tell me what to do because she wasn't my mother?" Our eyes meet, and I see the discomfort in his.

"We all do things we end up wishing we hadn't. Wait until you get to be my age. You'll see how much worse it can get." He stands by the door and waits while I check the coffee can and inside the freezer, my aunt's—my mother's—other favorite hiding places. They're both empty. Either she didn't have anything hidden, or somebody took it. I hate that I'll never know.

"Let's get out of here." I can't shake the feeling of closing a door on an entire phase of my life as I close the door to the trailer. I wish I'd been able to say goodbye, for real. I wish she hadn't died with so many questions. No matter how she ended up dead.

Lucas leads the way back to the car, and I walk with my head down, unwilling to spend another second staring into my past. I don't know what the hell the future holds, but I know wishing and wondering are a waste of time.

If life has taught me one lesson, it's that.

9

LUCAS

*I*t never takes much to wake me. I can't remember the last time I slept deeply—if I ever did beyond early childhood, and even then.

This time, it's the slightest shift on the other side of the mattress. Delilah has me sleeping lighter than ever. I doubt she'd do anything drastic, but there's never any telling. The idea of her giving in to despair while I lie here sleeping isn't one I can live with.

She must have rolled from her side onto her back, and that's what woke me. Now, she's staring at the ceiling. No pretense of trying to sleep. Her chest rises and falls evenly, but that's just about the only way to tell she's still alive.

"What are you doing awake?" I murmur, rubbing sleep from my eyes.

"I don't know. I've been this way since we lay down. It's not like I'm trying to stay awake."

"Did you try to sleep, though?"

How does a person *try* to sleep?" I don't like the way her voice sounds. How flat and almost dead it is.

"They close their eyes and try to relax."

"I did that already." She turns her head slightly, enough to catch sight of me from the corner of her vision. "Any other ideas?"

Yes, in fact. I know exactly what I would normally do in a situation like this. A way of releasing tension that always works. Something tells me she's not interested at the moment, and after what she's been through today, it wouldn't seem right to suggest it. I hardly recognize myself anymore. If Lauren was here, she might be able to help me make sense of it. Since when do I have a conscience? A sense of right and wrong, fair and otherwise?

"How about talking? I'm here. I have nothing better to do. What's on your mind?"

"Is that a serious question? No offense, but you know what's on my mind." She props the back of her head up on one folded arm before sighing. "Everything I ever thought I knew was a lie. I mean, I knew my father hated me just for being born. I wasn't another son like he wanted. He couldn't be bothered to love me for who I was, but it's not like I asked to be born."

"I know."

"But this? I never figured it was this bad. He threatened my mother. He told her he would kill me if I ever discovered who she was. Why would he do that?"

I'm not sure if that's a rhetorical question. I was never much good at those. "I wouldn't put anything past a man like that. I don't know why he made the choices he made when it came to you."

"I mean, I've always felt alone. I never really had friends. The more I think about it, the more obvious it seems that my mother kept me at arm's length so I wouldn't know how much she cared. She was determined to keep me safe."

"She loved you. She did what she had to do."

"Yeah, and look where it got her. Now she's dead, and somebody might have killed her, and I can't even apologize for all the times I was a real bitch. I didn't make things easy for her. I mean, I tried to stay out of her way as much as I could, but there were times she tried to reach out to me, too. I didn't want to hear it. I didn't care."

"That's not your fault. All kids are like that."

"It's not the same. You know, she probably could have had a much better life without me. All this time, I figured she was lazy and satisfied living in that shithole. Now I wonder, did he make her live there? What if she wanted to leave but was never able to because of me?"

It seems like the longer she thinks about this, the worse it gets. Every question leads to three more. "All you're doing is punishing yourself by dwelling on this."

"It's not like I want to. I'm not doing it on purpose."

She falls silent again, and I wait to see whether she has anything else on her mind. What am I supposed to do about this? How am I supposed to act? I'm not used to wanting to be helpful. Caring.

There's no way not to care after seeing her react to everything that took place in that grimy, grungy trailer. Learning her aunt was dead and that the woman wasn't her aunt at all. And this on the heels of Nathaniel and the whorehouse. How long until she shatters?

How is that any of my concern? Of all the times for me to grow a sense of empathy.

"I'm all alone. I mean, I was before, too. But there was always knowing she was there. I could go back to her if I needed to; if things were so bad that I didn't have any other option. Now I have nobody at all."

"You're young." What a lame fucking thing to say. It's better than blurting out something stupid like offering to be the support she needs. That would be a true mistake.

"What's wrong with me? Why don't I get to have friends and family like everybody else? Don't I deserve that? Why am I always alone?"

"It could be a strength," I point out. "When you don't need people, you can't be hurt by them."

"There's always a way to be hurt by people. They always find a way to surprise you."

It seems unfair for someone so young to be this deeply wounded. "But you're free now, too. No ties, nothing weighing you down. You can start fresh and be whoever you want to be."

I don't know what I expect in response to that. I know better than to think she'll be excited, not in her mood.

But tears? Not happy ones, either. She covers her face, shaking hard enough to shift the mattress under us. "That's a lot," she manages. "I've never been free."

"Now you will be. This is a good thing. You can work to forget all this past shit weighing you down. You're better than that, anyway."

"Since when?"

I can't pretend I don't understand what she means. "You deserve better than what you've gotten so far. That's the truth."

"You're the only person who's ever felt that way. I don't know where I'm going. I don't know what to do. It's too much, all at once. How am I supposed to sleep when I have to start making every decision in my whole life for myself? I've never been able to do that. And before you woke up..."

She lowers her hands with a shuddering sigh. "I'm ashamed to admit this, but I sort of wished things could go back to the way they were. At least then, I knew what was happening. I knew how to handle things."

"You don't want that, really."

"Easy for you to say."

There has to be a way to get her through this. Yet I can't help but ask myself, why do I care? It might be as simple as wanting to get some sleep without the question of whether she'll decide to off herself weighing on my mind, or it could be something else altogether.

"Follow me." I've made up my mind. Climbing out of bed, I pull her along with me.

"What are you doing?" She knows better than to try to fight as I lead her across the room and into the bathroom.

"Helping you relax." I run the shower before peeling off my shorts. "Come on. A hot shower will ease the tension." I have more in mind than that, but the shower is a start. She doesn't hesitate long before pulling Celia's nightshirt over her head, then dropping her panties.

Hunger stirs deep inside, and my cock twitches at the sight of her body as she steps under the steamy spray. By the time water begins running over and dripping from her luscious tits, I'm left battling between the desire to protect and comfort her and the desire to slam into her until we both collapse from exhaustion.

Instead, I soap up a mesh sponge and begin working it over her shoulders and arms. She closes her eyes, tipping her head back so the water runs over her hair and plasters it against her. I can't help but stare, transfixed, almost jealous of the beads tracing lines over her skin even though my hands are on her. Spreading suds, sliding over her firm, creamy ass cheeks, her flat stomach and full tits.

That's where I focus my attention, turning her in place and ditching the sponge in favor of using my hands.

"Mm... that's nice..." she whispers, the sound echoing in the stall. She leans against my chest, letting her head fall back onto my shoulder.

"Let go of everything," I croon in her ear while my hands travel in slow circles over her tits. Her nipples have tightened into peaks that practically beg to be stroked by my thumbs. She gasps when I do it, so I do it again, and again. Until she begins to whimper.

My lips find her throat, and I run them over the expanse of skin, my tongue darting out to lap at her.

"Yes," she whispers. "Yes, please."

My cock surges, pressing against her lower back, but I can't take advantage. My heart's not in it. This is about her.

With one hand still massaging her tits, I slide the other over her stomach. Muscles jump and flutter there, but it does nothing to keep her from spreading her thighs to make room for me. She moans helplessly when I cup her sex, jerking her hips ever so slightly in wordless encouragement.

"That's right." I nip at her throat and savor the way she shivers. "Take what you need. Help me make you come."

"I want to come…" She arches her back with a gasp when I delve between her swollen lips and into her sweet, wet heat. "Oh, yes… so good…" She bears down on my fingers, and I help her by working them in deeper, filling her with two digits and pumping them in and out while my thumb works tight circles over her clit.

"You like that?" I whisper, shoving my fingers as deep inside her as I can manage. Every thrust brings her up onto her tiptoes, the wet, sloppy sound rising over that of the shower. "You like it when I fuck you deep and hard?"

"Yes!" She repeats the word, falling into rhythm with my thrusts. She's mine, all mine, completely under my control. Like clay being molded by my hands, worked into a frenzy, thanks to the way I know what she craves. Complete release, a means of forgetting everything. I know that craving.

"Fuck, come for me." I breathe against her ear, my tongue moving over the lobe. I want to bite her and feel her tight pussy contract around me. "Take what you need from me. Use me."

"I'm… I'm going to…" She goes rigid, silent for a moment before spasming in the throes of her orgasm. Her muscles clench around my fingers, and they're soon soaked down to my knuckles. I keep pumping, rubbing her wall, coaxing more from her.

"Come on," I urge with a chuckle, knowing she's in the grips of sweet agony. "Give me another one before I lick up what's pouring out of that pussy."

"Ohhh... Lucas..." One of her arms snakes around my neck, her fingers threading in my hair and pulling. I reward her by increasing the pressure on her G-spot. "Oh, god, yes!" she sobs.

"Good girl." Her release drips to the floor and mixes with the falling water, and fuck me, there's nothing like this. Having this power over her body, over her soul. She's mine, shaking and moaning and senseless in my arms once the strongest waves have passed.

It isn't enough. I need her completely wiped out—not to mention the way a whiff of her arousal makes my mouth water. I need to taste her. To drink her.

I turn her around and lean her against the wall before lowering myself and draping her left leg over my shoulder. She barely rouses herself enough to open her eyes and cast a puzzled look down at me.

"More?" she whispers, still fighting to regain her breath.

I answer by extending my tongue and running it down the length of her slit. She flinches when the pressure against her sensitive flesh is too much, but I hold her in place and force her to take what I'm giving. Even when she pulls on my hair, her high-pitched whimpers giving away her desperation, I hold on. She's going to accept this. I know what she needs.

Seconds later, she relaxes into it, her jerking hips slowing, the motions sensual now. Instead of pulling my head away, she holds it in place, tilting her pelvis, so her pussy is wide open to me. I slide my tongue up inside her, past her quivering hole.

"Yeah, just like that," she pleads. "Fuck me."

I can't ignore my cock any longer. My hand closes around it, and I stroke in time with the thrusts from my tongue. She's wild now, humping my face, her heel digging into my back. My scalp is starting to sting, but it's good. It's all good. I wouldn't tell her to stop for anything. This is the only way we can connect now. In this place we've created together with our bodies.

She floods my tongue with endless musky sweetness a moment before I spray the wall with my cum. I swallow every drop of her while coming down from my high and stand in barely enough time to support her limp body before it slides to the floor.

"My god..." Her head lolls against me while I rinse her off, then myself. I turn off the water, open the shower door, and grab one of the towels hanging from a hook nearby. She hardly reacts as I dry her off before carrying her to the bed.

By the time I lay her down, she's out cold, a soft smile curving her plump lips. I stroke them with the tip of my thumb before toweling off and joining her.

This time, we both sleep soundly.

10

DELILAH

*I*t's still too weird being here. There's always tension in the air, no matter how nice Celia tries to be. And she does try. I can tell. Even when I don't feel much like smiling or sounding pleasant, the way she keeps trying to lighten things up at the breakfast table makes me feel like I should at least give it my best effort.

"You're going to want to go shopping for more clothes, I assume," she muses. I don't have the heart to tell her I've never equated shopping with good times, not the way other girls probably did.

Nobody ever handed me a credit card and told me to go crazy. Just the opposite. Having to add up the numbers on the tags to check whether I had enough to afford everything, even at the thrift store. Hunting around in hopes of finding a pair of shoes that matched on the disorganized shelves.

Knowing no matter how I tried, I'd never look good enough. That doesn't exactly equate to happy times.

I shrug. "Maybe. Though I have enough to get by for now."

Living in a house like this, I wonder if she understands what it means to have just enough and not a little bit extra. She moves and speaks and even eats like a rich person, the way I remember my family doing during the few visits I was permitted to go to.

She didn't come from nothing the way I have. Not that I hold it against her. None of us can do much about how and where we were born.

"If you don't have time to shop, I could always give you a few things. We're the same size, after all."

"It isn't that I don't have time. I don't know where the money is coming from, and I don't take money aimlessly."

"Then that's even more of a reason to take some of mine. Please, I don't need half of it."

She's trying hard to be nice. But dammit, I can't keep gritting my teeth. "I'm not a charity case." Pain is etched between her bunched eyebrows. Right away, I feel bad. "Sorry," I mumble.

"You don't have to apologize. I didn't realize how condescending that could come off." She sighs while picking up her coffee cup. "Sometimes, I forget what it's like to be where you are now. Like you're hanging in limbo."

"You know how that feels?"

Her head bobs up and down, her eyes wide. "Oh, yes. It's frustrating and scary when everything is moving around you so fast, and you don't know who you can trust. You might even feel like you can't trust yourself because you start liking things and even people you know you should hate. It makes you question who you are—the real you, deep down inside. It's scary enough when your life is in danger without all that confusion in your head."

"Honestly? It's hard to imagine you ever feeling that way."

She snorts softly. "You never saw the before. You're only looking at the after." There are footsteps outside the doorway, and her eyes seek out the source.

I watch as her face lights up and know it has to be Nic. It's hard to imagine a time when she didn't light up at his presence, but I'm not dumb. I can connect the dots. They didn't have it easy in the beginning.

Lucas is with him, and the way he drops into the chair beside mine tells me all I need to know about the conversation he had with his brother.

He takes food from the covered platters seemingly at random, filling his plate before sloshing coffee into his cup.

"Good morning," Nic murmurs after kissing his wife. "Sorry to have kept you ladies waiting." His tone is cordial, but he keeps shooting looks at Lucas, who's obviously going out of his way to pretend he doesn't notice.

He doesn't have me fooled. I see the way the muscles in his jaw keep twitching as he stares down at his plate, pushing food around with a fork before shoveling it in his mouth.

I can't shake the feeling this is about me. Nic's been civil toward me, but that's about as far as it goes. He'll have me in his house, but that doesn't make us friends. I'm sure there's liability involved with harboring somebody like me. He has a wife and a kid. He doesn't need my drama.

And it's like he can hear my thoughts. His gaze flicks over to me before landing on his brother again. "Word has already spread of what happened."

All of a sudden, the fresh blueberry muffin on my plate doesn't look so appetizing.

Lucas doesn't react beyond the flaring of his nostrils. I get the feeling this announcement is for my benefit, not his. "Preston made sure everyone knows about it," Nic continues, staring at his brother. If he looked at me the way he's looking at Lucas, I'd probably wet my pants. The man has turned glowering into an art form. He's even better at it than Lucas.

Maybe it's a family trait.

Celia shoots me an apologetic look. I know she feels sorry for me, the way any woman would. What would she have done in my place? Nobody would willingly let something like that happen without at least trying to defend themselves. Lucas is silent. I can feel the heat of his anger rolling off him.

"Have they used my name?" I murmur, dreading the response.

"They know it was you." My mouth opens when the next question follows, but he predicts it. "I don't know how. Nathaniel might've reached out to Preston after Lucas's first visit. For all we know, it could've been Preston's idea to get you out of there before we came to free you. Somehow, he knows it was you, Delilah, that his old man took from the whorehouse."

I hate that word. It's the least of my problems, but I hate that word. I heard some of those girls talking to their customers and to each other through the walls. One of them would sing to herself—the walls were so thin, we might as well have been in the same room. She had a nice voice. I wonder what happened to her. All of those girls were just like me, maybe even tricked into being there the way I was. Locked in. They weren't whores. They were victims.

"It's a good thing I'm not going back to Corium." I pick at the muffin, watching Lucas out of the corner of my eye. He's going to explode. I know it. It's only a matter of when. "Things were bad enough as it was before I killed someone. They'd probably put a price on my head."

"Actually. You are going back," Lucas announces.

I must've imagined it. No way did those words come out of Lucas's mouth. He messed something up in my head last night when we were in the shower. I had never come so hard, for so long. Maybe I popped a blood vessel in my brain or something? Because I swear, I just heard him say...

Unfortunately, Celia heard it, too. "But she—" I look at her and find her wincing at Nic. I guess she's not supposed to speak up. I'm sure women in this world don't get a lot of say over anything. My birth mother sure didn't.

Lucas finally decides to turn his attention to me. "That's how it's going to be. You're going to Corium."

My heart skips a beat. "But you said—"

"I know what I said. Things are different now that they all know what happened—sorry, Preston's version of what happened."

Nic leans in, scowling. "That's not what we discussed, dammit. You would dangle her in front of the rest of the kids there?"

Lucas holds up a finger. "No, committing murder. That's the only rule, and they know better than to break it."

"I see." Nic glances my way before muttering, "So I guess the plan for Aspen was to... what? Prank her while she was unconscious?"

"Don't do that." Lucas drops the fork onto the plate before shoving his chair back from the table. "Don't fucking make jokes about that."

"Who's joking? You know damn well what they would've done to her if Q hadn't followed her that night." Now Nic doesn't bother to hide his feelings, glaring at me. "What was the plan?"

"I didn't know anything about it. They were using me. That's all."

He snorts, but I think he believes me. How could he not? The whole plan is painfully obvious now that I look back on it. I was never a partner in it. Just a pawn. The way I've been my entire life.

"My point is, how do you expect to keep her safe when—" Nic's mouth snaps shut, but a second too late. It would've been better if he'd stopped himself before he started. Even I know what he was about to say.

How could you expect to keep her safe when you couldn't keep your daughter safe?

Lucas launches himself at Nic, hauling him from his chair while Celia and I look on in horror. "I warned you to watch your fucking mouth. You know it's rare to get a second warning out of me."

"You need to listen to reason for once." Nic doesn't look very worried about having Lucas's hands dangerously close to his neck. I guess this isn't the first time things have gotten to this point between them. Not surprising. They both appear to be hot heads.

"Since when do you give out advice about listening to reason? Since when do you listen to it?" He shoots a quick look at Celia, who shrinks back a little bit. "Last time I checked, you've made questionable choices in the past. And when I brought them to your attention, you weren't hearing any of it."

Nic snickers, looking Lucas up and down. "Finally. You're admitting it."

I have no idea what's happening. What Nic's talking about, or why Lucas lets go of him with a muttered curse. I only know those four words changed the energy in the dining room. Lucas sits back down and pulls his chair in. Meanwhile, Nic signals for Celia to follow him out of the room. He takes her hand in his and pulls her close to his body. I can see the love he has for her in his eyes, the way his features grow softer with her now in his arms.

"You need to think this one through again," he suggests in a quiet voice on the way past our chairs.

I'm so damn lost. And it feels weird sitting here with Lucas when he's clearly in the mood to damage something. Seconds tick by, and I remain silent, waiting for him to speak.

I don't know how much longer I'm going to be able to stay silent on this. Even if he's in a dangerous mood. His mood swings are enough to give me whiplash, and it's my life hanging in the balance. Don't I get a say in this? The courage builds, and from there, I finally gather up the strength to speak.

"I thought you wanted me to have a new start." I stare down at the plate, willing myself not to look at him. If I do, I might cry, and I'm tired of crying.

"I did—do."

My gaze escapes the plate, and I find myself staring at him. It's amazing I can understand him, his jaw is clenched so tight.

"But now I'm going back to Corium with you? Why?"

"Why do you need to know?" The way he looks at me brings back memories of those first days. He was so hateful and cold. How can he look at me that way again? Like last night never happened, like his gentleness after rescuing me was my imagination playing tricks. *No!* I'm not going to let him intimidate me the way I used to.

I lift my chin and somehow manage to speak even though I can't stop trembling under his cold gaze. "Because it's my life. You had me thinking I'd start making my own choices, and now it's all changed again."

He stands again, breakfast forgotten. "You were the one who wanted things to go back to the way they were before, right? You wanted somebody else to make your choices for you and all that, remember?" The gruffness of his voice slices right through me. "Well, you've got what you wanted."

I wince before I can help it and the darkness in his gaze lessens, becoming softer. He's said and done a lot of terrible things to me. He's hurt me deeper than most people ever have, which is saying something, but that was low. He took something I confessed in private and used it against me.

"Listen." He looks almost sorry, but I'm not stupid. I don't think he's capable of true remorse. "How am I supposed to let you go off on your own now when I know there are people out there who might want revenge for killing Nathaniel? I can't keep an eye on you and manage a school at the same time. Tell me you under-stand that you'd be safer at Corium?"

No. I don't. "Nic said it already. They could do all kinds of things to me there without actually killing me." Not to mention the way Aspen murdered Nash in the dorms. She's still there. Living like a queen, treated like her shit doesn't stink.

"But the chances of that happening are much slimmer than if you were in an apartment of your own. I'm sorry, but this is for the best." He marches out of the room before I can reply, but it doesn't matter. I wouldn't know what to say, and it would only be a waste of breath anyway. He has his mind made up.

It doesn't seem right that I'm not completely upset about the change in plans. I wasn't looking forward to living on my own, not only because I don't know much about navigating my own life. It was his idea to send me away in the first place. Not mine.

Now, there's a reason to still be around him. That was what hurt the most. Knowing he didn't want me around. Having to look forward to the rest of my lonely life without him. It's not right. I know it isn't.

But that doesn't change how I feel. I don't have to be alone, and I know he won't let anything happen to me at school.

Ironically, it might be the safest place in the world. `

11

LUCAS

*O*nce again, it's late at night, and one of us is wide awake. This time, though, I'm the one staring at the ceiling while Delilah sleeps peacefully.

That isn't the only difference. Rather than cuddling up close to me the way she's been doing since we got here, there's an ocean between us. Only a couple of feet in this king-size bed, but it may as well be a mile.

I don't have to wonder why. She's just as upset with me now as she was earlier today. I don't know what she wants from me. I'm handling this the only way I can: scrambling to adjust to each new twist.

One thing I know for sure. No way would I be able to function as anything close to a human being with the threat of her being in danger hanging over my every move and thought.

I doubt there's anywhere on earth I could hide her where the Brookshires wouldn't eventually find her and exact what I'm sure to them would feel like justice. As if a single one of them has the first idea about what justice truly means. If they did, they'd slink off into a hole and cover themselves with dirt. After everything that filthy, depraved family put her through, they'd have no right to blame her. But they would.

The worst part is, in another life, I would have done the same. Without knowing her, I would have made the mistake of assuming her guilt. I might have even enjoyed hearing stories of how she was brought to task for her sins. It would have appealed to the animal in me, the primal side of my nature.

And now I'm lying here wondering how many times I passed judgment and deemed the wrong party guilty. How much self-recrimination can a man take in one night?

Fuck this. The longer I lie here, the more I blame myself. I've never been one of those people into self-flagellation. If I'm going to hurt, I want it to be at the hands of another. I'd much rather take my frustrations out on someone else.

It's been a long time since I've done this but knowing it doesn't keep me from climbing out of bed as quietly as I can and leaving the bedroom to make a phone call. It's barely midnight—earlier than I would normally go to bed, but I was naïvely hoping to talk things out with Delilah before going to sleep.

There I was, assuming she'd be too upset to do more than lie there and dwell, the way she did last night. When am I going to learn it's a waste of time to concern myself with what I think others might be going through?

I touch a finger to a specific name in my contacts, one I haven't so much as glanced at in ages. A familiar voice meets my ear, and instantly, I'm transported back to what feels like another life.

"Lucas Diavolo," he grunts, sounding unimpressed. "To what do I owe the honor?" There's a lot of background noise, telling me I'm interrupting an evening on the town.

"It's great hearing your voice, too, Eli," I retort. "I need a fight. Tonight."

That changes his tune in a hurry. A fight for me means money for him, even if this is rather last minute. Once he sends out the heads-up, anyone familiar with his operation will come running. I've never disappointed a crowd.

"Why didn't you say so?" Now he is every inch the showman. "I can put something together within the hour."

I have no doubt. There are plenty of men out there desperate enough for a payday like the one promised by a fight like this. They'll jump at the opportunity to risk their lives, and that's exactly what they'll be doing. The fight won't end until only one of us is breathing. I hate to ruin anybody's hopes, but when all is said and done, I won't be the one getting dragged out and disposed of.

YES. This is what I needed. This energy, seething and roiling, is intense enough that it almost takes on a life of its own. That's the energy hanging over the old warehouse Eli reserved for this event. The smell of sweat and smoke permeates the air, and I'm brought back in time.

Charlotte didn't want to come. I had to force her into it.

"What?" I taunt her on the way to the fight, a bottle of whiskey in one hand while I use the other to drive. "You don't think you have the stomach to watch me kill a man?" I laugh when she turns her face away and wraps her arms around herself like she needs protection.

As if that would do anything to protect her from me.

"You don't have to do this," she whispers.

"That's where you're wrong. I do have to do this," I growl. She is always trying to find the good in me and make me into something I'm not.

The entire way into the venue—the basement of an empty apartment building—she hangs back, all big eyes and jumpy body language. It turns me on. Watching her shrink back and shiver at the sight of my world, here where I feel most at home. Most like myself.

Her golden head stands out among the rest in the smoke-filled space. Something about her being here—the perfectly beautiful, pure, sweet Charlotte—brings something out of me I rarely experience. A darkness I have only ever brushed against. I'm not only in it to win. I want to destroy and cause unimaginable pain and suffering. I want to tear my opponent to pieces with my bare hands while she watches. While I force her to watch.

As long as I live, I'll never forget staring her in the eye as I drove my fist into what was left of that guy's face again and again until I finally had to be pulled off the body, blood-soaked and unrecognizable. And still, I didn't look away from her. And she didn't look away from me, though I knew damn well that was all she wanted to do. She wanted to run away from me and never look back. But she didn't. Because she knew then that there was no escaping me once I decided what was mine.

A flash of golden hair in the crowd catches my attention, and I find myself following the girl's progress as she weaves through the bodies. The ache in my chest at the opportunity makes me want to follow her, just to see if it is, so I can demand she watches me slaughter another stranger.

It's not her, though. It can't be. She's dead.

Shaking my head, I let the thoughts blow like grains of sand in the wind. I need to get out of my fucking head if I plan to walk out of here alive.

Clearly, time spent away from this world hasn't done anything to lessen my reputation. As soon as I begin to make my way toward the empty space in the center of the floor, the crowd begins to part, all eyes on me. I hear my name whispered, the sounds overlapping. Like they heard I might have been one of the fighters tonight but didn't believe it until I walked in.

Eli is waiting, grinning by the time I reach him. "I hope you know I had to pull strings to get this together at the last minute."

"Bullshit," I growl while glancing around the room. There are people everywhere. People wait with bated breath for a fight like this, a chance to place a bet and make big money. This didn't take string pulling; all it took was a text telling them tonight could be the night they win big.

I shake off the negative energy and let my thoughts drift away.

My body is a live wire, my heart thunders in my chest, and adrenaline rushes through my veins. All I need is a look at my opponent to get an idea of my plan of attack.

I set my sights on a mountain of muscle, surrounded by a handful of women batting their eyes and looking like they want to take turns riding his cock. I've never met the guy before, but it's better in this type of thing when you've never met each other.

Before Eli has to tell me, I jerk my chin in his direction.

"Is that the guy?"

He nods. "Five fights in, and he's undefeated."

So he'll feel like he has something to prove. Especially against me since I'm undefeated as well—and I have many more kills under my belt. There's nothing like one of these matches to balance me out, and I needed a lot more balancing in the past.

He thinks this is the night that will make him a legend. And it might. Just not for the reason he thinks.

I strip off my shirt and toss it aside before kicking off my shoes. He's already done so, and now he begins stretching, staring at me the entire time. I return his steely glare while sizing him up.

He's big, telling me there's a good chance he'll rely on brute strength alone. His ham-sized fists can do a great deal of damage in a short amount of time. I'll have to avoid his punches, but then I've always known how to move smoothly and quickly.

Besides, there's more than pride pushing me to do this. That's what sets me apart and always has. Skill and experience.

That extra something, the quality that sets me apart, is the desire to exorcize my demons until there's nothing left but a dead body at my feet. A mass of bloody flesh that used to be a living, breathing man.

"Two minutes!" Eli calls out. "Betting ends in two minutes. Get yours in while you can." An obscene amount of money changes hands every time another spectator approaches him. I wonder absently about the odds he called. It doesn't matter, though the furtive glances I keep observing from those placing their last-minute bets make me think they expect to make a bundle on me.

I'm not in the same shape I was in the past, but I'm smarter and wiser. I've been down this road more than once, and even though I might appear to be an old man, I'm not.

Finally, Eli holds his hands up, standing in the center of the cleared space. He has guys positioned in even intervals, forming a circle around where we'll do our fighting. Just in case somebody decides they want to jump in and stop the fight—or if one of us decides they didn't bargain for this. Either way, there's no leaving or entering until the fight ends.

"Betting is now closed!" he shouts. "Our fighters know the rules. Only one man leaves. As usual, spectators are forbidden to enter the fight space." The excited murmuring quiets down until there's nothing but the sound of at least a hundred people taking a deep breath and holding it in anticipation.

Eli looks at me. He looks at my opponent, whose name I haven't learned and have no intention of learning. No sense humanizing the guy when he'll be dead in a few minutes.

"Fight!" Eli backs away, and my opponent wastes no time. He's not particularly quick, so I easily sidestep him before throwing a jab at his kidneys. He responds by pivoting, his fist cocked, as he drives it against my ribs before the other fist connects with my jaw hard enough to make me see stars.

Fuck, the man can hit.

I fall back a few steps, fists raised, shifting my weight from one foot to the other while waiting for the right moment. He throws another punch, but I easily block it, though not so for the jab to my right eye.

I recover quickly before landing a kick against his sternum that knocks the wind out of him. He staggers back a step, and I use his reaction to my advantage, bringing my leg up and around in a roundhouse that sends his head snapping to one side before he falls to his knees.

"Come on!" I bark along with so many others who made the mistake of throwing their money away on him. He gets on his feet, his face dark red with either rage or embarrassment. Which I'm not sure, nor do I really care.

The sight of it is like a white-hot knife sliding into my gut. He thought that was embarrassing? Now I want to punish him simply for thinking he was any match for me.

I wave him forward, grinning, and his rage makes him clumsy. He charges straight for me, and I reward him with another solid kick to his right knee. Even over the sound of my pounding heart and the cheering from the crowd, there's no muffling the popping sound his knee makes when I connect with it.

He goes down on that knee, and I do the same to the other. Rather than fall on his side helplessly, he wraps both arms around my calves and pulls me down with him. I land on my back but kick my way free before he can throw his considerable body weight on top of me. He sprawls face-first but rolls onto his back before I can take advantage.

This is almost too easy, and I hate him for it. I came here for a challenge, a way of clearing my head of everything getting in my way.

He's not even a challenge. He's nothing. A pothole in the road that I'll easily overstep. The sound of the crowd is a familiar one as their cheering takes on an almost sinister note.

They're just as thirsty for blood as I am. I jump to my feet and walk in a wide circle around my suffering opponent, the once powerful man now watching me like a hawk, looking to see what I'll do next. I'm a lion on the prowl, a predator ready to take out its prey and enjoy an evening with a belly full of food.

He has to know the end is near, doesn't he? I even let him try to stand while I catch my breath, and I watch in disgust as he barely makes it halfway before collapsing again. His eyes widen in evident fear as I charge toward him.

How dare he be this easy to defeat? He doesn't deserve to breathe the same air as me, much less to fight me the way he thought he could.

He shakes his head ever so slightly when I reach him, and somehow that only enrages me further, so much so that I take him by the head and press my thumbs against his eyes.

His screams ring out a moment later while he fights desperately to shove me off, landing blow after blow against my thighs, ribs, and arms.

The blows don't phase me. Nothing seems to matter more at that moment. Something has taken hold of me, the same something that always does at this moment. I hear nothing else but his screams. I see nothing else but his agony as I dig my thumbs deep into his sockets, feeling the warmth of blood on my hands as it begins to drip down his cheeks.

Finally, both eyes give way with a satisfying, if slightly stomach-churning, squelching sound, and his screams turn to high-pitched shrieks.

"Finish him!"

"Fucking kill him!"

"Get it over with!"

Not yet. Not until I hold his bleeding head in the crook of my left arm while taking hold of his mouth with my right.

I insert my fingers, then curl them around his lower jaw. He flails blindly, still shrieking, and the sound only intensifies when I manage to tear the lower half of his jaw away from the upper half. Blood pours from his mouth, splattering on the floor, splashing against my arm and up to my elbow.

The crowd's cheers have lessened as more and more of them react in horror. I take a long look around and find identical expressions of dismay on the faces that were, moments ago, flushed and glowing with excitement. And all the while, he screams wordlessly.

With a quick snap, I break the poor bastard's neck and let him drop into the pool of his blood. It splatters upward, painting my chest while I stand victorious over him, my chest heaving, his blood dripping from my hands.

What would Charlotte think if she saw me now? My gaze sweeps over the crowd, but I don't see that golden head anymore, the one so much like hers.

Eli steps up. "The winner!" He takes hold of my wrist and raises it above my head. There's cheering again, louder from those who've made money tonight. I'm panting, sore from the few blows he managed to connect, but for the first time in forever, I feel clean. My mind is crystal clear, unclouded.

I remember who I am now, and fuck if I've missed him.

12

DELILAH

"*No!*"

The sound of my cry is still hanging in the air when my eyes snap open. My heart's on overdrive, thumping against my ribs so hard each beat is an ache, and a cold sweat has soaked into my pillow.

I was dreaming about that place. That room. Only this time, there was nothing for me to use as a weapon. I was at Nathaniel's mercy. I shake my head, willing the nightmare away. He's dead. He'll never be able to hurt me again.

It takes a second for me to realize there's still something wrong here. I cried out, but nobody tried to comfort me. Nobody even reacted.

I roll onto my back to find Lucas's side of the bed empty. I touch a hand to the pillow. It's cold. He hasn't been in bed for a while.

"Lucas?" I whisper, climbing out of bed and tiptoeing to the bathroom door. Why do I feel like I have to be quiet?

There's something about a dark bedroom in the middle of the night, I guess. Besides, if he's in there because he's feeling sick or something, I'm sure he won't appreciate me being all loud and obnoxious about it.

Except the bathroom is dark when I reach it.

The already sweat-dampened hair at the back of my neck stands up while goose bumps pebble my arms. He's probably somewhere else in the house. Maybe he couldn't sleep and decided to watch TV, or he got hungry and went downstairs for a snack. I have to stop thinking the worst all the time. Just because my life has been pretty fucked up at times doesn't mean everything is fucked up.

Some good always comes with the bad, right?

I should stay here and wait for him, but I doubt I'll be able to fall back asleep. Besides, my side of the bed is sweaty and uncomfortable now. After a few moments, I make up my mind and decide to search for him before pulling the blankets back so the sheets can at least dry up and be more comfortable when I return. Then I head out into the hall, which is dark and quiet.

Something is unsettling about it. It must be my nightmare, and the little bits of it that still cling to my brain, that have me freaked out. By morning, I'm sure I'll forget it—the dream, if not the situation.

I just need to keep reminding myself that when the time came, I was my own hero. I will also need to remember that once I'm back at Corium and under the judgmental glares of so many people who don't have the first idea about what it's like to face what I faced.

I pad down the stairs barefoot, listening hard for any signs of him. There's nothing that sounds like a conversation. No TV or music. As I wander the halls, I can't shake the feeling of being an intruder. Maybe I should have brought breadcrumbs along with me to leave a trail back to the bedroom. The farther I get away from it, the more confused I become.

I'm not used to being anywhere this big, except for Corium. And it took me a minute to get the lay of the land there, too.

The only thing that keeps me moving is knowing he would never leave me here alone. I don't belong here as it is, but especially not without him. Still, why would he leave me alone in the middle of the night? What is he thinking?

I've just reached the kitchen and flipped on the lights when a noise coming from the front of the house seizes my heart and makes it stand still for a split second. I watch, frozen like a scared rabbit, staring down the hall toward the heavy door. It has to be him. No way could a random person wander in and out of this place at any time of the day, but especially not at this time of night.

Sure enough, I recognize his size and shape, backlit by the fixtures on either side of the entrance. His face is hidden in the shadows, so I can't get a look at his expression. I only know for sure he's locked his gaze on me. I feel it. Penetrating deep into my bones.

"The fuck do you think you're doing?"

My teeth sink into my lip as I weigh my options. Honesty seems the only way to go. "I was looking for you. I woke up from a nightmare and couldn't find you."

He closes the door before punching a code into the alarm system to keep it from wailing out his arrival. Maybe if I make a run for it, he won't be able to catch me. Where would I go? I only know there's something dangerous about him right now. I don't even know if I've ever seen this side of him.

Fear roots me to the spot by the time he begins stalking toward me. That's the word for it, too. An animal with prey in its sights. His hands are fisted, and he's breathing heavily.

What did I do this time? Why do I deserve this now?

It's only once he's close enough that the light I just turned on in the kitchen washes over his face, and the sight makes me recoil, my fear forgotten.

"What happened to you?" Reflex makes me reach up to touch his bruised jaw. The mark is dark purple, ugly, and covers most of his cheek. The eye on that side is a little swollen, too, with a big bruise forming beside it and a cut running through his eyebrow.

He slaps my hand away before I can make contact, then takes hold of that same wrist and squeezes hard. "You were just looking for me, huh? That's all you were trying to do?" Now that he's this close, I can smell the whiskey on his breath. It doesn't bode well for me. He's obviously not thinking clearly.

"Yes. You weren't there. I was worried."

"You were worried?" he taunts before laughing nastily. "You thought something bad happened to me? As if you could do anything about it even if something did happen. Try again."

There's no talking reason into somebody who's beyond this point.

"What else would it be?" I whisper. The sight of his hate-filled eyes makes me tear mine away. Only now, I'm staring at what's obviously dried blood on his hands and wrists. A lot of it, too.

He snickers. "What? You don't like seeing me bloody? What if I told you the guy who bled all over me is dead because I killed him in a fight?"

"You did?" I can barely get the sound out through my tight throat.

"And then I drank half a fucking bottle of whiskey because I could. Because I'm alive, and he's not." He hauls me close, and yes, the coppery stench of blood is all over him now that I'm up against him. "And what do I find when I get back? I find you trying to run away."

Fear trickles down my spine. "I wasn't! Where would I go?"

"You've snuck away in the past. How the fuck should I know?" I don't have time to come up with a defense for that before he makes up his mind, bending slightly and throwing me over his shoulder.

"What are you doing?" I try to kick out with both legs, but there's no budging the iron bar of an arm he's wrapped around my thighs.

"Taking you back where you belong," he snarls, bouncing me as he marches toward the stairs. Fear has me in its grip now. I know what's coming next.

On the way up the stairs, he mutters to himself, "Think you can leave me... you belong to me... ungrateful bitch..."

Tears fill my eyes, but I know arguing with him is useless. I'm not ungrateful. I wasn't trying to leave. I don't know where his mind is right now, but it's not here with me.

He barely takes time to close the bedroom door behind us before marching me across the room and throwing me onto the bed. I land hard enough to almost bounce off, but he blocks me with his body to stop that from happening. I manage to get on my hands and knees and start scrambling for the corner of the bed, but he's too quick for that, too.

"Running away again?" He grabs me by my ankle and tugs hard. I grab for the blankets, anything to stop this, but it's no use.

"Why are you doing this?" I'm talking to myself since Lucas yanks down my shorts and thong at the same time, his short nails breaking my skin and making me hiss in pain. Instead of stopping him, it seems to egg him on. He delivers a hard, unforgiving slap against the place where he scratched me, and I howl with my face pressed against the mattress.

"You can do better than that." He strikes me again, on the other cheek this time, and I yelp from the force. Blazing-hot pain radiates from that spot outward.

"No, stay that way," he growls when I try to lift my head. To help things, he puts a hand on the back of my neck and presses me farther into the mattress. Over the sound of my heart, I hear him lower his zipper.

"There's got to be a way I can teach you," he grunts, parting my thighs with his knee. "You belong to me. Your life is mine. Your body is mine. And this cunt?" He even slaps me there, hard.

"This is mine. Say it. It's mine. Your pussy is mine."

I'm delirious with need, with hate and rage.

He slaps that sensitive area again when I don't react last enough. It feels like it's on fire. "It's yours!" I shout. "It's yours, okay? Please, stop!"

"You tell me it's mine, but then you tell me I can't use it? What are we going to do about these mixed messages?"

I grit my teeth, my pulse thunders, and the burning rage toward him threatens to overflow. I don't get to answer him because suddenly, he's inside me, breaching my entrance and plowing ahead even though I'm dry.

I dig my fingers into the blankets. My body trembles, and pain ripples through my core, but that doesn't stop him. A sense of déjà vu overcomes me, and for a moment, I'm back in that cell, back to being helpless and used by a man supposed to protect me.

"Please, Lucas, it hurts."

"Not ready yet?" He spits, and his wet saliva hits my crack. He pulls out and drags his head through the wetness before entering me again. It's only slightly less uncomfortable.

"Asshole!" I growl, wanting to hurt him as badly as he's hurting me.

With the fingers of his other hand biting into my hip, he sets a rough, brutal pace. Unforgiving and unfeeling. I might as well not be here. I'm just a warm hole for him to fill. That is until he starts talking, and then I know he's speaking directly to me.

"I go out of my way for you... I risk everything, go against my family... and what do I get?" Every grunted phrase is punctuated by another thrust.

I can't answer him or even defend myself thanks to the way he holds me down, face-first. I start pounding my fists against the mattress, my lungs seize, the need for oxygen overcoming me.

When I'm sure he's going to kill me, the hand at the back of my head eases, and I gulp in a single breath before he pushes me down again. Is he trying to kill me? Death by sex might be a great way to go, but I'm not ready to die yet. As he continues to fuck me, a deep warmth fills my belly. Each stroke rubs against a spot at the back of my channel that I didn't even know existed.

The pain turns to pleasure, and the chaos of our rage becomes something beautiful. Intense pleasure threatens to consume me.

"Fucking beautiful." He laughs. "Look how wet you get once my cock is inside you. My cock. Only mine." Yes, only his because I can't imagine another one making me feel this way. Nobody ever has. Nobody ever wanted to.

Even though this is completely twisted and unthinkable, I still want him.

I even want this. The tension grows, the tightness building in my core until I have no choice but to explode. I press my knees against the mattress and use them for leverage, pushing back against him, deepening the pleasure.

"Oh god!!" I pant against the sheets.

The pressure against the back of my neck disappears only to be replaced a second later by a bright, stinging sensation that zings across my scalp as Lucas winds my hair around his fist and pulls. "You're going to come for me. I can feel it. Feel your pussy quivering and weeping for my cock," he declares. "And I want to hear it. Let it out. Come for me, slut."

I don't have a choice, nor would I want to stop.

Every deep thrust takes me closer to the edge until finally, he buries himself balls deep. I lose all sense of time and place and myself as a shattering orgasm races through me from head to toe, and I scream.

I scream in pleasure. I scream in confusion and anger toward Lucas, toward me. I don't understand myself. I don't understand what he does to me.

All I know is there's a deep satisfaction in feeling his hot cum splash over my ass and thighs. It's like he's marking me, and some fucked-up part of me wants him to. I want him to use me, mark me, but most of all, I want to be his.

When he's finally finished, he lets go of my hair and backs away, breathing heavily. I don't have the strength to even hold up my head. My whole body sags into the mattress.

"Go clean yourself up," he orders.

I'm still coming down from my high and shaking from head to toe, but I'm not about to argue with him. I hurry to the bathroom, closing the door behind me before I take a deep breath. *What the fuck just happened?*

Grabbing a washcloth from the cabinet, I soak it in warm soapy water to clean myself. Even with me going as gently as I can, the cloth feels uncomfortable against my swollen pussy lips.

When I'm all clean, I return to the bedroom with my head hung low, eyes downcast.

What happens next?

"Now go to bed." He walks past me, answering my unspoken question. He waltzes into the bathroom and closes the door without another word. A moment later, I hear the shower running and release a sigh of relief. Maybe he'll be in a better mood once he gets out.

But what about tomorrow, and every day after that? I don't know how much longer I can take being in the presence of somebody whose mood changes so quickly and with no explanation.

Don't I at least deserve to know why he does these things?

Rather than wait up in hopes of getting answers—I know I'll never get them—I crawl into bed and pull the blankets over my shoulders before closing my eyes. I'm not asleep when the door to the bathroom opens. I hold my breath, wondering if he'll have another episode of rage, but his steps are lighter. A moment later, I feel him slide into bed beside me.

The smell of his soap tickles my nostrils, and I suck a ragged breath into my lungs, letting it calm me. Despite our turbulent, Lucas is the only thing in my life that seems to be constant. After a moment, I feel him move closer, the heat of his body radiates through me, and I move closer out of instinct, the need to be cocooned by him.

"You're a light in this dark world. I just hope I don't dull that light," he whispers into my hair as he wraps his arm around me and pulls me close. I want to tell him my light shines through fractured pieces and that he can't dull me, but I don't. Instead, I succumb to his body's warmth and my mind's exhaustion.

13

LUCAS

She won't look at me.

I could probably set myself on fire, and she wouldn't look at me.

I'd do it, too, if it meant making up for last night. That's the part of life I hate the most. Having to face myself in the morning.

It was much easier back when I could drink it all away. I woke up feeling like the world's biggest piece of shit after using a woman for my pleasure. I'd pick up a bottle and blot out the memory until enough time passed that I couldn't remember what happened anymore.

That was then. Now I'm older, supposedly wiser. It doesn't stop me from making the same shit choices.

"Celia give you that?" I mutter, gesturing toward the leather tote and the folded garments inside. She's laid it on the bed and is now adding her own clothes to the stash. A short nod is the only response I get. Heat spreads in my chest and warms my face. Goddammit, can't she tell I'm trying?

Of course she can't. That would mean looking inside my head and seeing how much I wish things hadn't gone the way they did last night. If I could only make her understand. I don't have the words to do it. I've never been good at this kind of thing, apologizing and making amends.

Lauren would skin me alive if she knew I'd sunk so low again. I'm supposed to be better than this by now.

"I'm ready." Delilah zips the bag and lifts it from the bed before I can close a hand around the straps.

"Let me," I offer.

She shakes her head, then walks from the room. Message received. She knows how to put a man in his place, this one. Either that or I know I deserve it, which only makes things worse. There was a time I wouldn't have thought twice about my actions from the night before. I wish I could go back to that time, so brushing her off and dismissing her anger would be easy.

"You have everything?" Celia asks Delilah before looking up at me as I descend the stairs. She's obviously tense, rubbing her hands against her thighs. She's dreading this for Delilah.

"I do. Thank you so much for everything." She turns to Nic, who's standing by the door. He might as well shove her through it, he's so obviously ready to see us gone. "Thank you for finding me and for letting me stay here. I know it makes things uncomfortable for you."

"Don't worry yourself. That wasn't your fault." There's a great deal of meaning between the lines, and he damn well knows it. She might not hear his true meaning, but I do. It was my fault. I let her get away, to begin with, even if it was my daughter who freed her.

We still need to have a talk about that when I return. I make a mental note of it as I say my goodbyes. Celia gives me a quick hug before shooting me a plea with her eyes. I'm not sure who she's more concerned with, Delilah or me, and I don't know how to respond. I settle for an awkward pat on the shoulder before turning to my brother, who merely stands with one hand on the doorknob and the other in his pocket. Another message received.

"Let's go."

Delilah follows me from the house and out to the waiting car. Rather than leave her bag in the trunk, she chooses to hold it in her lap, both arms wrapped around it. A shield? Or a subconscious need to protect what little is hers? Probably both.

The silence between us is heavy. I stare out the window, knowing I ought to be thinking about Corium, and everything I'm sure has piled up on my desk since leaving. My thoughts shouldn't be trained on the girl sitting beside me. And I thought I'd be able to get her out of my life. I should've known better.

She's not going to be the one to break the silence. Nor should she be. What do I say? That I'm sorry I scared the hell out of her? Should I tell her if she thinks this is bad, she should have known me years ago? I doubt that will do much good, even if it's the truth.

But I have to say something. My conscience—what there is of it— won't let me get away with leaving this unsettled between us. I have to put it away before we part ways once we reach the school. And that's exactly what we're going to do. It's the only way to get through this.

HALLMAN & J.L. BECK

It isn't until we're on the plane that I clear my throat, sliding a glance her way. She goes rigid in anticipation of what's to come. "I, uh..."

Before I can finish stammering, she says, "Don't bother."

"You don't know what I was about to say."

"It was going to be some clumsy excuse for the way you treated me." To my surprise, she looks straight at me, her expression one of bland acceptance. "Well? Am I wrong?"

I can't even correct her on the clumsy aspect because it would certainly have been pitiful. "You deserve to know why."

"Like I said, don't bother. I don't need to know why. It doesn't change anything. People always have their reasons for what they do, right?" She turns away again, looking down at her hands where they sit in her lap. "I know I'm nothing. I can accept that."

"Who said you're nothing?"

"You mean besides everybody my entire life? Some things don't need to be said, anyway. Actions speak louder than words—isn't that how the old saying goes?"

Fuck me. She knows how to make a man feel roughly two inches tall.

"No." She sighs. "I know who I am. I know what I am. A hole for you to fuck. It doesn't even have to be a wet hole."

I'm burning with rage. Frustration. Yes, even shame. There's nothing like having a bright, unforgiving floodlight pointed at you to expose every last flaw. I'm at a loss for words. Nothing I say is going to make a difference, anyway. Such as how I wouldn't go to the lengths I've gone to for a mere hole to fuck. She might think she understands how things work in my world, but if she truly had a clue, she'd know the repercussions for sheltering her might be dire. I'm sure I don't have many friends right now.

She plotted to kill my daughter, yet she's still alive. That alone ought to prove she means more than a fuck toy.

The more I think about it—all the examples of what I've done for her, the risks I've taken, the enemies I might have made—the deeper my rage grows until I want nothing more than to hurt her. Why is that where my impulses immediately lead? Because there's no other way for me to vent this. Being underestimated, disregarded. Who the fuck does she think she is?

She thinks she's the girl I roughed up last night. Little does she know that was nothing compared to what I did earlier.

Things still haven't improved when we board the helicopter to Corium. Now I don't care to try to make amends. In fact, it's better this way. She might have done me a favor. I didn't know how to tell her what's coming once we arrive. Now, I almost look forward to it. The excuse to push her away for good, knowing she's too pissed at me to take it personally or ask for a bunch of explanations.

There's a reason we're doing this at night. I sense her apprehension as we step down from the helicopter. I led her through the snow and into the school not so long ago. It feels like years. Then I had righteous anger on my side. Disgust. I wanted her to suffer. I wish I knew what I want now.

At least the halls are darkened and empty by the time we step over the threshold and into the familiar entry hall. She does her best to pretend to be brave, but I know relief when I see it. Nobody is here to witness her arrival. Nobody to threaten or blame her. I'm sure that will come later, but it's her problem. I've already made the mistake of getting far too close to her. This is as good a time as any to remind her—and myself—of the way things should have gone from the beginning.

When I push the button leading to the dorm level rather than the floor where my apartment sits, she speaks for the first time since the plane. "Where are we going?"

"The dorms, of course. Where did you think?"

She stares at that lit button like it holds the answers for a moment. Her bottom lip disappearing under her teeth. "I didn't think…"

"What? You didn't think I'd let you stay in your own room? It's about time you did." We step off the elevator with me in the lead. She waits a beat as if afraid of running into anyone on this level. I can't blame her. But it isn't as if I would let anyone harm her in my presence. I doubt that would offer her much comfort at the moment, though.

"Come on. Your room is up here." Roughly halfway down the hall, I use my master key to unlock the door before swinging it open and stepping inside. "You should be more than comfortable here. It'll be an upgrade from having to share a space with me."

I keep my tone clipped, professional while I examine the space. It's typical of every other room—nothing more, nothing less. The notion of giving her bleak, shitty accommodations did occur to me, but I'm not a complete bastard. Besides, I allowed Aspen's mistreatment when she first came here, and I only ended up regretting it. Some lessons I manage to learn.

Still, there is a great deal of difference between making sure she has the basics and making things too easy for her. So while the room is clean and furnished, it's a step down from what she's accustomed to after staying in my apartment.

One glance at her tells me that's not what she's concerned with. "I didn't know I would be here alone. You didn't tell me I wouldn't be staying with you anymore." Her expression is one of horror.

"What? Did you think we'd play house? My brother wasn't kidding when he said everyone knows what happened with Brookshire. What did you think it would mean for me—and you—if word got around that I was giving you special treatment?" I continue when it looks like she's going to protest, "No, this is the end of us, in every way. We're never going back to the way things were. Understood?"

"So I don't get any protection at all? You know they're going to try to kill me. Even though it wasn't my fault."

I make a big deal of rolling my eyes so she knows just how tiresome this is. "Once again, this is the safest place for you. No one can touch you here."

"No. No one can kill me here—and your brother already said it. They still got to Nash."

The sound of my daughter's name coming from her mouth makes me see red. Before I know it, she's up against the door with my hand around her throat. I lean in close, snarling. "Don't you say her name. Understood? You don't speak of her, you don't see her, as far as you are concerned, she doesn't exist. Nod, so I know you understand."

Her face is deep red, and oh, there's so much hatred in her eyes to go with the rapid fluttering of her pulse under my fingers. Good. Let her hate me. Hate is easy, clean, and uncomplicated.

She jerks her chin in response, lifting her lip in a sneer.

And I smile. "Good. See? It isn't so hard getting through to you."

"You bastard."

My smile widens. "When you're right, you're right." I let go of her, and she slumps against the door, but that doesn't last long once I've opened it again. It's better this way. I have to believe it's better this way.

Without glancing at her over my shoulder, I say, "You're on your own." And once I've closed the door, she's no longer my problem.

14

DELILAH

So this is it. This is the room I'm going to die in. It's going to be my tomb. I won't even get to see the sun again, thanks to these stupid, windowless walls.

Because what's the alternative? Dying somewhere else? Either way, the result is the same. I won't be breathing air anymore. I might as well do it on my own terms, alone, with as little pain as possible. I'll slowly starve since I doubt anybody would go out of their way to make sure I get food.

Of course, I know there's no chance of leaving this life peacefully. I'm infamous. And I'm sure Lucas will find out if I don't show up for class after a few days or if I'm never seen in the cafeteria. He might not want anything to do with me, but I have no doubt he would drag me from this room and force me to face my fate.

He would probably get off on it. It wouldn't surprise me if he jerked off while watching my fellow students stone me to death or something barbaric like that. He'd finally have his revenge for his precious daughter, and nobody would ever have to know about our dirty little secret.

I touch the spot on my throat where his fingers pressed in. It's been hours, but I still feel it. Just like I still feel his anger, so intense I thought it might choke me before he ever laid a hand on me.

And I know a small part of that is my fault. I should have heard him out on the plane, given him a chance to explain himself. But I was hurting. He hurt me, and I was angry about that.

He wasn't just Lucas then. He was everybody who's ever used me, disregarded me, and thrown me away like I was garbage. I was lashing out at all of them. He just happened to be the person in front of me at the time.

I definitely shouldn't have brought up Aspen. I know better than that. But I was desperate, trying to convince him that leaving me here is a bad idea.

Now, he hates me just as much as everybody else. My only hope of protection around here, and I alienated him. I could have at least heard him out, maybe let him grovel a little. No, it wouldn't have changed anything, but he might not hate me the way he does now.

I don't know why I bothered trying to get to sleep. Great, now all I can think about is a few nights ago when I couldn't fall asleep. Our shower together. Not just that, but all the time he spent listening to me in bed. How could he be so thoughtful and considerate and generous, then try to choke me a few days later? Nothing about him makes sense.

But I need him. Not just physically. I need his support. I need people to know he's behind me.

"That's not going to happen." I roll over and punch my pillow before falling back with a groan. Even if he didn't hate me, he couldn't afford to let anybody know he actually cares what happens to me. That wouldn't do him any favors, not with the students nor their parents.

What a completely fucked-up bunch of people they are, all of them. When I think about it that way, I'm glad I didn't grow up close to this world. My father did me a favor by excluding me. At least I'm able to think like a normal person and not follow these strange, violent, archaic rules.

So what does he expect of me? Am I supposed to go to class like everything is normal? I don't know how I would. It was bad enough before this. Now I not only almost got Aspen killed, but I killed Nathaniel.

A knock on the door makes me sit bolt upright. Once my heart dislodges itself from my throat, it takes off at top speed. This is it. Somebody came for me. Funny how all of a sudden, the last thing I want is to die. Ten seconds ago, I was actually considering it.

There's another knock, softer this time. Am I making a mistake by getting out of bed and checking to see who it is? Then again, if somebody wants to hurt me, would they bother knocking? I'm sure if it was Quinton, for instance, he'd have a way of getting in without waiting for me to answer the door. Some people know how to get around the rules, no matter what the rules are.

"Who is it?" I ask. *Please, please, don't be Quinton.*

The door is thick, but with my ear pressed against the crack, I hear, "It's me, Dr. Lauren. I wanted to check on you now that I know you've arrived."

I almost forgot about her. Maybe she'll be on my side. She seems a lot smarter and more reasonable than the rest of these people. Like she might actually weigh the facts of a situation before deciding who was in the wrong.

She offers a tentative smile when I open the door enough to catch sight of her. It can't be much past five in the morning, but she already looks ready for her day. I wish I knew how to dress and groom myself like her. She's not flashy, nowhere close, but she always looks put together. Classy. Something that was in seriously short supply back at the trailer park.

"I'm sorry," she whispers after looking me over. "I'm sure I must have woken you up."

"You didn't." I back away, opening the door wider. "Come on in."

She takes a slow look around the room, nodding slightly. "This is nice. I'm sure you won't mind having your own space finally."

Sure, I might if it had been my choice. "If only I wasn't sure everybody would plot to be the first one to break in and murder me."

"That's not going to happen." She takes a seat on the foot of the bed, frowning. "I know what happened. And I know how to read between the lines. I also know you."

"No, you don't. Not really."

"Let's say I have a good instinct for people. I know you didn't have a choice."

I throw my hands into the air. "Thank you. I really appreciate it. But you and Lucas will be the only two people in this place who don't hold it against me. You're sort of outnumbered."

And I don't even know if I can count Lucas anymore. I can't tell her about that, though I sort of want to. This is the time in a girl's life when she could use a friend to confide in. The irony is, the only other person around here who's come close to that is Aspen. And that wasn't real, anyway—even if it was, she's not going to want to be my friend anymore.

"How are you holding up after what happened?"

I can't help but pace in front of her, and she doesn't try to stop me. "You mean besides not sleeping, and the graphic nightmares I end up having when I do?"

"You know, I can give you something to help with that. You'll go down hard and stay that way. No nightmares."

It's tempting. But... "I don't know if I should take anything like that. But thank you."

What happens if I'm out cold when somebody decides they want to break in and hurt me? I need to be able to react if there's a noise outside. Not to mention the whole 'my secret birth mother may or may not have died from an overdose' thing. I don't think I'd be able to take a pill without thinking of her. Not that I need an excuse to. She's never far from my thoughts.

"The offer's still good if you change your mind."

I like the way she doesn't try to push anything on me. That must be what loosens me up a little bit. "I don't know what to think about anything. I'm so confused."

"What do you mean?"

It might not be a good idea to confess all this to her, but I have to get it off my chest. I'll lose my mind if I don't. "Like Lucas. He saved me. I know it couldn't have been easy."

"He's never let anything like that stop him before."

"But the next minute, he's all cold and distant and acting like an asshole." I cover my mouth with my hand, horrified. "I'm sorry. I shouldn't have said that. Please, don't—"

She holds up her hands, laughing softly. "Trust me. You are not the first person to ever call Lucas Diavolo an asshole. Matter of fact, I call him worse to his face. And he deserves it. I know from experience."

I'm so relieved that I can't help but laugh with her. I'm so glad she came to see me. Not that this changes anything—I'm still scared out of my mind—but at least I can process things a little better.

"I'm really scared," I whisper. "I'm afraid to leave this room."

Her laughter dies. "I understand. But nobody is going to hurt you here. They can't."

"They'll find a way."

"And that's why if anyone so much as looks at you the wrong way, you're going to come to me, or you're going to go to Lucas. But either way, you're going to tell somebody."

I snicker. "Come to you, got it."

"There you go. You do have friends here. You aren't alone." She stands and takes me by the arms. "One thing you cannot do is let them win by locking yourself in here. You don't need to flaunt yourself, but don't hide either. The one thing you can't show is weakness."

I wouldn't expect something like that to come from her. She seems a lot more like the kind of person who would give me a bunch of happy little inspirational quotes. If you're going through hell, keep going. That sort of useless crap.

Then again, I guess working around these people means having to be a realist. She has to meet them where they are, good or bad.

"I'm lucky to have you on my side."

"And that's exactly where I am. Remember, anything you need. You come and see me. At least you'll have a day to get yourself settled before starting classes again tomorrow—call my office if you need to talk." She drops her hands and looks like she's about to go to the door when she stops herself. "One more thing. I know Lucas is prickly, stubborn, and contrary to the point where he sometimes makes you want to strangle him. But he's not all bad. And he's the kind of ally you want to have, too. He didn't put you in this room as a punishment. It's protection. It might be difficult to see it now, but I know that's where his heart is."

His heart. It's all I can do not to laugh at the idea of him having one. "Thank you. I appreciate that."

"I'll get out of your hair now." She leaves with a little smile, and right away, my mood sinks. I feel a little better but no safer. At least I know I can go to her when I start getting threats—and I know I will. That's not a question. It's only a matter of time.

I'm not leaving this school alive if they have their way. For all I know, Quinton and his buddies are plotting my demise as I pace my room, chewing my nails, wishing I had it in me to do what Lauren described. Having confidence and not hiding. Letting them know they can't break me.

At least that part is true. How can you break something that's already been broken?

15

LUCAS

Sweat drips down my face, adding to the puddle forming underneath me as I do another set of push-ups. I've lost count of how many it's been so far. I only know my shoulders and arms are burning from the effort.

But I welcome it. That's exactly what I want right now. To exhaust my body beyond the point of conscious thought. I need oblivion. I crave it. I even welcome the pain, gritting my teeth and pushing through though my body screams in protest. I deserve it. I need the punishment.

Since the option of finding a fight and snuffing out a man's life is off the table now, I have to do what I can to keep myself in check.

I can't remember the last time I was in this great a need. The sense of falling apart at the seams is like a shadow following me. No matter how I try to dodge it, there's no avoiding it. I'm losing control.

My growl fills the room, and I double my efforts, shouting out my pain, fatigue, and rage. Finally, my muscles reach the point of complete exhaustion and give out on me. Rather than fall face-first in my sweat, I roll to the side and stare at the ceiling, my heavy breathing filling the air.

All I see in front of me is her. Smiling. Crying. Finding her mother's letter. Staring me down when all I wanted was to watch fear spark behind her eyes.

What the fuck am I doing? This can't go on.

I should never have brought her here. Not to the school, definitely not to my apartment. I hate her. I miss her. I resent her. I want to protect her. She's become an obsession I resent and crave in equal parts.

She's brought back every one of my worst tendencies. And I don't know how to manage it. I feel myself slipping back into my old ways—that fight was the tip of the iceberg. I want to hurt something. I want to hurt it in hopes of ending my own pain.

Damn that Lauren. I'm talking to myself the way she talks to me, and I barely recognize the voice in my head anymore. I don't need to know why I do what I do. What I need is to forget. To disconnect. Here I was, thinking working out until I collapsed was the way to do it.

Lying on the floor isn't going to help anything, either. I drag myself up and grab a towel from the bathroom to wipe up the sweat before getting in the shower. Propping my forearms against the wall, I lean into the spray with my head lowered, so the steaming water runs down my shoulders and back. Normally, a strenuous workout leaves me feeling more alive. Right now, I'm tempted to wish I was anything but.

This has been the longest day of my life. As it turns out, there wasn't nearly as much work waiting for me as I imagined—what a shame since I didn't realize until it was too late that I was counting on that work to take my mind off Delilah. Instead, there was nothing for me to do after a few hours but wonder if she was safe. If she was afraid.

Of course she's afraid. I saw that much written all over her face before I put a hand on her last night. Anyone with a scrap of common sense would be scared out of their mind in her position.

I hardly made things better.

But that isn't my job, dammit. That's what I tried to remind myself of today, though it didn't work. She's not my problem. This school is my problem. Aspen is my problem. Not this damn girl.

No matter how much I want to go to her. It would be so simple to go to her room and let her know she isn't totally alone. That I crave her more than I crave air. I crave her scent. The sound of her voice. The tight clenching of her pussy around my cock in the split second before she comes.

To think I used to value my solitude. This apartment was always my escape, my refuge, the one place in this enormous structure where I could be myself. No mask, no need to be professional.

When I look around after finishing in the shower, I see is how empty it is. Devoid of life, bleak as fuck without her presence. I got used to her. How stupid can a man be? I became accustomed to her company and can't remember life before her.

A buzzing from the coffee table catches my attention. What a surprise. My brother calling to make sure everything is all right. In other words, he wants to check up on me and make sure I haven't managed to fuck something else up in the hours since we said goodbye. I'm surprised he didn't ask me to text when we arrived so he'd know we were safe. Sometimes, I think domestic bliss has castrated him.

Only it isn't Nic. I do recognize the number, though. My jaw clenches as I answer the call and raise the phone to my ear. "Xander. Hello."

He doesn't mince words. "Tell me it's a joke."

I have to take a deep breath before I lose it. This call was expected. I was hoping it would be at least twenty-four hours before it came since I haven't yet come up with a plausible excuse for bringing her here. "What are you talking about?"

"Tell me that girl isn't at Corium."

"And what if she is?"

"Then I'm inclined to believe you've lost your fucking mind. Have you forgotten what she tried to do? Are you unaware of what she managed to do during her little hiatus? Of course, you're aware of it. Everyone knows you are."

He has no idea he is fucking with the wrong person right now. I close my eyes, clench my teeth, and fight to keep myself under control. The man is an insufferable prick, but I can't alienate him. Not entirely.

"What would you like me to do?"

"Why do you ask stupid questions?" Before I can warn him against ever calling me or anything I say stupid, he charges forward. "I want her out of there. She can't be trusted, and you know she can't be trusted! Dammit! You have no business bringing her to Corium. She's more a liability than anything, a loose end."

I'm still fighting to hold my tongue when he adds, "I would think you of all people would want to keep her out of there. Unless you don't care that she nearly got your daughter killed."

This sufferable prick. As if he gave a shit about Aspen before she became involved with Quinton—and even then, it was only because he had no choice. Before then, he was as thirsty for her blood as anyone else.

"Don't talk to me about my daughter. I've got it under control."

"Are you sure about that? Because that's not what I'm hearing."

"Really? And exactly what are you hearing?"

"You know damn well what is being said, so don't pretend otherwise. Isn't it bad enough she slipped through your fingers and ran off once? You, of all people, should have made it your mission to keep her in a cell. Yet she traipsed off—and then what happened? Someone ended up dead. Someone very powerful. Someone with a lot of powerful friends."

"I'm well aware."

"Oh, so then you do know? I was beginning to wonder if you're capable of keeping your finger on the pulse of current events, the way a man has to be if he's going to succeed in your position."

"Are you finished?" I snarl. "Or would you like to continue beating a dead horse, Xander?"

"Excuse me?" he demands with a disbelieving laugh. "Have you forgotten who you're speaking to?"

That was a step too far. I grit my teeth against the rest of what I long to unleash on this son of a bitch, settling for, "Look, Delilah isn't your problem. I've taken full responsibility for her. The only place she is safe is here. She's mine to deal with, and I have it under control."

He's silent for a moment, which I know doesn't bode well. When powerful men are quiet, they're thinking, which is never a good thing.

"I see. Then I'll have to take care of things myself."

"Meaning?" I grit out.

"You've wasted enough of my time this evening, Lucas. I'm not going to answer questions to which we both know the answer."

Rage tints my vision. The thought of someone touching her, hurting her in any way, makes my stomach tight and my pulse jump. It makes me murderous.

"Leave her alone, Xander. I mean it. She's not yours to deal with."

"The time for that has passed. I'll do what needs to be done if you can't be bothered to do it yourself."

Before I can tell him exactly where to stick his worthless opinion, he ends the call and leaves me hanging. This asshole always needs the last word. I know I can't fight Xander. I'm not willing to go to war against my in-laws, but I can't let him hurt Delilah either. Even after everything, anyone with a brain would know she's innocent and merely a victim to the rage, greed, and needs of those around her. Before I know what I'm doing, I cock my arm and throw the phone.

It lands on the couch and bounces off, sliding across the floor. I don't bother checking to see whether it's broken. I don't give a fuck.

He's not a man who issues idle threats. Suppose he's ready to call me and announce his plan to eliminate Delilah. In that case, it means he's already got a strong idea of how to get it done—and if he doesn't, it's only a matter of time before he puts a plan together. A man like him has limitless resources, both in terms of financing and warm bodies willing to do his bidding.

He's going to have her killed. Just because he can. And I'm supposed to stand here and take it? Yes, you stupid bastard, that's exactly what you're supposed to do. I have a duty to the entire school, not this single girl who I have already gone too far for.

Fuck this. To hell with guarding against backsliding. I go to the cabinet and break out the whiskey bottle, uncapping it all at once and raising it to my lips. The first gulps race their way down my throat and into my chest, where heat blooms in their wake. My throat burns, but I even welcome that since it means I'm one step closer to oblivion.

She's a walking corpse. There's no other way of putting it. Xander's made up his mind, and there isn't a person alive able to foil a plan he's put in motion.

Meanwhile, here I am. Helpless against it. Knowing it's wrong—and not only because I've fucked the girl. That has nothing to do with it. This is entirely wrong. She saved her own life by ending Nathaniel's. And as for that piece of shit Marcel? He took advantage of her. She's never had anyone in her life, not a single person she could count on aside from the woman she never knew was her mother. A woman who was likely doing her best with the limited resources allowed her.

It's no surprise a vulnerable girl in that position would be willing to do just about anything if it meant finally belonging. Little did she know, the family she believed was her solace was really her biggest threat.

I take another long swig, then drag my forearm across my mouth. Dammit. She never had a chance. Why am I the only person who sees it? How am I supposed to protect her when no one wants to hear the truth? Now the warmth in my chest is bitter. White-hot. Murderous.

The world is starting to blur around the edges, but I welcome that. One step closer to having nothing to worry about. Nothing to regret. But I'm still aware enough to know something for sure: I'm not about to have this girl's death on my conscience. I might not be able to save her from what's coming, but I can at least give her a fighting chance by warning her.

16

DELILAH

I'm starting to wish I had taken Lauren up on those pills.

I can't get comfortable to save my life. It's not the bed's fault. It's my brain. All I've done for hours is lie one way and another. Arranging the pillows. Adding a blanket and taking it off not long after. Putting a pillow between my knees before changing my mind and hugging it to my chest. Moving from my stomach to my side and then back again.

I've done it all, and I'm still awake, no closer to drowsiness than I was before. Which sucks since I have to face my fate in the morning.

The less sleep I get, the more vulnerable I'll be. No, I don't think anybody will attack me the first day—that's not how they operate. I understand enough about the way they think to know they would rather torment me a little first, like a cat playing with a dying mouse before finally putting it out of its misery. That will be me, a dying mouse with so many cats surrounding me. Claws out, batting me back and forth between them.

I guess it's not surprising that I can't shut my brain down.

What's saddest is not having happy memories to think about as a way of relaxing. The few times I was sick as a kid, like really sick, my mother—it's still so weird, thinking of her that way—would try to lull me to sleep by telling me to think of something happy. Something I was looking forward to, something nice.

I don't have any of that. What's a happy memory? What does that even look like anymore? Great. Now I'm annoying myself on top of everything else. I squeeze my eyes shut and force my body to go limp, wiping clean all the thoughts in my mind.

It doesn't stay clear for long. A face begins to materialize in the darkness. Followed by the sensation of being held and caressed —protected.

Of all the times for me to think about Lucas. Am I ever going to free myself of him? It's obvious he wants to be free of me. I could at least have enough pride to forget him. Still, thinking about him takes my mind off everything else. I can almost feel his arms wrapped around me and his firm chest against my back. His heartbeat and the rising and fall of his chest as he breathes. I smile a little thinking about—

CRASH.

The door to my room flies open with a bang, slapping against the wall so hard it feels like the entire room is shaking. A high-pitched scream echoes through the space a moment before I realize it's me screaming. I sit up, pulling the blankets around my shoulders as if that could protect me from anything.

This is it.

This is how they're going to do it.

Why the hell didn't I try to get my hands on a weapon before now? They won't even let me go to class. I should have known they would rather get rid of me before anybody has to set eyes on me.

"You!" Lucas's deep voice booms through the room. The fog clouding my mind clears, and I realize it isn't a student standing in the doorway.

"Lucas?" I whisper, opening my eyes as wide as I can to adjust to the darkness. He's still standing there, only a silhouette of his wide shoulders almost filling the doorway, blocking out most of the light from the hall.

He stumbles into the room, slamming the door behind him and startling me once more. My heart is in my throat, and my instincts are telling me to get the hell out of bed and away from him. He's dangerous, like a grenade waiting to go off.

It's like one animal scenting another and knowing they're a threat. He doesn't have to say a word, I know he could hurt me, and part of me knows he wants to. He raises a bottle to his lips and throws his head back, emptying it before tossing it to the floor.

"You," he repeats. This time, I notice the slight slur in the single word. He is drunk.

"Me?" I whisper, wondering where this is going to go.

"Biggest fucking mistake I ever made." He sways, coming to a stop at the foot of the bed. I'm finally loose enough to lean over and turn on the lamp on the nightstand, so at least I can see him clearly.

Right away, I sort of wish I hadn't.

He's devilish looking with his dark hair an unruly mess like he's been running his hands through it. There is a wet spot on his shirt where he's spilled liquor on himself—whiskey, by the odor rolling off him. Even from here, I can smell it, clinging to him like a second skin. He's not usually sloppy like this. Something is wrong.

I stare into his bloodshot eyes. The darkness in them makes me wonder if I should run for the bathroom and lock the door. They're cold. Like a shark's, the pupils dilated to the point where they block out almost the entire iris.

And they're focused on me.

He raises his arm, pointing at me. "The biggest fucking mistake I ever made was bringing you here."

Am I supposed to say something? Or maybe I'm supposed to comfort him. Is that what this is about? Offering him a little solace?

"And now," he continues, his voice thick, "anything happens to you, and it's on my fucking conscience. Like I fucking need that. Like you're even fucking worth it." His arm drops to his side, but he's still glaring at me. Challenging me. Like he's jonesing for an excuse to get in a fight.

"I don't know what you want me to say," I whisper. "Am I supposed to apologize because you chose to bring me here? You didn't have to do that in the first place. But you decided I needed to be punished even more than I was in that awful place." And then, because I can't help myself, and I've never been good at making the right choices. "By your son-in-law."

His eyes flash, and suddenly, he's crawling across the bed. I scramble backward but don't get far before my back hits the head-board. In a breath, he's on top of me, one hand on either side of my head. Crowding me, reminding me he's much bigger and stronger than I.

The stench of whiskey is so strong I can hardly breathe. How much has he had to drink? A lot considering it looks like he can't even focus on me, his head tipping from one side to the other while he squints.

"Have you forgotten who you're talking to?" he growls. He might be a sip or two away from blacking out, but this is still a dangerous man. His nostrils flare as he lifts his lip, baring his gritted teeth. "Do you know how easy it would be for me to break you? I've taken apart men two, three times your size without hardly a scratch or a bruise on me. You saw how I was that last night at my brother's. All the blood. What do you think I'll look like after I take you apart?"

I hear his words. I feel his anger, so intense it's almost a tangible thing. Like there are three of us in the room now.

So why am I not terrified? Apprehensive, cautious? Sure. I'd be stupid if I wasn't. But stupidly, I'm not as afraid as I should be. He only wishes he could do to me what he just described. I'm not exactly sure why, but the desire is there. He can't bring himself to do it. That's the problem, at least from his perspective.

Perhaps that's why I'm able to speak without my voice trembling. Why I can look him in the eye without flinching back the way I know he wants me to. That's why he's here. To remind himself how powerful he is even when he doesn't feel that way.

"Who do you really want to take apart?"

He tilts his head back a little, his brows drawing together, his eyes narrowing. He pulls back his right fist and punches the wall so close to my head that I'm certain he's going to hit me. I flinch, drawing my shoulders up and tucking my chin against my chest. I remind myself that violence is all he knows and his only form of coping.

"Who the fuck do you think? Why else would I come here?"

I shouldn't push him, it's like provoking a bear and not expecting to get attacked, but I can't help myself.

"Then do it. Let your anger out on me. Use me. Hurt me. If that's what it takes to make you feel better."

"Is that an invitation?" He reaches for the blanket, pulling it off me with one harsh tug. He doesn't let me answer before giving his next command. "Take your shirt off."

Even in his drunken state, it doesn't take him long to free himself from his own clothes. With curious eyes, I watch him stroke his fat, throbbing cock. Thick veins run along his shaft like a roadmap leading to the precum glistening at the swollen head.

I'm so enthralled by the view that I yelp in surprise when Lucas grabs my cotton panties and rips them off me in one swift move.

"Spread your legs," he orders, and I follow his command without thought.

Cool air washes over my heated core, making me realize that I'm wet for him despite how he is treating me... maybe he has me so twisted that I'm welcoming it now. Or maybe I've always been fucked up.

"Should I fuck your cunt or your ass?"

"No!" My legs try to close on their own, but Lucas is faster, prying them open. "Please, not anal."

"You told me to let my anger out on you... to use you. And right now, I want to use your tight little asshole. Are you going to fight me? Because that would make it even better."

"You're sick."

"You're just now figured that out?" He presses me into the mattress using his body, keeping my legs spread for him. He grabs my wrists with one hand and pulls them over my head, holding them there like an iron shackle.

Real fear makes its way up my spine, settling into my bones. I try my best not to show him how scared I am, but I can't control how my body shudders and my bottom lip trembles.

"Mhh, I can smell the fear coming off you. It's so fucking sweet and makes my cock even harder." He slides his free hand between us, running his fingers through my folds, and gathering my wetness, bringing it down to my asshole. Without warning, he shoves his finger inside, making me clamp up on reflex.

"Please," I whimper, but Lucas is not taking mercy. He finger fucks my asshole until I have nothing left but to relax and let him in.

"You know this is my favorite part. Knowing I'm hurting you while I feel nothing but pleasure."

I'm starting to get that.

"You have no idea how good it felt to fuck you in that cell, to take from you without giving, to know how sore I left you. Were you reminded of me every time you moved after?"

He suddenly pulls his finger out, leaving me empty for one second before I feel the thick head of his cock sliding through my wetness. I clamp up again, preparing myself for the pain about to come, but instead of my ass, he pushes inside my pussy.

I wasn't prepared for the intrusion, but I'm wet enough for him to slide all the way in without any major pain. A moan falls from my lips, followed by a whimper as he does exactly what he promised —what I suggested. He uses me for his pleasure, fucking without a care for what I feel.

The worst part is that some depraved part of me enjoys this. He might be sick, but I'm not much better because as he is fucking me, my orgasm builds. Higher and higher with each forceful thrust. I'm so wet that the sloppy sounds my pussy makes are almost embarrassing.

My thighs quiver, my pussy tightens, and I'm about to come when he suddenly pulls out. "No..." I whine at the loss of him.

Lucas chuckles. "Greedy little cunt. But I told you what I want. I want this." He presses his thumb against my ass. "If you want to come, you'll have to do so while I fuck you here."

He replaces his thumb with the tip of his cock and presses against the tight ring of muscle. Instantly, I'm reminded of the searing pain he caused me last time. I try to relax, but fear has me in its clutches. My flight instinct kicks in, and I start to struggle in earnest. My feeble attempt at bucking him off only has him switching positions.

With ease, he moves me around. Letting go of my wrists, he grabs my thighs instead, pushing them onto my chest like he is folding me in half. Even with my arms free now, there is nothing I can do. His strength outmatches mine by so much that all I can do is lie here and hope he won't hurt me too badly.

Squeezing my eyes shut, I turn my head into the pillow and prepare myself for the pain. I feel the head of his cock sliding between my cheeks once more. He presses into me surprisingly slowly, almost gently. He forces himself into my ass until his entire length is buried inside me and his balls are touching my skin.

This position and my wetness let him use my back entrance without much pain. He slides in and out easily, and though I feel uncomfortably full, it doesn't really hurt.

"That's it. Be my good little toy and take it."

And that's exactly what I do. I close my eyes, but this time not in fear but in pleasure. I let him use me, and I find a way to enjoy it.

He fucks me in long deep strokes. Plunging into me over and over again until there is not an ounce of discomfort left, and I'm on the verge of my orgasm once more. Lucas must feel it, too, because his fingers find my needy clit, and he rubs it with his thumb until I come apart.

"That's it. Squeeze my cock with your ass."

We come at the same time. My body is convulsing from the intense release while Lucas, stills deep in my ass, shoots his cum inside me. I feel weightless, my limbs are numb, and I couldn't move a muscle if I wanted to.

Lucas slips out of me before he unfolds my body, letting my legs fall back onto the mattress. I'm so spent that, for a moment, I think I'm going to pass out, but there are too many things bothering me. Most of all, I don't know when I will see Lucas again, and I can't let him go without talking.

My eyes are still closed when I ask the question burning in my mind. "So what did I do this time?"

"What the fuck are you talking about?"

I blink my eyes open and find him staring at me with genuine curiosity.

"I'm lying here, trying to get to sleep. I haven't set foot out of this room since you put me here. What did I do that made you want to punish me? You can't be this mad at me just because I'm breathing."

There's a long pause, his eyes bleeding into mine. "What if I am?"

"Then I know any good thing you ever told me was a lie. When you said, I didn't deserve what happened to me. That was a lie. And you rescuing me? Telling me I was safe? That was a lie, too. Unless all you wanted was to save me for yourself to kill one day."

He's breathing harder than ever, his face flushed, and his body is starting to tremble like he's barely holding himself back. I'm standing at the edge of a cliff here. This could go either way—I fall back, where it's safe, or I plunge forward, and that's the end.

It's all up to him. Once again, my fate is in someone else's hands. I hold my breath, the air in the room electrified with energy. A moment later, he makes his choice. He falls back, clumsily rolling to the side and plopping down, legs splayed, and his head falling back.

Now I can breathe again, and I do, as quietly as possible. The man can barely see straight, but I'm not kidding myself. He'll know if he has me scared, which might pour fuel on the fire, so I can't afford to show it.

"I fucked it up. I fucked it all up."

I shouldn't care. I really shouldn't, not after everything he's said and done. I've never heard anyone sound like they're in this much pain.

Not even me, and I've been in pain most of my life, but he's talking like a man with so much weight on his chest that he can barely breathe.

"What did you fuck up?" I whisper a little more gently.

"Take your pick." He snickers bitterly. "My whole life. One fuckup after another. And you know what? I never cared much. It didn't matter. What the world thought of me, none of it."

He sighs, staring at the ceiling like I was not so long ago. "And it bit me in the ass. I let them do whatever they wanted to her, and I told myself it was right. That's the way we handle things. It's how we take care of filthy rats and their families."

Aspen.

I should have known this wasn't really about me. I guess I should be relieved.

"I fucking failed my own kid. I should have seen it coming. I should have known."

Dammit! I can't help but feel sorry for him. What is it about this man that makes me like this? If anybody else in the world had hurt me the way he has, over and over, I wouldn't piss on them if they were on fire.

But him? I let him get too close to my heart. He's under my skin, the blood in my veins, and the air in my lungs. He's inside me, and I can't escape him.

That's why, instead of telling him to get the fuck over it, I murmur, "You couldn't have known. You thought she was somebody else's kid. And like you said, her "father" was a rat. There are rules in this world—even I know that, and I wasn't raised in my father's household. I know there isn't any mercy shown to traitors, and that's what you thought she was."

"When I think of her suffering. She needed me. She needed a protector, and I was right there, but I didn't do a damn thing to help. How am I supposed to build anything with her now? How am I ever supposed to get her to trust me?"

And there I was, thinking I was never supposed to talk about her. I guess the rules change after you drink a bottle of whiskey.

"She's a forgiving person," I offer, and he snorts. "You know she is. She has a good heart. She was probably the only person who wanted to give me a chance. She even helped me get away, and she was the last person who should have wanted it that way. In time, things will be good between you two. But I think you have to let that happen. You have to stop telling yourself you did everything wrong. Forgive yourself a little and move on. I think that's when you'll be able to build a real relationship. You can't move forward if all you're doing is looking back."

I didn't mean to say all that, and now I'm a little embarrassed.

His head swings to the side, his unfocused eyes landing on me. "And how are we supposed to move forward? What am I supposed to do with you?"

And that is the million-dollar question. "I thought you didn't want there to be anything else between us?"

"I'm not supposed to. How am I to mend the relationship with my daughter when I also want to fuck the woman who tried to kill her."

"I didn't—"

"What you did was enough," he growls, growing more agitated by the second. "I want to torture you for that. I want to make you suffer. I want to see the pain in your eyes when I'm the one inflicting it."

I swallow, trying to get the words to pass the huge lump in my throat. "But you also want to protect me from others?"

"Unfortunately... yes. I want to punish you for what you did. I want you to hurt in every way possible, but I want to be the only one doing it."

"I should probably try to get away from you." His confession should have me running away as far and as fast as I can. "Yet I want to be with you. It doesn't make sense after everything you said and did to me. But I still want you to touch me."

Now both confessions are hanging in the air, one worse than the other but equally insane.

"How do you do that?" he mumbles.

"How do I do what?"

"How do you see any kind of light in me? All I see is darkness, but you keep finding the good; even if it's as small as a grain of sand, you still find it and hold it up like a diamond. How do you do that?"

I shrug, at a loss. "How do you see me as a real person when everybody else sees me as an enemy? You've seen right through it. People use me and then blame me for their choices, like what they did to Aspen. And the situation with Nathaniel. You understood right away I was only trying to defend myself. Nobody else ever wants to hear that, but you get it."

For a moment, all we do is stare at each other. I don't quite understand what's happening. He's not mad anymore, at least not at me, but then I don't think he ever was. He was mad at himself and looking for somebody to take it out on, as always.

"Everything is all fucked up."

"I know what you mean."

He nods slowly, then starts sliding down the bed until his head hits the pillow. "I'm so fucking tired, Delilah. I'm so tired."

"Then rest. Let it all go for now." I lie down beside him, cautious. I don't want him getting pissed because I got too close.

His eyes slide shut almost instantly, and it's not long before he starts to snore. I turn out the light and settle in, pulling the blankets over him before taking a chance and resting my head on his shoulder. His snoring doesn't skip a beat, and I smile to myself.

He'll hurt like hell in the morning, but for now, his presence has a soothing effect. I don't have to imagine having him here with me. He's here right now, and I can touch him, and even though I know the whole thing is completely fucked, it feels good. The first thing that's felt good in days.

I don't just drift off to sleep. I drop into it all at once.

And by the time I wake up to the high-pitched beeping of my alarm clock, he's gone. His side of the bed is cold.

17

LUCAS

*I*t isn't until my desk phone rings and startles the shit out of me that I realize I was zoned out again. No surprise there, of course. I've been zoned out for a week. No matter what I'm doing, my head is always somewhere else.

Per usual, I don't want to talk to the person calling.

"Can you get that?" I call out to my assistant. "I'm busy."

I know Lauren won't accept that excuse forever, but as far as I'm concerned, that's her fucking problem. She needs to take the hint before I end up saying or doing something I can't take back. I hear the excuse my assistant gives, regretful but firm. That's one problem taken care of.

For now. She'll find another way to remind me of her existence before long.

I don't need her right now. I doubt I ever did. All the so-called help she's given me has done nothing but make things worse.

I already know I'm a fuckup. That bringing Delilah to Corium might have been the biggest mistake in a life full of them.

And that I can't backslide into destructive habits.

Frankly, I don't give a fuck about what I'm supposed to do or what I shouldn't do. I've tried all this time to turn things around, be a better man, and look where it got me. What a waste of time.

I was already prone to hurting others. Destroying lives. Ending them. I still have that ability within me. Now, I get to feel bad about it after the fact. If all this therapy didn't change anything about who I am, what's the point?

Like that night in Delilah's room, it's a miracle I didn't kill her—or at least hurt her badly, as I was close to doing when I first threw open the door. I wanted blood. Her blood on my hands.

How did things end up? With me passing out after blubbering like a fucking moron and spending the night in her bed. We were here for all of twenty-four hours at that point, and I went against my own ground rules.

What's worse, I never got around to warning her about Xander.

Now, I don't want to. I'm afraid of what will happen if I spend another minute with her. What is it about her that gets into my bones? I can't shake her no matter how I try, and I'm struggling.

The temptation to go to her rather than sit at this desk and pretend I'm paying attention to my work is stronger than the temptation to drown my sorrows in a whiskey bottle. Considering the way I'm struggling with that, it's saying something. She's stronger than any addiction or craving I've ever known. The release she's brought me is on par with the release I get during a fight. I don't need to beat anybody to a pulp to earn it either.

Though I can't pretend watching fear spark in her eyes isn't a turn-on. Even now, sitting here, my cock stirs at the memory of her short, shallow breaths. The way she backed up against the headboard as I crawled to her like a lion prepared to devour his prey.

Granted, the memory is a little fuzzy. Considering everything I drank that night, it's amazing I made it to her room in the first place. There are things I remember clearly, though. Being close to her. The way she flinched when I punched the wall hard enough to leave my knuckles aching the next day. There's a satisfaction in that that I can't deny.

But I also can't indulge it. Because indulging in it means accepting everything that comes with being close to her. The temptation to do more than terrify her, hurt her. The temptation to hold her. To open my cracked, blackened heart and pour everything out. I'm a disease, a cancer that will eat her alive, and I can't allow myself to do that. She's been through enough, and even I'm not selfish enough to do that.

Despite everything, she sees me. Understands me. And like she said, it goes both ways. Maybe because of Aspen, maybe not. Maybe I don't want to fuck up again by punishing somebody for someone else's sins.

As far as I know, she's all right—there aren't any reports to the contrary, at least. Not like I've gone out of my way to ask anyone about her, of course. That would be too obvious. And I don't need word getting back to her somehow that I was interested. I need to be strong. I know I can be. No matter how much it makes me feel like tearing this school down around me.

Here I am, shuffling papers. What a pathetic joke. I might as well be in a cage as I place yet another file folder in my outbox. It's a gilded cage, comfortable and even impressive, but it keeps me locked away when all I want is to break free and be who I was before.

I didn't like that man, but at least he knew who he was.

There's a knock on the door. My head snaps up, and my heart begins to race. Like Pavlov's fucking dog, salivating on cue. I disgust myself.

I stare at the door, wishing I could see through it. If it's Delilah, I'd rather avoid answering. I've been so strong all week. A single glance at her and it will have all been for nothing.

You stupid prick. How many students are in this place? She's one of many. Right, not counting staff on top of that. I'm going to lose my mind before much longer.

"Lucas?" Another knock. This time, I stand and cross the room, recognizing the voice of an annoyed student.

Quinton is waiting for me, arms folded.

"What can I do for you?" I ask, glad for another distraction. Even if I'm not in what anyone would consider a conversational mood, I'm glad to see him. I'd like to know how my daughter is doing at the very least. She hasn't gone out of her way to visit me, but we didn't leave things on good terms. I still don't know how to deal with her deception.

"Can I come in?" He glances over his shoulder and out the open door to the hall. Now I see his apprehension for what it is.

I open the door wider, inviting him in without a word. My fighting experience taught me the ability to read body language. Everything about him is tense, nervous, and jumpy. The way he flexes his fingers, his gaze darting around without lingering on any one spot for too long.

Obviously, there's only one question on my mind. "Is it Aspen? Is something wrong?"

"No, she's fine. She's in the library with Brittney, doing whatever they do there." He waves a dismissive hand, though the fond smile he tries to hide tells me I don't have anything to worry about. He only pretends to be dismissive of how she chooses to spend her time. It's probably more habit than anything else by now, mirroring what would surely be his father's attitude in the same situation.

As it turns out, Xander is the reason Quinton paid a visit.

"I can't fucking do it. I don't want anything to do with this whole situation."

Rather than jump to take the bait, I play it cool. Knowing Xander, this could be a means of testing my position. "What situation?" I ask, returning to my chair and watching as he paces in tight circles.

He rolls his eyes at me before scoffing loudly. "You know what I'm talking about. Let's cut the bullshit, okay?"

"Careful, now," I warn. "We might have my daughter in common, but I'm not somebody you want as an enemy."

"I know. But I mean it. We're past that point. I know he called you. I know he told you what he wants to do. He wants her gone. Out of here, out of our lives, out of everything."

This doesn't come as a surprise—I knew from the beginning he wasn't making an idle threat. Men like him never do. That doesn't mean I'm happy to be proven right. "And how does he plan to do that?"

"I still don't know." I lower my brow, staring at him. "I don't. I swear. You know how it is. He wouldn't tell me until the last minute. He doesn't want me spilling to anybody and fucking with his plans."

I believe him. "But you don't want anything to do with it?"

He scrubs his hands over his head, still pacing. He reminds me of myself, angry and uncertain, full of energy he can't vent how he wants to. "Listen. You know there's no love lost between that girl and me." Something dark stirs in me when he lifts his lip in disgust. "But she's not some criminal genius either. The only reason she'd have to get that close to Nathaniel Brookshire would be if he forced her. She didn't seek out and murder him in cold blood, though that's what everyone wants to make it sound like."

Yes, they would. Yet another thing I've always known would be the case. "So he's going to try to get to her while she's here?"

"He's dead set on it."

Fuck! I force a few deep breaths to calm myself a fraction. The fresh whiskey bottle in the cabinet is calling to me, its sweet song tickling my ears and promising release. Something tells me there wouldn't be any measure of control once I got started drinking, and I can't have Q knowing about that. He's not the kind of person who'd run off and tell everyone I'm spiraling, but that doesn't mean I want him to see me like that. I'm not exactly proud of myself right now.

He rambles on, oblivious to my reaction. "I don't know what to do. I don't even know why I came to you. I can't talk about it with Aspen because we both know how she'll feel about it, and the last thing I want to do is make my wife upset, but when my father is set on something, he's set on it."

"We don't need her helping Delilah escape again," I murmur.

"Good luck if you think she'll ever truly be sorry for that, though she feels sorry for what happened to Delilah afterward. She knows if she hadn't freed her, things would have gone a lot differently, but still thinks she should never have been locked away in the first place."

"Hindsight is 20/20." Is it ever?

"What a shame foresight can't be." Again, he scrubs his hands over his head, blowing out a sigh that puffs his cheeks. "What am I supposed to do about this? It feels wrong, and I never thought I'd say that about anything involving Delilah."

There's only one thing to say. "Don't worry about it."

He looks at me like I lapsed into Greek. "Really? That's all you have to say? Don't worry about it?"

"I'll take care of it. All I need you to do is worry about yourself and Aspen. Enjoy being together, like you should be. You shouldn't have to worry about what your father may or may not do."

"But—"

"That's an order." I know how impossible it is to be in his position. It's one thing for me to tell Xander to fuck off, but his own son? That's a very different story. And while Quinton is fearsome and even dangerous, family loyalty is what matters most in this world. He loves Aspen, and I know he'd kill anyone who thought to hurt her, but he can't go to war against his father. It's not possible.

He shakes his head as he leaves, obviously perplexed. Let him be. That's better than going against his father and possibly jeopardizing Aspen somehow. I wouldn't put it past that son of a bitch to hurt her somehow in retaliation against his own son. He's that cold-hearted.

I'm about to close the door when Quinton doubles back before reaching the hall. "I don't know what you plan on doing with Delilah, but you'll regret it. I just know it."

It's all I can do not to burst out laughing. "I already do."

He scowls, puzzled, before leaving for good.

Like he has to teach me about regret. Like I don't have enough regret to fill a book. Maybe a library full of them.

Now that I'm alone again, the temptation is too much to resist. I read once not long ago that the human brain only has so much room for willpower on any given day. What I read was in relation to self-improvement and physical conditioning. Get the hard shit out of the way early because you might not have the willpower later after exercising it all day long.

My willpower? It's all being spent on avoiding Delilah. How can I be expected to resist the urge to drink, too? My fingers close around the bottle, and I unscrew the cap, skipping over the simple act of pouring it into a glass in favor of pouring it down my throat.

The familiar heat races through me, spreading across my chest. I take another gulp, and another, connecting with the pain burning in my throat. Relishing it, even.

The jangling of the phone makes me snarl. That goddamn Lauren. When is she going to take the hint? I storm over to the desk and consider tearing the whole phone from the wall and smashing it, but instead, I lift the receiver and bark into the mouthpiece. "This better be good."

There's a moment of silence that jars me. A look down at the screen tells me it's an unlisted number.

"Hello?" I mutter, listening hard.

"Lucas? Is that you?"

It's the strangest thing. Like a spark shoots out of the receiver and travels straight to my brain, lighting up the synapses until they glow like a fucking light bulb. It's the voice. That vaguely familiar voice.

"Yes. Who is this?" I ask though part of me knows. But it's impossible. Something somewhere in the back of my mind tells me to hang up and forget about it. Nothing good can come of it.

Before I can do that, she speaks again. "It's me. It's Charlotte."

18

DELILAH

*T*his has been a hellish week, but at least it's Friday, meaning I'll be able to hide out in my room for the most part over the next two days. But I still have to get through the second half of today in one piece.

That's what my life is now. Divided hour by hour. I can get to the next one if I just make it through this class. Then I can go to lunch, which I dread all morning long, from the moment I open my eyes. Because at lunch, there's less structure. No instructor at the front of the room glaring at anybody who dares to speak out of turn. We're supposed to at least pretend to pay attention, even though so many people don't. What do they care? They're from rich families. They don't have to pretend they want to learn how to navigate the underworld. They'll have people to do it for them.

But lunch is like being thrown into a swamp full of alligators just dying to take a bite out of me. Anywhere I look, somebody is glaring at me. Snickering, laughing. Muttering insults and gossip or flat-out threatening me. Bitch. Traitor. Cunt.

I wish I could say I've started to grow a thicker skin after a week's worth of it. That I can ignore the worst of it because, after all, not one of them knows me. They don't know what I've been through. They weren't in that awful room with that disgusting little costume. They weren't about to be raped.

I wish I could say it doesn't bother me, but I've never been big on lying to myself. I want to scream at them, smash my tray over their heads, and shriek in their faces. I want them all to know every humiliating, filthy detail, even though it would mean embarrassing myself.

Then again, they wouldn't believe me because they don't want to. It's easier to hate me. Like a group activity that brings everybody closer together. All thanks to me and the horror show my life has become.

I navigate my way between tables, moving quickly but carefully. I have no doubt somebody will trip me, elbow me, or shove their chair out from their table to make me drop my tray and spill everything. Or worse. They want me to get hurt. They want to see me fall.

I am not going to give them the satisfaction. I won't do it. And they can all go to hell.

It's easy to think that. But it's another story when I take a seat and feel the weight of so many stares on me. I want to ask what the hell they think they're all looking at, but of course, that wouldn't get me anywhere. Instead, I pick up my sandwich and take a bite, glad that at least the kitchen staff isn't trying to kill me.

All I have to do is eat quickly and get the hell out of here. I wish there was time to get back to my room to eat alone before going to my next class. I don't know how I'm going to eat over the weekend —maybe I'll have to come down early, like as soon as the cafeteria opens, and grab enough to get me through the day before running back to the dorm. If it means not having to deal with being on display like this? I'm fine with it.

"Hey, traitor. Murder anybody today?"

It's rare for someone to get so close to me. Most of them insult me from a distance. I look up from my tray to find Ren because he would be enough of a dick to do this. I'm sure Q put him up to it. I try not to stare at him. He's got secrets in his dark eyes, and I can tell from a mile away he hates me. The way he watches people, the secretive things he does. He's either very quiet or training to become a serial killer.

"No, but it's only a little after noon. Still plenty of time." I force a brittle smile before taking another bite of what is suddenly dry and tasteless. I chew it anyway, slowly and deliberately, staring up at him.

His mouth pulls up at one corner. White teeth appear, and I'd say he's smiling if he didn't look like a fucking shark ready to bite me.

"Funny."

"I wasn't trying to be."

"No. Comedy isn't your thing, is it? More like blunt force trauma."

My hands start to tremble, and my heartbeat skyrockets. I see the droplets of blood pooling on the floor. Like rubies, weren't they? And that heavy bookend covered in blood and hair. I'm about to lose what just entered my stomach.

No. Do not give him the satisfaction. Anyway, even if I did throw up, I'd want to get it on him, but the table is between us, so it'd be a worthless vomit.

He leans in and lowers his voice until it's a menacing growl. "In case no one let you in on it, I'll tell you what everyone else in this room is thinking. You. Don't. Belong. Here." He enunciates every word like I'm stupid and don't know what he's saying.

"I belong anywhere I want to be. Corium houses the offspring of all criminals." I wish I believed that, though at least it sounds like I do. I'm almost impressed with myself.

"You think so?" The look in his eyes makes my skin crawl. "Rules were made to be broken."

I arch an eyebrow, quaking inside but blank-faced as I can manage. "Is that a threat?"

"If that's how you want to see it." He shrugs, smirking. "If you ask me, it's more of a warning. An appetizer of what's to come if you remain here."

He grabs the apple off my tray and takes a bite out of it; the crunch of his teeth sinking into the skin reverberates through me. *Asshole.*

"That's my apple, douchebag."

"*Was.* Your apple. It's mine now."

"I didn't do anything wrong, so I don't know why everyone hates me so much," I growl.

Ren huffs. "It's obvious from a mile away, but I understand how your small brain may interpret it differently. You killed a man and got away with it, and now people are out for blood. You're a liability and a loose end."

"I was defending myself!"

He takes another bite of *my* apple, and I'm tempted to grab it from his hand and chuck it at his head. "That doesn't matter. Someone died, and you must pay the price."

I snarl my lip, ready to say something else, but there are already too many eyes on us, and now they're snickering, pointing, and basically taking no pains to even pretend they're leaving me alone.

"Just leave me alone!" I tell Ren, who takes a step back, a stupid smug look on his arrogant face. I force down every last bite of my sandwich because fuck them. Then I waste no time gathering my things, getting up, and leaving the cafeteria.

I guess this is what Lucas meant when he said he wouldn't do anything to protect me. In the grand scheme of things, it hasn't been that bad—threats and insults, they hurt but won't kill me.

Knowing how much worse things can and probably will get has me deciding to skip my next class. I did my best, but I can't take any more today.

I could go back to my room, but I'll be spending the entire weekend there anyway. Instead, I head for the library. I'll get lost there, deep in the stacks. I wonder what the odds are of hanging out there this weekend, come to think of it. The way Brittney and Aspen made it sound, nobody ever goes there. It might at least be a change of scenery.

The pressure in my chest eases when I step over the threshold. I know my mind is playing tricks on me, but the air feels sweeter and cleaner. Easier to breathe. The silence is delicious. The lack of anybody watching and judging me, waiting for me to screw up somehow. It's freeing.

"I'll grab the other stack from your desk." Oh, shit. I forgot about her. How did I forget about her? I start backing up, suddenly regretting this decision, but it's too late. Aspen has already seen me.

She stops short, frowning. "Hi."

That's about the nicest greeting I've received all week. "Hi."

"I heard you were back."

"Yeah, well, I've kind of been running from class to class and trying to stay away from as many people as possible." Why am I pouring my heart out like this? Maybe because it seems like she wants to listen.

"Yeah. I know what that feels like." Her gaze drifts toward the stack of books on Brittney's desk, which I guess she was on her way to pick up when she ran into me. "Can you help me with those? I might not be able to carry them all by myself."

That's bullshit, of course. Part of me wonders if this is some kind of trick. But I'm the one who did that to her, aren't I? Am I projecting by expecting her to double cross me the same way? Or did her husband put her up to it?

I can't keep overthinking everything. I'm going to drive myself insane. "Sure." I pick up half of them, all thick hardbacks, then follow her to where Brittney is waiting.

Her eyes widen a smidge like she's surprised to see me. "Hi, there. I'm glad you're here. I was hoping you would stop by."

Are these people for real? Why would either of them be glad to see me?

"This is maybe one of two places in the whole school where there isn't anybody threatening me—no, three. Dr. Lauren's office." I don't count Lucas in that because I don't think I can. I'm sure he's come up with a new reason to hate me by now. Otherwise, how could he go a week without checking to see if I'm okay?

"You can always come here," Brittney assures me. I believe her, too. I'm not used to people being so sincere, with nothing in it for them. That's how it is, too. I have nothing to give her, nothing to give either of them. But they're so nice to me anyway.

Before long, Brittney makes an excuse to go back to her desk for something or other, leaving Aspen and me to finish shelving the books they cataloged. She slides a look my way before ducking her head, her hair falling on either side of her face, so I can't see her expression. "I'm sorry for what happened. After you left here, I mean."

"Everybody knows about it, huh?"

"If I hadn't helped you leave, it never would have happened."

"Yeah, well, it did." But then, because I feel bad, I add, "It wasn't your fault."

And because I don't want to talk about this anymore, I pick up a historical fiction book featuring a woman in a gorgeous ball gown standing with her back to me. It's so beautiful I don't want to put the book down.

"Oh, that's a good one."

"Have you read every book in this library?" I ask with a laugh.

She doesn't take it as an insult. "Maybe I have. Maybe there was a long time when I had nothing else to do. I know what it's like to have to hide out."

I wish it wasn't so easy to like her. It would be a lot easier if she was the snide little bitch I imagined her to be. Maybe it's my need for friends. I'm just that desperate.

155

"What the fuck is this?"

I drop the book on the floor, where it lands with a loud bang. Quinton is glaring at me, his breathing heavy enough to remind me of a bull about to charge. Like the very sight of me standing anywhere close to Aspen is enough to make him crazy.

"It's all right. We were just putting books away. Nothing to get upset about." Aspen places her hands on his chest. He only grunts, glaring at me. "She was helping Brittney and me."

"Right. Just like she was only being friendly before." I hear his frustration with her, and I almost feel sorry for him for a moment. He loves her—that much is obvious. He's a complete prick, but I do believe he wants what's best for her, and as far as he's concerned, I don't fit the bill. I can't blame him for that after what I've done. I wish I could go back and undo it, but then, I wish a lot of things were different.

"I don't want you anywhere near her, got it?" He even pushes forward and gets in my face, the jerk. "Tell me you understand, Delilah."

"Would you please stop?" Aspen hisses, tugging on his arm. "It's not worth this big deal you're making it out to be. She didn't do anything to hurt me."

"Maybe not yet, or this time. But we all know what she's capable of." Funny, but I'm not scared the way I used to be. Maybe I'm beyond that point. Too numb. Too tired.

"Let's get out of here, okay? I can always come back later." I almost feel sorry for Aspen as she steers him from the row we're in, casting a sorrowful look my way.

He turns, his eyes blazing as they pin me in place. "You don't belong here, and I think it's time you realize that before someone makes you."

Terrific. Not like I didn't know he put Ren up to that little spectacle in the lunchroom, but I didn't need to be proven right. I hear the two of them quietly bickering as they leave the library, their whispers fading into silence.

I finish shelving the books for lack of anything better to do, taking the historical fiction Aspen recommended before mumbling an excuse to Brittney and heading out again. I don't belong anywhere.

There's not a place in this school where I'm safe except in my room, and even then, there's always the chance of somebody with a master key finding a way in. Like Lucas, though, I'm not sure if he's the worst or least of my problems anymore. He insisted I come here. I hope he's satisfied when they find me dead.

My eyes are turned toward the floor as I round a corner—just in time to smack straight into somebody.

"Watch where the fuck you're going," she snarls. I look up to find Anja glaring at me. Sure, I crashed into her, but she barely stumbled. All we'd have to do is mumble an apology and walk past each other. But nobody in this fucking place is particularly sane or reasonable.

"Sorry." I try to sidestep her, but she mirrors my action and ends up in front of me again. This isn't one of those situations where two people laugh it off, and one of them asks if they want to dance. That would be corny, but better than this.

"Excuse me. I have someplace to be." I try again, and again she places herself in my way. At least nobody is around to see what I'm sure will happen next. Something snaps in me. There's only so much a person can take, after all. She just so happens to be the straw that breaks the camel's back.

"What the fuck is your problem?" I grit out, glaring at her. "I didn't do anything to you."

Her eyes light up. "You're my problem, you pathetic bitch. Haven't you figured it out yet? Nobody fucking wants you here. You don't belong in this school."

"Yeah, no shit," I fire back. "Do you think I'd stay here if I had a choice? Who would put themselves through this? I don't want to be anywhere near you assholes."

"Then, by all means, get the hell out." She shoves me with both hands against my chest, and I fall back a few steps but manage to stay on my feet.

"Don't put your fucking hands on me," I warn.

"Um, looks like I just did. What are you going to do about it?"

I'd think they would want to stay out of my way, seeing as how they all call me a murderer and know how I killed Nathaniel. Why would anybody want to pick a fight with somebody capable of taking down a man of his size?

I don't know, and I don't care. I also don't care what happens after I raise the book I'm carrying in both hands and whack her with it. She must not have figured I would strike back, so she didn't defend herself. Her head snaps around, and she raises a hand to her lips. When she lifts her fingers, there's blood on the tips.

Damn, it feels good. Like I took a little bit of myself back.

"You bitch!" She backhands me before I know what's happening. My head snaps back, and pain radiates across my face. I lick my lips, the coppery tang of blood exploding against my tongue.

I'm about to drop the book, ready to beat the shit out of her when something shiny catches the light. She raises her arm, and I get a good look at the knife in her hand.

In utter shock, I watch the blade heading straight for my chest. Raising the book, I block the attack, using the momentum to bring the book down on her hand. She loses her grasp, and the knife falls to the ground between us.

Tightening my grip on the thick novel, I use it as a weapon, hitting Anja over and over again. At this moment, I'm not only beating her but I'm also beating everybody who's ever hurt me.

"Hey! What do you two think you're doing?" Footsteps pound our way as we both back off, flushed and guilty. It's one of the instructors, Mr. Daniels, and he's pissed as hell. "Don't try to deny that you were fighting. I can see the blood on both your faces."

He sighs, shaking his head. "You're going to have to see the headmaster about this."

Terrific. Just when I didn't think the day could get any worse.

19

LUCAS

"You're going to have to explain this to me slowly." It's a good thing I already picked the whiskey out of the cabinet since I'm going to need a stiff drink after this. Maybe the entire contents of the bottle. How often does a man hear the voice of a woman he believed was dead?

"I know you must be confused."

"Confused? That doesn't begin to describe what I'm feeling."

"I know. I'm sorry. I didn't want it to happen this way."

Her voice is the same: sweet, filled with apology. She did a lot of apologizing when we were together, for reasons I don't remember anymore. Maybe there weren't any reasons in the first place. Maybe I wanted her to be wrong, wanted a reason to hurt her.

"You make it sound like you didn't have any choice but to pretend you were dead."

"I didn't. Her adoptive parents sent me to Europe and made it look like I had died. They wouldn't give me details. I didn't know anything about it. I didn't disappear because I wanted to. I disappeared because they made me. They didn't want me to have anything to do with her and were afraid I might try to have a relationship with her."

"And you couldn't be bothered to reach out in all these years? Let somebody know you were actually alive?" My jaw tightens. "Your daughter, for instance?"

It seems like I still want to hurt her. There's pain in her voice when she murmurs, "I tried to get in touch with Aspen. I even tried to get in touch with you. It's not that easy. I don't have the kind of resources you have."

I suck in a deep breath, reminding myself that I'm not innocent in all of this. We never would have been in this mess if it wasn't for me. "Start from the beginning. You gave her up for adoption, but you tried to stay in touch with them?"

"She was a little girl, and I wanted to hear her voice. You have no idea how many nights I spent crying with nobody to hear me, wishing I knew what my little girl sounded like. Do you understand what that's like? Loving somebody so much and knowing there's no way to be with them?"

I hear her words, but I refuse to let them sink in. I can't think about that because it would inevitably take me down paths I don't want to travel. "What happened when you tried?"

"At first, they ignored me. Then after a while, she was getting older and saw the people she lived with as her family. I didn't want to drop a bomb on her, so eventually, I convinced myself it was in her best interest to stay away. But not a day has gone by that I haven't thought about her—you don't have to believe anything else I say but believe that. There have been times when the thought of her is the only thing that has kept me going."

I believe her, and not only because she was never a liar. If there's one person I could always see through, it was her. She had a quiet strength I couldn't appreciate back in the day, but I see it for what it is now.

And I hear it in her still. The years might have changed a lot of things for both of us, but that's remained the same.

"Why now?" I'm still gripping the bottle tight but haven't put my lips on it since before answering the phone. I want what's left of my good sense intact for this.

"I started trying again when she turned eighteen. I found her social media, but she wasn't active online. I was worried and dug deeper, leading to new articles about Aspen's father being arrested. Since then, I've been trying to find out where she is now."

"And how exactly did you figure out she is here?"

"Well... I don't really know. I kept hitting dead ends, and suddenly I got an anonymous email telling me that Aspen is at a university in Alaska and that you are the headmaster. I thought it was a cruel joke, to be honest."

"Well, I felt the same when they offered me this position."

"I know she's there, with you. Please just tell me she is safe."

"She is safe, and she is happy. She's been through a lot, but she is in a good place now."

"Does she know you are her father?"

"Yes. She hasn't known for long, neither have I, but I guess that's my fault."

"For what it's worth, I tried to tell you when I first found out I was pregnant."

"I know that."

"I would like to come to Corium to meet her."

Of course she does. "I don't know if this is the right time." How much more can she handle? Aspen has hardly had time to get over the shock. So much has happened.

I have such a fragile relationship with her. How can I expect her to believe I didn't know about this all along?

That damn bottle. Promising so much. All I have to do is take a sip, which will be easier to deal with. Just one sip will inevitably lead to another. Eventually, I'll be able to forget.

"Why?" she prompts. "If not now, when can I see her?

"She has been through a lot recently. I think we should give her some time to adjust before we throw something else at her."

"I guess you know her better than I do."

Do I? On paper, certainly. I've actually come face-to-face with her recently, unlike her mother. That isn't the same as really knowing someone. "First things first, did it never occur to you that you could reach out to me? Let me know you were alive?"

I know what she's about to say before she says a word. All it takes is her faint chuckle. "How was I supposed to know you would care? The last time I came to you, your friend almost raped me while you were passed out in the living room."

Fuck.

"Were you even aware that I was supposedly dead?"

"Yes. I've known for a while."

"Lucas, I'm sorry about that. I really am."

"I wish you would have told my brother about your pregnancy. He could have helped you."

"I thought about it. But I wasn't sure if I could trust him, and let's be honest with each other. Would you have wanted a baby? Think back to who you were then. I understand you've come a long way but try to remember."

I do remember, and it isn't as difficult as she might think. I've come a long way. Maybe I have, but I've also slipped back quite a bit. I'm more in touch with that side of myself than I've been in a long time, maybe because I'm not pretending he doesn't exist the way I tried before.

And no, that version of me had no interest in being a father. "I know you're right. I'm sorry you didn't think you could tell me about her."

"More than anything, I don't want you to think I've been gallivanting around Europe, avoiding my responsibilities."

"I don't think I could ever imagine you doing something like that." Me, on the other hand? It's a lot easier to imagine.

"I miss her. I really would like to see her as soon as possible. She needs a mother in her life, and I've needed her all this time."

"Why don't you let me talk to her first? I don't think it would do her any favors, her birth mother appearing out of the blue. She deserves a warning, at least. Some time to process it." Right now, I know all about being given no time to process things. I'm still trying to wrap my head around the conversation I'm having with this woman. She's alive. My past, alive and well after all this time. Yet another reminder of who I used to be.

"I'm sure you're right. She doesn't need me showing up and upsetting her. But please, could you talk to her soon? I hate to be pushy, but…"

"I get it." I need to get off the phone. I need to drink this away. I can't stand how thirsty I suddenly feel.

"Thank you. You don't know how much it means to hear you say that."

"I'll get back to you soon—"

"Wait! Don't hang up yet. I just want to know… is she happy? I mean, now, at Corium?"

"Yes. I think she is happy here. She wasn't at first, but now she is with Quinton, and he treats her well."

"I'm glad." Charlotte sighs, and I can hear the relief in her voice.

"Where can I reach you?" She gives me her number, and I promise to call as soon as I've had the discussion with Aspen. Then I have to hang up. I can't keep it together anymore.

Alive. All this time, she's been alive.

How am I supposed to tell Aspen about this? Where do I begin? I'm nobody's idea of cool or calm, and tact has never been my strong suit. There's nothing to prepare me for this. I'll find a way to fuck it up, I'm sure.

I can't believe how much I care about how she'll take this. I want to do the right thing by her, which means forgetting about my apprehension, getting over how awkward and painful this will be, and finding a way to frame this in a positive light. She thought she'd lost her parents, and now she has them both back. We might not be what she bargained for, but there's plenty of time to make up for the years we've lost.

All I can do is hope she'll buy it.

Fuck. I take a swig of the whiskey, but now I can hardly taste it. It might as well be water. I can't think of anything, but what I know will be shock and amazement and maybe betrayal on her face.

How am I supposed to explain why her own mother stayed away? How can I expect her to believe it? That's not my problem, though, right? That's the thing about having a kid, I've realized. All of a sudden, their problems become your problems. I want to spare her any additional pain.

I've drained nearly a third of the bottle when my phone rings again. I yank the receiver from the cradle, prepared to scream for my assistant to hold my calls for the rest of the day once I'm finished.

"What?" I bark, noting the extension to the history department on the screen.

"We have a problem on the dorm level. Two female students were fighting. One had a knife."

As if I need to deal with this piddly bullshit. "Deal with them."

There's a shuffling noise, then his voice drops to little more than a mumble. "Don't you think it would be more effective, coming from you?"

He's right. This is part of my job, like it or not. "I'll be there in a minute." I cap the bottle and set it aside before standing and straightening my shirt and tie. There I was, hoping to lay low for the rest of the day while I piece together a plan of action for Aspen. I should know by now there's no rest for the wicked. I make my way to the office, hoping I don't smell like a distillery or look as pissed off as I feel. The last thing I expect to find on reaching the office is Anja—and Delilah, standing in the corner with her arms folded.

When I enter the room, her jaw juts out, drawing my attention to her bruised, bloodied lip. My mood swings violently from relief at seeing her again to something much darker. Much more dangerous.

My chest goes painfully tight, and for a long moment, all I can see is that blood. She's bleeding. Anja made her bleed. If anyone is going to draw blood on her, it will be me. Who the fuck does that girl think she is?

Delilah's eyes widen, and I realize almost too late that the fury building inside me has begun to show itself. It's one thing for her to see that, but we aren't alone. "What happened here?" I ask in a strained voice.

"I happened to find these two in the middle of a brawl."

"It wasn't a brawl," Delilah mumbles.

"You were putting your hands on each other, which is bad enough. Having a weapon is unacceptable."

"I hit her with a book, not my hands," Delilah adds, digging herself a deeper hole. "She's the one who pulled a knife." Doesn't she know when to shut up? Meanwhile, I can't take my eyes off her lip. I want to taste it, run my tongue along its length, and savor the coppery taste of her blood. I'm losing all semblance of myself, aren't I? All because of her.

All eyes are on me. Right, I'm the headmaster. They expect me to be a leader. If only they saw what was in my head. They would want no such thing from me.

"There's a simple solution to all this." Instead of being repentant, Anja doesn't bother trying to hide how she glares at Delilah. She looks as if she's disgusted at her mere presence. "She could leave, disappear from Corium. She doesn't belong here or deserve to use this place as a sanctuary to hide from her demons."

I need to get her out of my sight before I do something I'll regret. "That's not your call, is it?" I turn to her, frowning. I know Delilah. She wouldn't pick a fight and wouldn't engage in one unless she was given no choice. I can hardly share that with this haughty, snide little bitch sitting in front of me with her arms folded. "I think it's best if you leave Corium for a while. You are suspended until further notice."

Anja's face falls, her smug grin turning into an opened-mouthed O. "Are you serious?"

"Very. Now get out of here, pack your shit, and head back to Russia."

Anja stays frozen in shock for a few more seconds before she shoves out of the chair and marches from the room.

Delilah stares at the floor, sullen, scuffing the tile with the toe of her shoe.

I make a big deal of turning toward Delilah, keeping my voice grave. "You stay out of trouble. I don't want to hear anything about fighting, not ever again."

I still need to put on a good show. "Thank you for calling me, Mr. Daniels. I'll escort Delilah out." What I have to say to her can't be shared in his presence. For his part, he looks relieved to get the whole thing over with.

After ensuring we're alone in the hallway, I turn to her and study her face more closely. "You should put ice on that."

All she does is roll her eyes. "What, are you trying to do a good deed today?"

"What does that mean?"

"You're anything but dumb, Lucas. Figure it out." She heaves a sigh before turning away. "And please don't look at me like you give a shit, okay?"

My mouth goes dry, I want to tell her I do, but I can't. I can't physically or mentally make my mouth say the words, but I can react.

Reaching for her, I brush away the stray strands of hair that linger on her face. She's beautiful, not in a supermodel way but in a natural way. There is no filter with her, making her unique, a breath of fresh air. I cup her cheeks tenderly, and she lifts her gaze, her long lashes flutter, and I can't help myself. I have to taste her lips.

I lean in and gently graze her lips with my own. I know the risk I'm taking kissing her, but I don't care.

I don't care what anyone has to say. She lets out a low whimper from deep in her throat, and the sound goes straight to my cock.

Her sweet taste, mixed with the copper tang of her blood, touches my lips, and I'm like a shark who just had a taste of prey. I kiss her a little deeper, wanting more, needing more. Before I get the chance, she pulls away, her eyes big, her lip bruised, and a hint of sadness in her eyes.

"We shouldn't," she whispers. All I can do is watch her as she retreats, wishing I could tell her how much I care.

How I'd love to break that little bitch's hands for daring to lay them on someone so obviously above her. I want to punish Anja as much as I want to punish anyone and everyone who's ever made Delilah feel less than. Worthless, useless, alone.

The thing is, I don't know if it's all a matter of protecting her or saving her misery for myself. So I can savor it, knowing I'm the only one with that sort of power over her.

And I think I'm ever going to make a decent father? Who am I trying to kid? There's nothing for me to do but retreat to my apartment. My day is fucked, my already sparse concentration destroyed by the call from Charlotte and the unplanned contact with the girl I've avoided all week. At least now I've seen her with my own two eyes, so there's no question of whether or not she's in one piece—but it also means knowing firsthand what she's going through. She can't walk down the hall without being hit.

At least she gave some of it back. Anja was bleeding, too.

"There you are."

Son of a bitch. Is the entire world conspiring against me today? I reach the floor where the apartments sit. I'm halfway down the hall before I notice Lauren waiting for me, leaning against my door like she has all the time in the world and nowhere else to be. It's too late to avoid her now. Besides, it would look like I was running away. I might do just that, but I don't want it to look that way.

"Don't you have something better to do?" I grumble.

"Presently? No. I have been waiting for you to come in for a session, which you know very well since you've been avoiding my phone calls like they're the plague."

"If I were avoiding you, that would imply this is important enough for me to avoid. Really, I don't have the time or the inclination."

Her head bobs up and down slowly. "Sure. Tell me another good one."

She won't move away from the door, and the fury blazing within me leaves me wanting to warn her.

"Lauren. This isn't the time. For your own sake, get out of the way."

"Are you going to come in for a session?"

When all I do is growl, she steps aside. "You can't avoid yourself forever, you know."

"Who said I was avoiding myself?" I ask as I unlock the door. "It's just that I've figured out what you haven't."

"And what is that?"

I barely spare her a glance over my shoulder. "I'm past saving, so please stop wasting your time and mine."

With that, I slam the door, ending the conversation.

20

DELILAH

Two weeks have passed in slow motion, and each day seems to take longer to get through than the last. Lucas has fallen off the face of the earth, and I'm struggling to understand what I should do. I hate it here, and there isn't a single soul that makes me believe this place is safe, except Lucas. I can still feel his kiss on my lips if I shut my eyes. It's the last thing he did. I knew what he was trying to do, but I needed more.

I close the book I'm reading, realizing it's impossible to focus on the words when my mind is elsewhere.

It only frustrates me the more I try to concentrate. How am I supposed to concentrate on reading anything when I always feel like I'm waiting for the other shoe to drop? I can't settle down. I can't clear my mind.

It's been way too quiet these past couple of weeks. Things have calmed down since the fight with Anja, and it's damn near creepy.

Maybe it's paranoia, but I can't shake the idea they're planning something. I don't know who *they* are exactly. Whoever they are, they're not giving up out of nowhere. Not when they're so committed to hating me. That kind of thing doesn't fade away overnight.

Maybe this is part of the plan now that I think about it. Making me wonder. Making me wait, dread, and look over my shoulder everywhere I go. Even here, in my room. I never settle in before checking under the bed and in the bathroom in case someone is hiding. I'm that afraid.

I'm also lonely. Extremely. As much as I would like to go back to the library and hang out with Brittney and Aspen, I can't risk pissing Q off worse than I already have. It's not so much that I'm afraid of him but of what he'll set in motion. I don't need to tempt him to hurt me or to have somebody else do it for him. I don't need to give him any excuses.

But I'm starting to lose it a little. Always staring at these walls when I'm not in class. Having nobody to talk to, not a single soul. Not even Lucas, which hurts worse than anything.

He looked concerned, genuinely upset after the whole thing with Anja.

But I was right, wasn't I? He didn't actually care. How could he? He never checked in on me after that. I haven't set eyes on him since.

I guess I was right when I accused him of not giving a shit about me. It doesn't mean I want it to be right. I was hoping he would argue or try to prove me wrong. His kiss was a small reprieve, but it wasn't enough. I needed to hear him say it. As always, the memory of that night here in my room makes me feel a little sick. Not because of what he said or did, but how he was. Practically unhinged, wasted out of his mind. And that day, after the fight. I smelled the whiskey on his breath and saw how glassy his eyes were starting to get. He was drinking in the middle of the day, probably sitting alone in his office.

He's not doing well. I can only imagine it's gotten worse since then.

I can't believe I care, but I'm not going to waste time telling myself I shouldn't. I have a fucked-up relationship with him. Arguing with myself about it isn't going to change anything. I have to accept that, for some reason, he's taken hold of me. No matter how much I wish it were possible, I can't free myself.

I have to see him. Not because I think he'll help me, but because he needs help. The thought of him being in pain causes me pain—my chest hurts just imagining it.

It's late enough that the halls should be pretty much empty. What's the worst that could happen? He'll tell me to mind my own business. But at least I'll be able to see him and maybe get through to him that there's someone who cares whether he drinks himself to death or not.

It's as good an excuse as any to get up and sneak into the hall. It's not like I haven't wanted to do this for weeks, but at least now there's a plausible excuse for it. All I have to do is dart over to the elevator and take it to Lucas's floor. I don't hear anything out here —no voices, footsteps, or even any loud TV or music coming from the other rooms.

I jog over to the elevator and press the button, bouncing up and down on the balls of my feet, waiting for it to arrive. The last thing I need is for somebody to see me out here and wonder why I'm—

It happens so fast. There are no footsteps, no noise at all. One minute I am standing, and then suddenly, I'm on my knees. Pain radiates through my head from the back, and black dots appear over my vision. My entire body sways like a branch in the wind, and I fall against the wall, hitting the floor before even realizing what's happened. Nausea grips me tight, but the pain is worse.

My vision blurs, and I'm afraid to put a hand to my head since I don't know what I'm going to find.

I don't even think to look up and see who did it. I'm too busy trying to catch up with what's happening. My thoughts are all jumbled. I can't think straight. I can't even see straight. Everything is all swimmy and blurred.

I've barely caught my breath before I hear, "Delilah! Oh, my god. Are you okay?"

I blink and find Aspen hovering over me, holding my face between her hands. "What happened?"

I can't believe how long it takes me to make my tongue work. It's so heavy. "I... don't know. Somebody hit me."

"I thought I heard somebody running, but they were going in the other direction." She tips my head down to take a look at the back. "Shit. You're bleeding. We have to get you down to medical right away. Do you think you can walk?"

"I'll try."

She helps me stand, and I have to take a second to lean against the wall when the hallway doesn't stop tilting back and forth. It does eventually, and I lean on Aspen as we get in the elevator and take it down to the medical wing.

"Did you see anyone?" she asks along the way.

"No. They came at me from behind and ran off. I was too dazed to get a look at anyone."

"What a coward," she mutters. I can only grunt in agreement. Even nodding my head hurts too much.

Who would do this? I knew something had to be coming, but a sneak attack? Even I didn't expect that.

"YOU'LL BE FINE." Dr. Lauren peels off her gloves before tossing them in a wastebasket. Despite her warm assurance, she looks downright pissed. "It looks like you have a slight concussion. I'm going to give you something for the pain. Other than that, it's nothing but a shallow laceration. You'll have to be careful for a couple of days while your scalp is tender."

"Thank you." I'm on a gurney, the bright examination light glaring down at me. She's kind enough to adjust it, swinging it to the side, so I don't have to squint anymore.

"I'm sorry, Delilah. I'm sorry this happened to you." Aspen insisted on staying, and now she's standing by my side, her arms folded, her eyes blazing with rage.

It's still hard to believe she cares, but I guess she must. I'm lucky she found me. For all I know, whoever hurt me saw her coming and ran off. They might have kept hitting me if it hadn't been for that. I could be dead right now.

I don't want to think about it.

The doors burst open and in rushes Quinton. He immediately gathers Aspen into his arms like she's some piece of precious porcelain.

"Are you all right?" he murmurs, holding her tight to his chest. I was only slightly nauseated before. Now? I'm a kiss on the forehead away from puking.

"I'm fine. Nothing happened to me." She even looks slightly annoyed, but he doesn't seem to notice.

Quinton didn't come by himself either. Lucas storms in on his heels—and his rage only flares up when he sets his eyes on Aspen.

"What the hell were you two doing together, and why the hell are you here?" he demands, glaring at her. At least he sounds sober. I guess that's a good sign. Then again, what do I know? I have a concussion.

"I found her in the hallway. I didn't do anything wrong." She tips her head to the side, looking back and forth between the two men. "What's this all about? Why are you acting like this? Like I have something to be afraid of."

Instead of answering, Lucas turns his attention my way. "Who did this to you? What happened?"

I can't come out and tell him what I was doing, not with everybody else on top of us. "I was out in the hallway, and somebody hit me from behind. I didn't even hear them coming, and I never saw them."

Before anybody can ask her, Aspen pipes up. "Like I told her, I heard somebody running away, but I never saw them."

"She might have saved my life." To think, she was the one who saved me. Life has a funny way of playing tricks on people.

If there's one thing I've come to expect from Lucas, it's the unexpected. By now, nothing he does or says should surprise me. But when he whirls on Q and takes him by the shoulders, I gasp along with Lauren and Aspen.

"Why the fuck would you let Ren do this to her? Are you out of your mind? What about what we discussed?"

Quinton shoves him away. "It wasn't Ren. My father hasn't given the order yet, so I know he had nothing to do with it."

"Wait a second." I hold up a hand, whispering since my head might split open if I try to speak any louder. "What are you talking about? What order?"

"Yeah. I would like to know, as well." Aspen's hands land on her hips. "What do you two know that we don't?"

The two of them wear identical expressions of guilt. "Let me explain," Q begins, reaching for Aspen like he wants to gather her in his arms before she runs away.

She slips out of his grasp. "No. That's not how this is going to go. What aren't you telling me? What order are you talking about? What is your father doing this time?"

He grits his teeth, flushing like he's either furious or embarrassed. She must really have his nuts in a vise.

"You know it's not simple with him. He got it in his head that he wanted to make Delilah pay for what happened. She's a loose end, and he wants her gone." The coward. He won't even look at me when he says it. "I don't know what he wants to do. He won't tell me. I only know he hasn't made up his mind yet. So this wasn't him."

All I can do is stare at Lucas, open-mouthed. "And you knew." I don't have it in me to scream the way I want to, the way I am inside my already aching head.

On the other hand, Aspen isn't the one with a splitting headache.

"You knew something like this could happen, and you would let her die and not do anything about it! How could you?" She backs away from both of them. "How could either of you?"

"You know it isn't that simple, dammit," Q growls.

"It seems pretty simple to me. You could tell Lucas about your father's plan, but not Delilah? Not even me? I'm your wife, dammit. Why would you keep this from me?"

"That's easy," I whisper. Even that is enough to take it out of me. I'm so tired. "He wouldn't want to get in the way of his father's plans."

He glares at me for a second before softening a little. "It's not like that. You're underestimating me."

"How so? It would have been pretty simple to give me a heads-up. I already know there's a target on my back around here, but I didn't think he'd be sending somebody to kill me."

"But this wasn't him."

"Enough. I don't want to hear it anymore." I close my eyes, fighting the tears threatening to well up in them. I won't give any of them the satisfaction of seeing me cry. I'm so tired of being hurt.

"Both of you, get back to the dorms. It's late." Lucas turns to Aspen and Q.

It's obvious Aspen doesn't want to listen to him any more than she wants to be near her husband, but she goes anyway after shooting me one last look. "Let me know if you need anything, okay?"

"I will. Thank you."

Lauren clears her throat. "I have to do a couple of things. I'll be nearby if you need me." She shoots daggers at Lucas before leaving the two of us alone. I really wish she wouldn't. I have nothing to say to him now.

Actually, that's not quite true. "I can't believe you. How could you do this to me?"

"I meant to tell you the night I came to your room."

"But you didn't. And that was, what, three weeks ago? How many opportunities have you had since then? Or was this the kind of thing you could only tell me that night, and that's all?"

His face scrunches up, and he rubs the bridge of his nose like he has a headache. Like he has any idea what a headache is right now. I'm the one lying here suffering. "You're not making this any easier."

"Oh, excuse me. I would hate to inconvenience you. I'm sorry you had to take time away from whatever you were doing just to come down here."

"You know it isn't like that."

"I don't know anything, do I? Here I was, thinking you actually cared about me at least a little. All these weeks, there was the chance I could be killed. And you couldn't say a word about it. What if I died tonight? And you could have stopped it, but you didn't?"

His mouth works like he's trying to come up with something to say, but I know whatever it is will be a lie. "Just forget about it. Go away. I don't want you here, and I don't want your shitty excuses." I turn my face away from his, even though moving my head is agony.

It's still preferable to having to set eyes on him. The liar. The coward.

At least he takes the hint, retreating slowly. Now I can let the tears fall, and I do, allowing them to course slowly down my cheeks.

21

LUCAS

*I*t has been a while since I felt this way. I almost forgot the way my skin crawls as the walls seemingly close in on me. With each second passing, the walls inch closer, and the air in my lungs becomes more sparse.

I hate it. I hate the feeling of drowning, suffocating slowly while the rest of the world moves on like I don't even exist. It took me years to get over this feeling, and just when I thought I had figured it out, Delilah came along and ruined everything. I was doing great without her. Maybe I wasn't happy, but I wasn't miserable either.

Looking over at the empty bottle of whiskey sitting on my nightstand, I quietly curse to myself. I'm out of booze, and it's not like I can walk down to the nearest convenience store and pick up something else. I don't even know when the next shipment is coming in. Unless it's today, it's not soon enough.

Briefly, I think about sending out the helicopter. But Xander is already on my case, and I'm sure I'd never hear the end of it if I used his precious school money to get me more alcohol. I would roll my eyes at him if my head wasn't pounding already. But my killer headache makes me sit up slowly instead.

It's not until I'm upright that I realize how bad my hangover really is. Ugh. This is literally straight from hell. I squeeze my eyes shut and wait for the room to stop spinning.

Putting my feet on the floor helps ground me. My equilibrium balances out, and it doesn't feel like I'm about to fall off the earth.

But that's only step one. This isn't my first rodeo, as they say. I've been through worse than this, though this is bad enough.

I'm sure age doesn't help things. Back in the day, I'd wake up feeling like shit, down some black coffee and a couple of aspirin—if that—and I'd be back in action.

Nowadays, the thought of the aftermath is almost enough to make me avoid drinking in the first place.

But not quite enough. Because here I am, feeling like absolute dogshit with an entire day ahead of me. A day in which I'm supposed to at least appear to be in charge of things around here.

I get on my feet slowly, cautiously. When the room generally stays the way it should, with everything upright and nothing spinning, I take the slow, painful walk to the bathroom. This is almost bad enough to make me swear off drinking for good. The only thing keeping me moving right now is knowing it will pass.

If only I had the hair of the dog to get me through it. But no, I had to go and drain the entire bottle last night. Fucking idiot.

Somehow, I manage to make it into the shower. This isn't the time to comfort myself with anything warm. Cold water hits me like a million little razor blades, digging into my skin, into my very skull.

But it's what I need now. It wakes me up and gets my blood pumping. I stand under the spray for as long as I can stand it before adding enough hot water to make it bearable. By the time I'm out, I feel substantially more human, but I still drag ass into the kitchen to make coffee. A lot of very strong coffee.

I know this has to stop. Every morning, it's the same thing. I can't keep doing this. It won't end well. I'm not the kid I used to be—there's no bouncing back. At this rate, I've set myself up for a day of doing nothing but trying to keep my head from hitting the desk. I ache from head to toe and can't hold a thought that doesn't have to deal with fatigue or pain. I force myself to chug a bottle of water while the coffee brews, then head into the bedroom to pull out my clothes for the day before grooming as best as I can.

There's going to be a point when I hit bottom. It happens to everybody in my position. Shit gets out of hand to the point where there's no continuing in the same vein any longer. If this isn't rock bottom, I don't want to know what is. And frankly, I don't know that I have it in me to claw my way out of this. This might be where I stay.

Eventually, I'll get used to staggering through my day. That's another difference from my old life. I could afford to nurse an especially bad hangover until I felt up to facing existence. Now, I have no choice. I have bullshit responsibilities and people counting on me.

A look at my reflection as I'm shaving tells me I'm in serious need of eye drops. My eyes have that bloodshot, haggard look of a drunk. There's a bottle in the medicine cabinet, and I use it liberally once I've finished rinsing my cheeks.

I also make liberal use of ibuprofen, downing a small handful before cracking open another bottle of water and gulping half of it down. Greasy food used to be a cure-all, but the concept of having so much as a bite of food pass my lips makes my stomach churn. That might have to wait until later.

I fill a travel mug with coffee, pack my laptop into my briefcase, and head to my office. At least my gait is steady, and the murderous pounding in my head has lessened to something closer to a dull throb. Every footstep isn't agony, so I can afford to offer a brief smile to the few people I cross paths with.

Always in the back of my head is whether they know. Whether they see what's happening inside me. Has it started showing itself in my face? I don't think so, not yet, but I know it's inevitable. Nobody lies to themselves quite like an addict. Most of the time, they're the last to know everybody's been able to see through them for ages. I never wanted to be that person. I still don't.

But, my god, what I wouldn't give for a drink.

I'm in my office before my assistant arrives, and that's a small blessing since I'm not in a place where conversation is a good idea. By the time I've finished my coffee, I might be able to consider it. I close my door for the sake of suffering in private, then sink into my chair with an exhausted sigh.

My brain is full of cotton candy, and my limbs feel heavy. I manage to pull out my laptop and boot it up, but I can't bring myself to concentrate on any of the emails awaiting my attention. I would happily delete my entire inbox if I thought I could get away with it.

I force myself through them, one by one, even the piddly bullshit I shouldn't have to concern myself with. Signing off on purchase orders and emails from parents about their children. At least it's nothing too challenging, nothing I have to expend any brain power over. Sounds from outside my office tell me I'm not alone anymore, but at least she doesn't invade my privacy. Thank god for small favors.

As it turns out, someone else wants to invade my privacy, only he uses the phone. I'd swear the man has a hidden camera trained on me at all times. He always seems to know exactly when I want to talk to him the least.

I can't get away with ignoring him the way I've done to Lauren all these weeks, so I pick up the phone on the fourth ring. "You know better than to hit me up first thing in the morning," I tell my brother. I actually sound pretty clear-headed and energetic, at least to my ears.

"I figured I'd grab you before the day gets too busy."

"Considerate of you." Something's up. He sounds too smooth, too even.

My suspicions make me sit up straighter and push the pain and fatigue away. I know how to rally, and something tells me that's what I need to do now. "What's on your mind?" I ask.

"How are things going there? I haven't heard anything about Delilah."

"That's because there's nothing to hear."

"I got word Xander Rossi took it on himself to deal with her."

Of course. My brother has his finger on the pulse of just about everything. It's enough to set my teeth on edge. "Took it on himself? He takes nothing on himself. You know it means giving the order to someone else."

"The result is the same. But she's okay?"

"For now, yes." She came so close to being anything but. And it's my fault. She's right. I didn't warn her. I didn't even give her that much.

"And how are you?"

"Fine. Since when do we check in with each other and talk about our feelings and stuff?"

"What gave you the impression I was concerned with your feelings?" He snickers. Now disappointment leaks into his voice. At least he tried to keep it out at first. "You know I hear things."

"Maybe you should see a psychiatrist if you're hearing things."

"Enough," he snaps. "Knock it the fuck off with the games. You're falling the fuck apart. Tell yourself all you want that you're able to hide it, but I think you know better. You should by now. It's not like this is the first time you've gone off the deep end."

"Deep end? Who the fuck are you talking to? I'm just fine, thank you very much. Deep end. As if I'm not sitting here at my fucking desk right this very minute, going through my inbox even though it's the most boring fucking thing in the world. Deep end. You don't know what you're talking about."

"And whenever you start throwing out these protests, I know you're trying to cover something up. Have you forgotten who you're talking to?"

"Have you? I am a grown fucking man. I don't need you checking up on me."

"I'm worried about you."

"You're wasting your time." I slam the receiver down before he can hand me more of his bullshit. Like I need that today or any other day. His fucking concern. I know what he really wants. An opportunity to say I told you so. I'll be damned if I'm going to give it to him.

It's not another two minutes before there's a sharp knock on my door. I'd scream if I had the energy. "Mr. Diavolo? You have a visitor."

I recognize the kid when he strolls in. Enzo Moroni, sullen as ever. He hands me a folded, stapled note. Obviously, whoever gave it to him to deliver wanted to make sure he didn't open it.

It's from his math instructor. I glance up from the page, lifting an eyebrow. "Contraband?"

"It's not that big a deal. It's not like I'm peddling meth."

"Meth wouldn't be as serious as bringing a gun. What else do you have?"

He reaches into his pockets with a heavy sigh and pulls out three prescription bottles. Xanax. Adderall. Percocet. "So you raided the family medicine cabinet the last time you were home, huh?" I ask, picking up the painkillers and examining the label in his mother's name.

"So what? Nobody notices it's gone. They'll just get more."

I turn the bottle over and over in my hand, watching him. He's a cool one. That much is for sure. Doesn't look the slightest bit sorry.

I slap the bottle down on the desk, which at least gets a reaction out of him. He jumps, his gaze snapping up and locking on mine. "I don't care much about the drugs. I do care that you brought a gun in here. Why? Don't you feel safe here?"

He shrugs. "I mean, I guess. A lot of shit has been going down."

"You know you can get canned for this, right? We have a zero-tolerance policy on weapons."

"Like the zero tolerance you have on killing a student?"

"Don't be a smart-ass. That was handled accordingly. This is about you."

"So what?" Another shrug. "I don't give a shit. I don't want to be here, anyway. You kick me out? That's fine."

I don't have it in me to get through to this kid—and frankly, I don't care enough, either. "You realize I'm confiscating these, right? Get back to class, and don't ever let me hear about you having shit you are not supposed to have. Because if anything like this is found on another student, I'm coming to you first. And there are worse things than getting kicked out of Corium. Don't make it so you have to find out firsthand."

He blows out a heavy sigh and comes dangerously close to testing the limits of my patience but is smart enough to spin on his heel and stroll out of the office. This fucking kid. All these fucking kids. Not that I would be that much better, but good luck being successful in our world—and not ending up in federal prison—if you aren't smart enough to wait until after class to sell pills to your friends. Dipshit.

Pills which I quickly stash in my desk drawer. The kid did me a favor by being so stupid. A couple of five-milligram tablets of Percocet might be just what the doctor ordered, come to think of it. And it might help me get through the rest of the day.

Though, now that my email is taken care of and my to-do list is pretty much cleared off, I'm of half a mind to get the hell out of here for the rest of the day. I can make up an excuse, not that I should have to. Who's going to question me?

I have my hand on the laptop lid, prepared to close it and announce I can be reached in my apartment if anything comes up.

As if on cue, there's another knock on the door. The entire school is conspiring to kill me today. I'm sure of it. "What is it this time?"

I look up as the door opens, prepared to get rid of whoever it is as quickly as possible.

The sight of a familiar pair of eyes knocks the breath out of my lungs and sends me slamming back in my chair. She's older, but then so am I. She still has that quality of pure, natural beauty. Beauty I tried so hard to destroy.

She's standing in front of me after all this time.

And, my god, does she look like our daughter. How did I not see it from the very beginning?

"Charlotte."

22

DELILAH

"*T*hank you for taking the time to see me."

"You don't have to thank me." Dr. Lauren wears a funny look when she pushes her chair away from me, rolling backward so she can toss her gloves in the trash after examining the cut on my head. "This is my job, don't forget. And I told you to come in and follow up with me, remember?"

"I remember. But I'm fine. It seems like you're going out of your way."

"I'm not." She hits me with an appraising look as she stands. "You need to get used to people giving a damn about you, girl."

That only makes me laugh. I know I shouldn't. I know she means it. But there comes a time when a person has to get real. "You're one of the few who ever have."

"That was the past. This is now. You have to give yourself a chance to be cared for."

Right. I thought Lucas cared about me, and look where I ended up. Alone. Hated. Maybe Aspen wants to be friends—I still can't imagine why—but her husband won't let her. He acted like I was a leper or something when he saw us together in the medical wing. Freaking out because, oh no, his precious Aspen was spending time with a girl who wouldn't be alive much longer.

Let's not help the girl with a death sentence hanging over her head or anything. Let's avoid her, instead. Wouldn't want to get any blood splattered on us.

"Caring for me is too dangerous," I remind her. "It's probably not safe for you, either. You're better off pretending I don't exist, like everybody else does."

"It won't always be like this. I'm sure..." What else is there to say? It's a waste of breath to tell me everything will be okay. I know it won't unless the people with a thing against me all change their minds for some reason. I can't think of what that reason might be. I doubt such a reason exists, anyway. Once people get ideas in their heads, they don't easily let go of them.

"Thanks for checking up on me." I hop down from the examination table. "I'd better get to class."

"How are classes going, by the way? Have you been able to concentrate on your work?"

Her penetrating stare tells me she already knows the answer. It isn't easy lying to her when she's so friendly and caring. So I don't bother. "No. Not at all. But it's not like I actually want to be here. I learn more from reading books in the library."

"Keep doing that. You're a smart girl. I would hate to think of you not learning anything all this time."

What's the use? I'm not leaving here alive. "I'm doing my best." At least that's not a lie. But my best isn't exactly a whole lot, either.

I don't particularly feel like going to class. I'm sure nobody will care if I show up or not. It's a complete joke, being here in the first place. Like being on death row, but people expect you to go through the motions of an ordinary day as if you have a future worth preparing for. It's like everybody around here operates under the same mass delusion.

I don't want to go to the library, either. I might see Aspen there, which means her guard dog will eventually come sniffing around. He can't be too far from her for too long. She might make the grave mistake of speaking to me, and then where would we be?

It's Lucas I want to see. I want to know more about why he was ready to let me die. That pathetic excuse about wanting to tell me the night he came to my room. What was that supposed to be about? Am I supposed to think he's a good guy for considering giving me a heads-up? Let's gloss over the weeks between then and now. What a coward.

I doubt that's a word he'd ever use to describe himself. Coward. He thinks he's strong and vicious and all that. The sort of man who makes things happen. He snaps his fingers, and everybody sits up straight and waits for his instructions. He barges into a girl's bedroom, and she lies back and waits for him, trembling, anticipating his touch.

At least, that's what he wishes was true.

I know the truth—and maybe that's why he hates me. Because I know the truth about him. I know who he is, the sort of man underneath the mask he wears. He has actual feelings. A conscience. He wants to do right by his kid, even though he doesn't have the first idea of how to show emotion. He wants to be nice to me, but it would mean going against everything that's supposed to matter in this fucked-up world of his.

He feels things. He wants things. He's afraid to show it, and he doesn't understand that fear makes him weak. Not feeling or wanting things but being afraid to show it.

He would have warned me if he hadn't been afraid to show how much he actually cared whether I live or die.

That is, if he actually does care. Which part was the lie? The caring, or the pretending not to? I'm so tired of all these questions, never knowing what's real and what's not.

I guess that's why I'm halfway to Lucas's office before I know what I'm doing. This was always where I was going to end up. I can either sit and stew with all these questions, or I can force him to answer me.

His assistant isn't at her desk. That's probably not a bad thing. She doesn't need to hear what I have to say. His door is open a crack, far enough for me to see him at his desk.

"What are you doing here? I told you I'd call when the time is right."

Whoever he's talking to, he's not happy with them. I press myself against the wall, holding my breath. I should probably get out of here, or at least wait further away until his conversation is over. Right? That's what a normal, sane person would do.

Nobody ever called me normal, did they?

"I know. I was too eager. I've been waiting so long and couldn't wait any longer."

I have to clamp my hand over my mouth in hopes of silencing my gasp. I figured he was on the phone. From where I'm standing, I can't see much of the room's interior. Only his arm, his shoulder.

But he's definitely talking to a woman. And of course, now I want to know who she is. It can't be Lauren since I just left her. It's not Aspen, either—she sounds older, more like Lucas's age.

Of course, idiot. What, did you think you were the only woman in his life?

I watch the side of his fist pound against the desk. Even at a distance, it makes me jump. "You know how complicated this could make things? There was a reason I didn't want you showing up here unannounced. You've made this a lot more difficult than it was already going to be."

My stomach is churning, and my palms are sweaty, and I really, really wish I could get a look at whoever he's talking to. There's only one explanation that makes any sense. She's a girlfriend. Somebody he doesn't want people to know about. Maybe they were supposed to meet up somewhere away from Corium, something like that.

"I couldn't stay away. And I couldn't keep waiting for you." Oh, fuck, she sounds so desperate. Like she's in love with him. Can this get any worse?

"I have work to do here, you know. I can't afford to let personal things get in the way all the time. This kind of thing has to be worked out carefully. How am I going to explain why you're here? And how exactly did you get here anyway?"

I'm going to be sick. Just when I thought I had already heard every possible lie come out of his mouth. Then again, is a lie of omission the same as a regular lie? I never came out and asked him if he had a girlfriend. He conveniently never told me.

And why would he? Why do I matter? I don't. I'm somebody to keep his dick wet and his balls drained while he's waiting for his girlfriend to show up. I wonder if she knows who he really is. What he's been doing with me.

More than anything, I wish I had the guts to go in there. Swing the door open and announce myself and insist on a little truth. Does she know what a coward he is? How he was willing to let me die? I wonder if she'd feel so desperate to be with him if she heard about that.

I have to fight to hold myself back. What would it make me look like, going in there, freaking out? That's not who I want to be. The spurned side piece who loses it once it becomes clear a guy isn't interested in her anymore. That's pathetic. I've already lost so much, but I'll be damned if I lose what little bit of pride I have left.

I can't believe how much it hurts, though. I can't believe I still had a little shred of hope in my heart, either. Shouldn't I know better by now? But it's gone, burned up. One more thing for Lucas to take from me.

One thing is for sure as I tiptoe out of the assistant's office, then rush back to my room to be alone—he's not going to get away with this. I won't throw a fit in front of his woman, whoever she is, but I'm not going to pretend I don't know she exists. Maybe I'll rub it in his face a little bit, even. His little secret isn't a secret anymore. He's not as good a liar as he thought he was.

Has he somehow been fucking her all this time? What if she comes in every once in a while and wasn't supposed to be back until after this? The next time he called her or whatever? I can just imagine it. Sneaking her in, sneaking her back out. No wonder it's been so easy for him to stay away from me these past few weeks. The bastard. The lying, callous bastard. Pretending. Making me think he cared.

And dammit, I should have known better. How many times am I going to let him hurt me?

My fists slice through the air at my sides as I walk, and I imagine driving them into his face again and again. He knows what things have been like for me. He's seen it. He's been there. He knows practically everything about me, how I've never been able to count on anybody. And still, he lied. He used me, lied, and then threw me away.

Where's the big surprise there? He couldn't be bothered to warn me about Xander. What's a little thing like a secret girlfriend compared to that?

At least I can be alone for a little while. I can cry in private, maybe get it all out of my system before I see him. Maybe I'll wait until later while he's in his apartment. I'll have him send his little girlfriend away and pretend it's a school-related thing. The way it would be if I hadn't let him get to me the way I did.

I'm prepared to do my usual checking under the bed routine when I reach my room and open the door.

But I can't move once I get a look inside. I don't want to, either. I'm afraid to.

My eyes dart all around the room, landing on one thing after another. The mattress hangs halfway off the bed frame. The pillows ripped open, stuffing everywhere. The broken lamp. The books are torn to pieces, pages strewn from one end of the room to the other.

Clothes, torn to shreds. Everywhere. Even the clothes Celia gave me. All of it pulled out and torn up and thrown around.

But it's the wall above the headboard that holds my attention once I've taken in the sight of everything else. It's what turns my blood to ice. Two words are scrawled in what looks like blood.

YOU'RE DEAD.

At first, it feels like this is happening to somebody else. This can't be my room. I see it, but I don't feel connected to it. My brain won't let me.

But slowly, a little bit at a time, I've come to realize somebody broke into my room and tore it apart. Just because they could, and maybe because they were expected to.

In other words, the sneak attack wasn't a fluke or an accident. They want to make sure I'm aware of what their intentions were and still are. Just because they couldn't finish the job the first time around doesn't mean I can breathe easy.

And knowing there won't be repercussions for anything they do, things are only going to get worse.

"*I*f you know what's good for you, you will not step foot outside this room until I tell you to."

"I told you I wouldn't, and I won't," Charlotte fires back and closes the door in my face. I put her in an empty staff apartment. It's close enough to mine that she can get to me if she needs anything without revealing herself. As far as I know, she's fine and better stay that way. The only way she wouldn't is if she left the apartment.

Knowing she's there will eat away at me all night, and it will render me useless all day.

Then there is the fact that I have nothing to drink. No means of blotting out reality. There's nothing to do but face it. Stare at it head-on.

What makes matters worse is the text I get.

Aspen: I feel like I could use a session. Do you have time?

Her timing is impeccable. If I didn't know better, I'd bet on her knowing more than she's supposed to. But no, it's just another joke on me by the universe at large. The gods fucking with me, seeing how far they can push me this time.

Me: Sure, meet me at the gym.

A few minutes later, I head to the gym even though I can hardly keep my eyes open. I'm not sure what's worse, pretending not to have a hangover or pretending not to be half dead from lack of sleep. Fighting to find a way through the tangled disaster my life has become.

If anything, I tell myself as I walk down the hall on the way to the gym, this could be a blessing in disguise. Now I have no choice but to come clean with her. No excuses, no avoidance. It's the simplest thing in the world. All I have to do is get the fucking words to come out of my mouth.

Aspen, your mother is alive, and she's here.

DAMMIT. I don't know if I can do it. Why do I always go cold inside at the thought of telling her? I'm not at fault here. I didn't keep Charlotte from her.

I had no idea she was alive until recently. It's all a matter of telling the truth: I didn't know how to explain it. I didn't want to upset her. All I know is that this will hurt her, and that's the last thing she deserves.

I don't have the first fucking clue how to relate to my own daughter.

I'll probably leave that part unspoken, though it's no less true.

This isn't one of those old sitcoms where the parents and kids sit down for a heart-to-heart. There will be no swelling of music. No canned laughter from the invisible audience. That's not me. Never has been, never will be. I'm out to sea here, fighting to keep my head above water. Fighting against everything ingrained in me my entire life, and there isn't a boat or life vest in sight.

Once I arrive at the gym, I find she's already waiting for me. Of course she is. So eager. So ready to put the work in once she sets her mind to something.

Pride somehow leaks its way into my awareness, pushing aside exhaustion and hopelessness for a moment. I stand back and watch, amused at the way she attacks a heavy bag like she has a grudge against it.

"You keep leading with your head," I point out.

She jumps and spins to face me, her face flushed from the exertion.

"You could let a person know you're here. *Jeez.* I almost had to use my ninja moves on you."

I barely manage to hide the smirk pulling at my lips. "I thought that's what I was doing when I offered instruction just now. And if that's your version of ninja moves, I think I'll be okay. If you keep doing what you're doing, you'll never be able to hold your own against someone else."

"What do you mean?"

I feel a sudden rush of relief. This, I can talk about. This, I know.

"When you throw a punch, you can't push your head forward the way you do." I demonstrate, bringing to mind a pigeon with my head bobbing back and forth.

She snorts, and it turns into a giggle. "Was I doing that? I didn't know I was doing that."

"It's a surefire way to strain your neck. Not to mention, you're leaving yourself wide open for a crack against the jaw." I stand behind her and gently take her head between my hands. "Now. Throw a punch." She does, this time with me holding her head steady. "Do you see the difference?"

"Yeah, I guess I do. I still have a lot to learn."

"And you have me to teach you." There are moments like this when it almost feels like we're a real father and daughter. I wonder how much of her desire to train is real and how much comes from a desire to spend time with me. I can't imagine why she'd want to. I know I don't want to be around me, and I don't have a choice.

"What did you have in mind today?"

She turns away from the bag, shrugging. "I don't know exactly. It just seems like…" Her gaze drops to the floor.

"Out with it."

"I'm just saying, if things are starting to heat up around here, I would like to be able to defend myself if I have to."

Right away, I bite my tongue against the worst of what wants to pour out. "You have nothing to worry about, and I mean that. Don't let yourself think otherwise."

"That's easier said than done." We head over to the mats, where we normally practice hand-to-hand combat. I'm not sure I have it in me today, but then she never presents much of a threat. Over time, she's gotten better, but physics is still on my side.

"There's no reason for anyone to go after you. So long as you keep your head down and mind your business, that is."

Bullseye. She looks away, chewing her lip. "I can't just ignore her the way everybody else has."

"That's exactly what you can do. And it's what you have to do."

"But don't you see? I know some of how she feels. I know what it's like to be alone and to know everybody hates you. She needs a friend."

"It's not going to be you." When she opens her mouth like she wants to keep arguing, I snap, "Enough, already. Quit it."

Her eyes widen, and once again, I'm left knowing I fucked up.

"You have to know there's nothing more important than your safety," I remind her in a calmer voice.

"You know how much that means to me. But sometimes, I have to make my own choices, too. And I'm getting a little tired of trying to get that through your head—and Quinton's."

This is all wrong. How am I ever supposed to tell her what needs to be said if all we're doing is bickering over Delilah? "Let's put it aside for now. We're already here, and I'll never deny you the opportunity to learn more about how to defend yourself." We go through a few practice moves, both loosening up and getting into the rhythm of things.

That is, Aspen gets into the rhythm of things. "What's the matter?" she asks, standing with her hands on her hips, hardly out of breath, while I pant for air. Son of a bitch. I haven't had a drop to drink in almost forty-eight hours, and I still feel like I got run over.

"Nothing. Why?"

She tips her head to the side, smirking. "Come on. You're never off your game like this. And no offense, but you don't look well."

"I don't remember asking how I look."

Rather than smart off some more, she reaches out and places a hand on my arm. "Seriously. What's the matter? Do you need help with something? Is there anything I can do?"

The sincerity glowing in her eyes is murder. Would it be there if she knew what I'd kept from her? She has a right to know her mother is alive. I know that's how she'll take it, too. Her sense of justice doesn't allow itself for much of a gray area. Either I told her, or I didn't. It doesn't matter what the reasons were.

"No, I don't think there's anything you can do," I lie. *You can forgive me for what's about to happen.*

"What's on your mind? Did you get any sleep last night? You know, we didn't have to do this today. It would have been okay if you'd said no."

"I don't want to say no to you," I rattle off before thinking. It's the truth, but rarely have I been so open. I'm too busy trying to figure out how I'm going to drop the bomb to give much thought to what tumbles out of my mouth otherwise.

She offers a tiny smile. "Thank you. That's nice."

"I'm nobody's idea of an ideal parent, am I?" We circle each other slowly, occasionally feigning a lunge to draw the other one out.

"What's an ideal parent?" she asks with a chuckle. "I wouldn't know."

I'm about to clumsily segue into her having another living parent, but she speaks over me. "Besides, knowing I have you here is pretty nice. Like there's still somebody watching over me other than Q," she adds. "There's somebody I can go to who's not going to bullshit me, and that means everything."

If only I had spoken faster. Because now my tongue is tied. She couldn't hit me any deeper if she tried.

"You know, I don't have to be the only one... I mean, there might be more than just me."

"I know. I have Brittney and Dr. Lauren. And I know Quinton would never let anything happen."

"Of course. We're all here for you." You coward. You fucking coward. The opportunity was right there, but now a trio of kids saunters into the gym for a workout. My golden opportunity fizzles into nothing.

"You know what? I forgot about a call I have a little later. I better get back. I'm obviously no good to you right now, anyway."

"Make sure you get some rest, okay? You look really tired."

"Which one of us is the adult here?" Because it's easier to be sarcastic than to admit her concern is both a blessing and a curse. If she knew me, really knew me, she wouldn't give a shit. She'd hate me, and I wouldn't blame her.

Here I am, running from my daughter, retreating to my apartment like the damn coward I am. Running away from everything the way I've been doing for weeks.

Every day that passes makes it worse. It's one day further from when I should have finally opened up and been honest. One more opportunity to do the right thing, which I squander. If I only had the words. Why is it so impossible to find the words?

There aren't any answers in my apartment, either. No one to talk to, no one whose advice I can use. I'm alone, the way I deserve to be. The way I was always going to be.

More and more lately, it seems I want it this way. I must, or else I wouldn't insist on making one wrong decision after another.

My hands flex, clenching and unclenching. I need to hurt something. Someone. Nothing else will do. Only a good fight would ease what's burning its way through me. A way of forgetting everything, venting all my ugly thoughts and unwanted emotions. Cleansing myself. Punishing another person in lieu of punishing myself.

But I can't even do that. I'm trapped here, in this fucking apartment, in this goddamn school.

Before I decide to do it, I pick up one of the chairs around the kitchen table and hurl it against the wall. Delilah sat here with me. We ate meals together. I learned what it's like not to feel so damn alone, if only for a little while. And now I'll never be able to get rid of that memory. Everything that happens from now on will be tainted by the experience of being seen. Understood. Hell, even accepted, something I have no right of hoping to be.

One chair isn't going to cut it. I smash another against the floor and send wood flying everywhere. One of the legs is fully intact, so I pick it up and use it as a club, smashing it against the counter before sweeping the surface.

There's something about this that appeals to my darkness. Destruction, chaos.

Destruction I now have to live with. Clean up somehow. Explain away. In other words, once again, I'm fucking myself over.

I can't bring myself to care much. Not when it feels so good to let it go. I strike the counter hard enough to snap the wood in half and stand here panting, craving more. More release. More destruction. More of the sense that I can control something.

A knock on my door makes my head snap up. "Who is it?" I bark, marching to the door. Charlotte is the last person I want to see right now and the only one I can imagine coming straight to my apartment. She'll want to know if I spoke to Aspen, how much longer she'll have to wait to see her precious little girl. She's going to find out I don't much care what she wants.

And I'm so convinced I'll find Charlotte standing in the hallway that the sight of Delilah knocks me off-balance. "What are you doing here?" I whisper once the surprise wears off. "Don't you know it'll only make things worse if somebody sees you here?"

Now I see her. I really see her. The disgust is written all over her face. The rage in the fists clenched at her sides. The fear shining in those wide eyes.

"Does it even matter?" she mutters. "Do you know what I did today? I spent the entire day putting my room back together after somebody broke in and trashed it yesterday."

"They what? Why didn't you come to me before this?"

"Don't pretend you care," she scoffs. "Stop insulting me. At least now I know why you got tired of me. Because you had somebody else."

"What the fuck are you talking about? Get out of here, now. Or do you want a bigger X on your back than you already have?"

"I thought it would be easier for you if you could get me out of the way. Now that you have somebody else to fuck, why would you care if I live or die?"

"You're not making any sense." I look up and down the length of the hall, which is thankfully empty at the moment. "I don't know what point you're trying to prove here, but this is neither the time nor the place. I'm going to tell you once more. Get out of here, now."

"Not until I say one more thing." She tosses her head back, eyes narrowing. "It's over. For real. I'm sick of you using me. I'm sick of the lies. I'm sick of being hurt. You're going to let me die anyway, so at least I'll take back my dignity. And I'm going to tell you I'm sick of you. I hate you. And when I'm gone, and you did nothing to stop it, I hope it's on your conscience until the day you die."

And then she backs away.

Which is her mistake. Thinking she'll have the last word. Thinking I would let her get away with this on her terms.

Here I am, wishing for some way to vent my anguish.

A means of doing just that delivered themselves to my front door.

"Oh, no," I whisper, hauling her close. "It's not going to be that easy. This doesn't end until I say it does."

With that, I pull her inside and lock the door.

24

DELILAH

*N*ow I've done it.

I'm not only observing a predator. I'm trapped in the cage with him.

The worst part is I walked up to the cage myself. Nobody forced me into it. The only person I have to blame is myself.

Lucas takes me by the wrist in a flash and pins my arm behind my back. He's breathing heavy, each burst of air hot against my face. I try to turn away from it, away from him, but he only digs his fingers into my cheeks and forces me to look at him.

"You are not the one calling the shots here, Delilah." He hardly even sounds like himself, like somebody I've never met before.

Somebody unhinged, wild, and dark.

He's capable of anything, and somehow, the only thing I can think is: would anybody hear me if I screamed?

Do I even want to?

He trails his fingers over my jaw and down my throat. My breath hitches, and he smiles. "That's right. We both know the things that I could do to you right now. It would be effortless. It might even solve my problems. Hell, it would definitely put your mouth to better use than it's currently being used for."

"Let me go," I grunt, still wiggling even though it doesn't do me any good.

"Didn't I already tell you once that you don't get a say in what happens next?" He pulls my wrist a little farther up my back, and pain radiates down my arm. When I gasp, his smile widens. "I could snap your arm like a twig, and there's nothing you could do about it. Say it. There's nothing I can do about it."

"There's nothing I can do about it, Lucas." The words taste sour in my mouth, but maybe that's my fear.

"And if I take this." He jams his other hand between my legs and squeezes until tears come to my eyes. "As many times as I want. As often as I want. There's nothing you can do to stop me. *Say it.*"

"I can't stop you. There's nothing I can do," I whisper the words, hating the way my voice sounds as they come out.

His grip tightens, and the pain intensifies, causing me to whimper. "You're hurting me, Lucas."

"Good, but surely not as bad as you hurt me," he growls and continues, "I want your pain, Delilah. I want your fear, your sadness. I want it all."

A shiver works its way down my spine.

Does he really want to hurt me?

He pushes me against the door and holds me in place with his body. His teeth graze my earlobe. "Come on. Fight me. Try to stop me."

I don't know what to do. My thoughts are racing, and adrenaline pulses through my veins, making it hard to think. I don't know how I hurt him, and I don't know how to fix this without it ending badly.

Do I give him what he wants? Will he hurt me more if I don't try?

He squeezes my pussy again, and this time my whimper is louder. "Are you going to fight, or are you afraid?" Now both my wrists are pinned above my head, held in place by one of his hands while the other travels down my side and over my hip. He touches me like a lover, even when the rage inside his eyes resembles something like hate. His lips skim my throat, and I almost lean into his touch until I'm reminded of the monster he is when his teeth sink into my flesh.

It makes me jump and struggle purely on reflex, my body bucking until he laughs against my skin. "You can do better than that." I raise a knee and try to make contact with his balls, but he maneuvers them out of the way before holding my legs in place with one of his. He's that big and powerful. His presence is like a mountain, and there is no moving a mountain.

And while I struggle, I remember the dried blood all over him that night at Nic and Celia's.

What if he did that to me? Whatever it took to make the blood flow.

"You're disappointing me." He lifts his head before lowering it again, his lips descend on mine, and we struggle until I open my mouth, allowing him entrance. His tongue caresses mine, and I feel his hard cock as he moves his hips, rubbing himself against me.

There must be something wrong with me because the feel of him doesn't scare me. No, it's more like fireworks going off in my head —and pulsing all through my body.

My pussy is hot and wet, and every thrust of his tongue makes me wetter. He wants me to fight, but all I want is to give in. To let him take what he wants because it's what I want, too.

No matter what I've told myself, this is all I really want. Dread, fear? I'm too relieved to be getting what I need for any of that to even enter my thoughts.

"What do I have to do?" he pants after breaking the kiss. His eyes are locked with mine, the blue in them dulled out by the inky black center threatening to take over. "Tell me, do I have to hurt you? Will that be enough?"

A moment of silence drags on between us, and then a bubble of laughter escapes him, but it's not the cheerful kind.

It's the kind that says I'm a complete psychopath.

"Or maybe that's what you want? Maybe you like the pain? Maybe you want to see how far you can push me before I fall off the ledge?" He presses against me, and I feel his beast threatening to break free. "Spoiler alert, I've already fallen off the cliff edge, baby."

This time I grit my teeth and do the only thing I can manage in this position. I pick up my foot and bring it down on his as hard as possible.

It couldn't have hurt too much, but it surprised him enough that his grip on my wrists loosened. I pull them free and start giving him what he wants.

I slap his face, then smack away his hand as he tries to take hold again. When he grabs my wrist, I let him, then pull his hand close to my mouth and bite down on the digits.

"Fuck!" He lets go, and so do I. I catch sight of bright red marks embedded in his skin before he shakes his hand. His psychopath laughter echoes around us.

"All right. So you do have some fight left in you." He takes me around the waist with one arm and begins pulling me toward the bedroom. My hands and feet are flying. I'm not sure where the hits land, but it doesn't seem to phase him. He doesn't even bat an eye or grunt, and it's terrifying.

Just as we reach the bed, he reaches into the nightstand. I fight harder than ever, screaming now. I'm like an animal, frantic, my voice breaking from the strain, sweat rolling down the back of my neck.

I'm angry and terrified. I want to hurt him. I want him to know what it feels like to be discarded.

"That's right. Tire yourself out." He laughs.

I land on the bed with a thud, and not even a second later, he is on top of me. No matter how much I struggle, he still manages to tie my wrists together, almost as if I'm not moving at all.

"I hate you!" I spit the words into the air, and he flips me onto my stomach. I try to push onto my knees, but he shoves me down with a hand to the center of my back.

Then he binds the silk cord to the headboard.

"Hate me all you want, but this ends when I decide," he snarls into my ear.

My heartbeat skyrockets as I try to fight against the ties. It's useless, but I don't want to go down without a fight.

His knuckles drag along my hips as he yanks my leggings down around my knees, followed by my thong. I know he's going to see what this is doing to me. Even if I don't want to admit it, even though every part of me hates how he makes me feel when he takes me by the hips and pulls them back, exposing me, I feel the air hit my wet lips. Through this whole thing, I've never been more turned on by the man in my entire life.

"If you thought I didn't give a shit about you before, wait until the night is over." There's a promise of pain and so much venom in his voice.

He acts like I'm the one who hurt him.

"I'm done with you, Lucas! I'm done doing whatever the hell we're doing," I yell, my voice cracking with raw emotion.

"Lie to me again; lie and tell me that the arousal dripping out of your cunt isn't from me." He delivers a sharp slap against my left cheek like he's punishing me. I bite down on the pillow under me to hold back a shout. "You can't, you fucking can't, and it's because I spark something in you. I douse your fire with gasoline. Even if you hate me, I doubt, you still want my cock inside you." Another slap, harder this time. Blistering pain spreads through me, throbbing in time with my racing pulse.

Like the sinister bastard he is, he slips a finger between my lips, dragging my arousal from my clit to my asshole. Regardless of my feelings at that moment, I can't help but moan while my body gives me away, my hips lift, and I push back against his finger.

"I knew it was true." He chuckles like a mad man. "You don't want this to end. You're just angry and maybe a little jealous, but you still want my cock deep inside you."

I don't say a word, answering instead by kicking my feet at him. I hit what feels like his thigh, and he delivers another slap against my right cheek. The next time I kick, he moves out of the way and spreads my thighs wider before positioning himself between them.

Now I'm trapped, no longer able to kick him and spread wide for his pleasure. He grabs me by the hips and pulls upward, tilting me so my pussy is bare to him. Instead of lapping up my juices, like I anticipated and hoped, he first drags his teeth over where he slapped me. The skin still burns and throbs in the aftermath.

A scream rips from my throat, but because the sensations are so intense, I don't know what else to do. It's like I'm so sensitive even the slightest touch is enough to drive me out of my mind. He does it again and again until I'm close to the edge, teetering on it, about to fall over.

Then the bastard flicks my clit.

Only once, with the very tip of his tongue.

I explode, shrieking when the tension hits its height before breaking. It goes on and on, my body spasming, my arousal drips down my thighs, flowing freely, and Lucas laps them up greedily, grunting like an animal once I can finally hear him over my dying moans.

His fingers dig into my skin with bruising force, and his teeth graze my clit, making me feel both pain and pleasure all at once. After teasing my clit for what feels like an eternity, he plunges his tongue deep into my pulsing pussy like he wants to claim every last drop of my orgasm for himself.

I can't help but respond again, my body betraying my mind. I'm just as greedy for him, just as hungry and desperate and in need of somebody who gets it. Who gets me. If this is the only way we can connect, then maybe it's enough.

But he's not thinking of anything like that. Not right now. He's too busy claiming and owning. And oh, yes, I want him to.

Whatever darkness is in me wants the darkness in him. It calls to him, like the sun and the moon. I thrust back against his tongue, then grind my hips, begging for more without saying a word.

Giving myself to him not because I have to but because it's all I want. No matter what I say, no matter what I tell myself, this is what's real.

"You taste so fucking good," he grunts on withdrawing his tongue, which he then drags up my slit once again to my delight. "This pussy is mine. So fucking juicy and delicious. I could eat it all day long."

Out of nowhere, he smacks me right in my pussy, right over my clit —each slap is sharp, but when the pain fades, my entire body flushes, the pleasure builds deep in my belly with each slap, and I know I shouldn't enjoy this. I know I shouldn't want to beg him for more, but I never want it to stop.

As if he knows this, he unties my wrists and rolls me over onto my back. My entire body is boneless, and it feels like I've been hit by a truck. I'm too weak to move at first, unable to even pretend to fight as he pulls up my shirt and bra all at once, taking them both off over my head, then removing my shoes and leggings. He takes a moment to look at me, his gaze is hungry and intense, and I watch through half-lidded eyes, splayed like a starfish, all his to claim.

"What, you think we're finished? You think I eat your pussy, and that's all that's going to happen. That I'll let you lie here and enjoy yourself?" He slaps my cheek, and I snap fully awake before slapping him back.

"You've got to know that just turns me on more, don't you?" He begins spreading my legs again, forcing them open, his fingers dig into the flesh, and I know there will be bruises tomorrow.

I fight, kick, and groan, if only to see what he'll do next.

"That's right, try to stop me. Try to keep me from fucking *my* pussy."

I pull his hair, sink my nails into his shoulders and scratch, dig my heels into his calves and thighs while he sucks and licks and bites anything he can reach. I plant my heels on the mattress and push up as hard as possible, knocking him off-balance. Then I shove hard with both hands and manage to knock him onto his side.

But he only snakes an arm around my waist and slams me back down before climbing on top of me again. I bring my arm up, my fingers curled into claws that I drag down the side of his face and neck.

He hisses through his teeth, pushing up in time for me to watch blood begin to seep from the scratches. He seems to forget everything for a second, raising a hand to the spot, his eyes drawn to the blood on his fingers like he's never seen such a thing before.

When his eyes meet mine, the look in them sends a shiver down my spine. *Rage.* Red hot rage reflects back at me.

"Nobody makes me bleed without paying for it."

And now there's no amount of fighting that will save me. Not once does he reach between us and pulls himself free from his pants.

Nothing can stop him from impaling me, and he does without warning, spreading my thighs like he's trying to break a wishbone. Driving himself deep inside me, the momentum is hard enough to make me yelp.

He covers my mouth with one hand, using the other to squeeze my breasts painfully, almost brutally. I almost wish I hadn't provoked him.

"Do you know how fucking hard I fought this?" he grunts, his ass bouncing, while the bed squeaks every time he crashes against me. And that's what he's doing. He's branding me, forcing himself deep inside me. "Every day. Wanting you. Hating you for it. Hating me."

Every thrust drives me into the mattress, his body crushing mine until I can barely breathe between that and his hand covering my mouth. I drag my nails across the back of it, but he only digs his fingers in harder.

My eyes fly open wide, and I scream behind his palm. Our gazes collide; he must see the fear there because he eases up, and I gulp in a breath. I'm thankful for the reprieve, but he only covers my mouth again and pounds into me harder than before, hard enough I'm afraid he'll break me.

"Why are you doing this? Why? Why? Why?" Every repeated question is punctuated with another merciless thrust that makes me whimper in pain and, yes, pleasure. I can't tell the difference anymore. The two are so wrapped up together that they become one thing, this thing he's creating, using my body. A shattered, beautifully broken masterpiece.

I can't tell him I don't know what he's talking about, and I don't think I'd be able to speak if I had the chance.

I don't want to talk.

I don't want questions.

I just want him, all of him. I want him to take me and break me and turn me into something that belongs to him, only to him.

If he only knew. But would that change anything?

It all runs through my head at once, that in so many other things —this is wrong, we shouldn't be doing this, he has somebody else, and so many other warnings and fears but none of them matter. All of that can come later.

"I hate you for this," he growls before lowering his hand to replace it with his mouth. This time I kiss him back hard, rough, our teeth scraping together, my lips stretching and bruising.

I manage to bite his lip, and he stiffens in surprise—then lets loose in a furious barrage of deep, crushing thrusts that make me squeal in mixed pain and excitement because yes, yes, he's going to make me come again, he might shatter me into pieces, but I'm going to come first.

His cock touches something deep inside me, something that makes me go off like a rocket. There's nothing for me to do but scream into his mouth, scream out all my fear and pain and loneliness and jealousy and even my hate because there's so much of that, too. I let it all out until tears start to roll down my face, and there's nothing left in me but blissful aftershocks.

Then he goes stiff, pulling his mouth away from mine to cry out a single word. "Delilah!" he roars with his head thrown back, tendons standing out on his neck while his cum spills onto my stomach.

For one moment, he's not an animal or a murderer or a monster.

He's mine, locked with me, lost in what only I can give him.

And then it's over, and he collapses on his side with an arm draped over my stomach. Now I can breathe, and I do, taking deep gulps while little aftershocks ripple through me. I ache all over, but it's a good kind of ache. There's a satisfaction that goes along with it, something deeper than physical pleasure.

I slowly turn my head to the side, nervous to look over at him. His eyes are closed, and his breathing is beginning to slow. I don't know what to say. I don't know if there is anything to say.

As it turns out, nothing I could say would be better than him drawing me close, wrapping his arms around me. He doesn't say anything.

He doesn't have to. I understand him. It's me I'm worried about because right then, I realized the one thing I was hiding from, running from.

I love him. Oh, my god. I love him, and there's no way for me to let go. I can feel the tears fill my eyes, and I blink them back, not wanting him to see me cry. He has no idea, or maybe he does, and we're both hopeless causes. All I know is I can't unfall for him, so what do I do now?

25

LUCAS

I must have slept like the dead.

My head's in a fog when I open my eyes, but it's a different sort of fog than the one I've experienced lately. Too many mornings in a row, I woke to a pounding head and a sour stomach. This is something entirely different. The fog results from a deep, heavy sleep. I can't remember the last time I slept so well and completely sober.

Maybe not completely. There are all sorts of drugs for a man to indulge in. Not all of them come in a bottle or a baggie.

Like the sleeping woman in my arms.

I never thought I'd find something as cleansing as fighting. Last night with her brought me a peace I've never known. I felt whole, if only for a moment or two. She wiped me clean. She took everything I poured into her, and she stayed. She didn't run away. No, on the contrary. She curled up beside me and slept with her head on my chest most of the night.

How am I supposed to stay away from her?

How am I supposed to give this up?

I'd stay here with her forever, but certain things can't be put off. I gently disentangle myself, leaving her curled up on her side—her favorite sleeping position, I guess. She's still out cold, not so much as stirring when I get out of bed and draw the covers over her shoulder.

It's a blessing, her being fast asleep like this. I'm not sure what to say, which is increasingly the case with me. I never considered myself someone afraid to say what was on his mind.

But what is there to say, after all? We both know this shouldn't be happening, that there are rules, and we're breaking every one. It's wrong. It could mean a lot more grief for both of us.

Yet there's no stopping, and we both know that. She proved it to me last night. The way we connected—I didn't think such a thing was possible. I thought for sure I would scare her away. I showed her the darkest part of myself, a part I'm hardly proud of. Even that wasn't enough to make her want to disappear.

I pull on my pants from last night before wandering out to the kitchen, where I stop short at the sight of the carnage I caused. I even forgot about that. I was going to make coffee, but the machine was one of last night's casualties.

I haven't yet decided whether to wait until Delilah wakes up to start pulling shit together when there's a knock on the door. I'm getting sick of visitors. I ignore whoever it is and pretend I'm still asleep, but that might only make them knock harder and thus wake Delilah. All I need is someone to see her here—or Charlotte, if it's her in the hall. *Shit.* She's been quiet all this time; of course she'd eventually come knocking.

I rush to the bedroom door and close it quietly before crossing to the front door, where another round of knocking has begun. "Okay, okay," I mutter. If it is Charlotte, I sure as hell can't let her in to see the apartment like this. Or Delilah.

I intend to only open the door wide enough to look through—whatever this is can wait—until I see who's on the other side, and my stomach drops.

"Lucas." As always, there is a smug note in Xander's voice. The voice of a man who thinks he owns everything and everyone. And if he doesn't yet, he will eventually.

It's only when he scowls that I remember what I must look like. "Good morning," I murmur and rub my chin with my hand. "It's a surprise to see you."

"Evidently." He looks me up and down. "I would like to speak with you, and I don't have time to wait around." In other words, he's coming in whether I like it or not.

It's like being in one of those old nightmares from when I was a kid. Showing up to school in my underwear or being forced to give a presentation in a class I had never attended. Then I could wake up, relieved none of it was real.

No such luck this time. I have no choice but to open the door wider and take my medicine.

He says nothing about the splintered wood and random small appliances strewn over the floor, settling on lifting his eyebrows until they nearly disappear into his hairline.

"I thought I saw a rodent running around here." I don't expect him to take me seriously, and I'm right.

He snorts, eyeballing the mess. "It must have been a big one." He makes a big deal of stepping over one of the larger pieces of the chair I smashed.

"What can I do for you?"

Jesus Christ, I must reek of pussy even at a distance. My neck stings where Delilah raked me with her nails—I'm sure there's dried blood there.

She managed to land a few solid punches, and my hair is probably sticking straight up from the way she pulled it. Even my lips sting from her vicious kisses, swollen and raw. I know what I must look like. A man who either brawled or fucked himself half to death last night. Not the headmaster of Corium.

Xander lifts an eyebrow. "You can tell me what the hell is going on with you. You know I don't make this trip because I find it pleasurable."

"I'm sorry you felt you had to come all this way. A phone call would've told you everything you needed to know."

"Would it have? Some things a man has to see for himself. Especially when he can't always count on people to give him the full story."

There's a creaking, the sound of a door opening. What an ideal time for Delilah to make an appearance.

I may as well be watching my life end in slow motion as the disheveled Delilah peers out while Xander's eyes widen as understanding settles in.

"I'm sorry," she murmurs. Her cheeks go pink while her gaze darts from him over to me. "I heard voices out here."

Xander's face hardens. "So this is what you're doing in your off hours nowadays." His eyes are cold, and his mouth twisted in a smirk. "No wonder you have no time to handle important matters."

"I'm sorry," she repeats, staring at me. Her chin trembles like she might be tearing up. The sight of it sends every protective instinct I possess into overdrive. I'll be damned if I let anyone make her feel small and threatened.

"Like you said, these are my off hours, so I can't see how it's anyone else's concern." While Xander continues to sneer and snicker, I turn to Delilah. "Clean yourself up. Get dressed. Then stay in the room until I come and get you."

There's no room for questions, though it doesn't seem like she'd ask any if there was. At a time like this, it's a good idea to make a quick exit. She's smart enough to do so.

"I have to say, I'm disappointed. For a number of reasons." He has the nerve to shake his head at me, mournful. "Especially when you know what she's capable of."

"Leave her out of it. Whatever you're here for, she's no part of it."

"Not part of this? She is the entire reason. Did you forget the conversation we had?" He looks me up and down, his lip curling in distaste. "Don't bother answering that. I wouldn't be surprised if you did. You're falling to pieces in front of me."

"Feel free to explain at any point why you visited." Despite my bare feet, I begin picking items up from the floor. Anything is better than being forced to look at the man another second.

"In a way, the theme is the same. Why haven't you done what you need to do?"

Leave it to him to bring this up with her in the next room. "I told you. I'm not going to—"

"I'm talking about Charlotte and Aspen."

He could've taken a swing at me and surprised me less. I straighten up, forgetting the mess again. "How did you know she was here?"

"Does it matter? What I want to know is, have you told your daughter her mother is alive?" He directs a very obvious glance toward the bedroom. "Or have you been too busy doing other things? Like Delilah?"

I can barely get the words out with my teeth gritted like they are. "As I said. Leave her out of it."

He shrugs blithely like it doesn't matter. I suppose to him, it doesn't. "Well? Have you?"

"What business is it of yours?"

"Considering how special she is to my son, let's say I have a vested interest. Especially because I know Quinton. If he finds out Charlotte is here, he won't be able to keep from telling his wife. But you and I both know you're the one that should come from. She deserves to hear it from you."

He's right, the arrogant bastard. I want him to be wrong more than I want a drink, but there's no changing the truth. If there's one person my daughter deserves to hear this from, it's me.

Here I am, cursing myself for letting her down in the past. I'd only let her down again if I let Quinton do the dirty work for me.

"I'm working on it."

"Exactly how much work does it take? Simply tell her."

"I will, Xander."

He waves an arm around, indicating what's still spread over half the apartment. "This can't go on. You know that, don't you?"

"I don't exactly make a habit of breaking the place up."

"You don't need to make a habit of it," he retorts. "Once is enough. But don't act like this came out of the blue. You're unraveling. A man in your position can't afford to unravel."

"I appreciate your concern." It takes everything in me to keep from taking one of those chair legs and beating him to a pulp with it. A man in my position can't afford to unravel. What the hell does he know about it? Who is he to tell me what I can and can't afford to do?

That sort of reaction might fly if this were nearly anyone else but the man standing in front of me, wearing what looks like a touch of pity in his eyes. Anything but pity.

"So you're going to deal with this before it escalates, and I end up with a devastated daughter-in-law and a furious son?"

"I said I would."

"And you're going to pull yourself together? Because you need to, badly."

"I will," I grunt.

"Just the same, you will understand if I stay around for a while. I, erm, think it might be wise for me to keep an eye on things." He needs to get out of here before my fist finds his face and rearranges it.

Right now, I'd agree to anything short of castration if it meant getting him out of here before I snap. "Whatever you think is necessary. If you'll excuse me, I have to get my day started."

With another pointed look toward the bedroom door, Xander mutters, "Yes, it appears you do."

He shakes his head, wearing a grim smirk. I'd love nothing more than to wipe off his face. I only have to withstand another ten seconds or so of this. He'll be gone soon. I'm strong enough to hold on until he's gone. Still, he steps out of the room not a moment too soon. Immediately, I turn away from the door, charge across the room, and flip the coffee table, scattering everything on it.

It's not enough, so I turn to one of the end tables and pick up the lamp, which I then throw to the floor. The sound of breaking glass is discordant music to my ears.

But it isn't enough. It's never going to be enough. It won't wipe out the memory of Xander's judgment. Being told what to do. The sense of nothing about my life being private. Belonging only to me.

The familiar craving begins to build deep inside. The desire to break someone. To make them suffer. Bleed. Die.

And there's no substitution for it.

26

DELILAH

X ander Rossi. I didn't need to be formally introduced. Quinton looks just like him, although he hasn't yet achieved the level of haughty asshole his father has. But there's time. He's still young.

Of all times for him to show up, this is the worst.

Lucas isn't at his best, not even close, and then there's the mess in the apartment! He must be dying from embarrassment.

Not that my being here makes things any easier. I know it's now awkward for Lucas. I shouldn't have popped out of the bedroom. Why couldn't I just wait? They're still talking by the time I'm finished rushing through washing up and getting dressed. I was feeling sleepy and foggy when I first got out of bed—if I hadn't, I might've thought twice about opening the door.

Amazing, really, how receiving a shock like coming face-to-face with somebody you know wishes you were dead can wake you up all of a sudden.

I hear the front door open and close and let out a sigh of relief. At least he's gone. How much apologizing will it take to make up for the way I stuck my foot in the middle of things?

I reach for the doorknob, then remember Lucas's instructions. I'm supposed to wait for him to tell me to come out. It seems kind of silly to wait, but I already made a mistake this morning. I don't want to make another one if I can help it.

The shattering of glass makes me jump back a step, and I cringe. Something heavy hits the floor, and I back farther from the door, wrapping my arms around myself. It continues, with Lucas grunting and shouting words I can't make sense of. He might not even be trying to speak. Like his rage has to come out somehow, and he can't form words around it.

I know the smart thing would be to stay here. It's probably the safest place to be. I don't want to get in the way of whatever he's going through, but my heart aches. Glass breaks again, and I jump. He wouldn't even have to try to hurt me. I would only need to be in the room as he shatters one thing after another until it feels like there's nothing in the world but that jarring, ear-splitting noise.

It eventually stops, which somehow scares me more. Has he worked out whatever started this? What if he hurt himself?

Now I want to go to him if only to make sure he's physically okay. He'll probably hate me for checking on him, but I can't stand here and eat my heart out with worry forever.

I turn the knob slowly, then just as slowly open the door.

I almost wish I hadn't because the sight of the wreckage makes my chest tighten and my stomach drop.

The living room looks like a tornado went through it. I guess it did, one named Lucas Diavolo. The coffee table is overturned and cracked down the center. I guess that wasn't enough for him because he broke a lamp. But there's more glass on the floor than makes sense. I tiptoe through the space and find the kitchen cabinets open and half empty. So that's what he kept shattering. Plates, dishes, anything he could get his hands on. I'm afraid to step any farther into the kitchen—I'm wearing shoes but don't want to track glass all over the place.

Yet when I set eyes on Lucas, leaning over the counter with his head in his hands, something propels me forward. I can't see him like this and not try to help. It's enough to break my heart, watching him suffer. Doesn't he know he doesn't need to suffer alone?

When I take a step, glass crunches under my foot. He stiffens, lifting his head from his hands but staring at the backsplash instead of looking my way. "You need to go."

"But you—"

"I said, you need to go," he insists, carefully enunciating every word. "Now."

"I don't want to leave you alone. Let me help you."

At first, all he does is breathe heavier. Louder. Like there's a beast inside him, and it's trying to get out. Or he's trying to hold it in. "There's nothing you can do to help, dammit. Who do you think you are? What makes you think you could do anything to help me?"

He doesn't mean this. I can't believe he means it. "I can help you clean up, at least. Let me do that."

"Did I ask you to? I didn't ask you for a damn thing. Only to leave. You want to help me? Get out of here."

It's enough to stir up actual pain in my chest. "I don't want to leave you like this. I'm worried."

He pounds his fist against the granite counter, and I jump. "Go!" He finally turns to me, and what I see leaves me holding back a sob. He's broken and in so much pain. He doesn't have to say it. It's written all over his face: anguish, heartbreak, and frustration.

Behind it all is the rage, blazing like a fire that wants to become an inferno. The beast I hear in his voice. I'm almost drawn to it, like a moth to a flame, but some deeper wisdom tells me to back off. One more little push might send him over the edge. Might bring the beast out.

"You need to leave," he grunts, his shoulders rising and falling in time with his quickened breath. "Before I hurt you. I'm not myself right now. This is me trying to be decent. Trying to save you. Okay?"

"Okay," I reply in a teary whisper. "I'm sorry, but you don't have to save me. Not from yourself."

He only snorts before turning away. "Right. That helps things."

I ignore the sarcasm since I know it's masking something deeper and step carefully through the mess before ducking out into the hallway. This is the last thing I want to do, but he's too unbalanced to be reasoned with now. I'd only make things worse by sticking around.

There's nothing more painful than watching somebody I care for so much go through this torture and being unable to do a thing about it. He doesn't even want me to be with him. I'm useless, helpless.

I'm also a sitting duck. It's just as dangerous out here as it is inside. Thankfully, nobody is walking around right now. My heart is heavy and tears sting behind my eyes, threatening to spill over, but I dart for the elevator and pray it gets here fast.

It's almost too late by the time I hear a man's voice coming around the corner up ahead, close to the elevator shaft. I double back at full speed, running flat out until I reach the next corner and duck around it. I don't think he saw me, whoever he is. And guess I'll have to take the stairs, which is probably a better idea. I won't have to stand around in the open and wait.

I'm halfway to the stairwell and about to turn yet another corner before reaching the door when I hear more voices, two of them.

"You know this can't happen, Scarlet. It's hard enough without you making it worse. I wish you could let it go."

A student, for sure. Not old enough to be an instructor. And the voice sounds vaguely familiar, but I can't place it.

"Why not?" the girl—Scarlet—demands. "You keep giving me excuses, but that's all they are. I know you want this as much as I do, Ren."

Oh, shit. So it's Ren and some girl he shouldn't be with. I must have a death wish because instead of backing away and finding another route to the dorms, I creep closer to the corner before peeking around to see what's happening.

She's standing with her back to the wall between the stairwell and me, with Ren leaning close to her. She's pretty, and everything about her body language—the hand on his chest, the other one on the back of his head so she can run her fingers through his hair—screams out how much she wants him. I can't say I understand why since he's repulsive and disgusting. Lucas hasn't always treated me well, and I still want him desperately.

"Excuses?" He sighs, shaking his head. "You think your brother killing me if he ever found out is just an excuse? Because that's what he would do. Literally."

"Please. He would never kill you. You're his best friend. Besides, I wouldn't let Quinton hurt you."

Quinton! Just when I thought this couldn't get any better. Or worse, considering how I look at it. It's all starting to make sense now. That's Quinton's sister, and she's got a thing for his best friend.

They have no idea I'm here, and I should use that to my advantage. I'm dead if he finds me here. But there's something about watching him struggle, hearing him groan as she runs her fingers through his hair before letting her fingertips trail down the back of his neck, that pleases me more than it should. So he knows what it's like to fight between what he wants and what he knows will get him hurt. I feel slightly vindicated even if he has no idea I know what he's going through.

"Ren." She cups his cheek, drawing him closer, and he groans again. "You know I want you. I always have. I always will. Doesn't that mean anything? How much we both want this?"

"Scarlet, please..." Yet even as he murmurs it in desperation, he lowers his head an inch at a time.

Finally, it's clear he can't control himself anymore. He kisses her fiercely, crushing her against him before pressing her against the wall and holding her in place with his body. She runs her fingers through his hair before dragging her nails over his shoulders and back while he runs a hand down her thigh, then lifts it and hooks her leg around his hip.

When he starts working his hand under her skirt, I make my mistake. I gasp in surprise at how far they're going in the middle of the hall.

And just like that, the moment's over. Scarlet gasps, clamping a hand over her mouth. Her face goes beet red, her eyes wide and full of fear over the top of her hand.

Ren only glares at me, his chest heaving. "Run along." Only two words, but they're full of meaning.

I know better than to ignore them. I back away without saying a word, then turn on my heel and take off running. Looks like I'll be getting on the elevator, after all. It's better than facing Ren right now.

"Wait a minute." I didn't hear him chasing me over the pounding of my feet—and my heart. He grabs me by the arm and pulls me to a stop before turning me around to face him. "So you're not just a murderer, are you," he snarls, pulling me close. "You're also a spy."

"I wasn't spying," I whisper. "I swear!"

"Then why were you standing there? Why were you watching and listening? Tell me!" His fingers bite into my flesh, and I want to beg him to let me go, but I know that would only make it worse.

"I don't know. I wasn't trying to spy. I don't care who you date."

"You're so fucking pathetic," he mutters, his lip curling in disgust. "Dating. Like that has anything to do with it."

"You know what I mean. I don't care what you do. Just let me go, all right? I'm not going to tell anybody." I try in vain to yank my arm free, but he only squeezes until I grind my teeth together to keep from screaming.

"Oh, I know that. Because even though your life is worthless, you still want to keep it, I bet. Though I can't understand why. I'd rather pitch myself off a roof than be you."

"Yeah, I got the feeling. But that doesn't have anything to do with this. It's none of my business. Let's just forget the whole thing."

"Oh, I'm not going to forget." I suck in a pained gasp when he shoves me against the wall hard enough to rattle my bones. "If you fucking betray me, I'll kill you. Do you understand? If you tell anyone what you saw, I'll know you did it. And there won't be a place on earth you can hide from me. Tell me. Do you understand?"

I do—and I'm damn sick of it. The threats and the cruelty. "Then I guess I might as well tell somebody," I retort. "My life means nothing at the moment since you're planning on killing me, anyway."

I've never seen a smile so chilling. "Who knows? There's a chance that might not need to happen. But I promise, you breathe a word of this, and I'll kill you without blinking. Or do you doubt me?"

"I don't doubt you," I say while looking him straight in the eye. I refuse to beg for my life, especially not to him.

"Good." He shoves me away, then wipes his hand on his thigh like I soiled him. "Get the fuck out of here and pretend you never heard or saw a thing."

I'm so glad to be away from him that my feet start moving before I make the conscious thought to flee. I hate letting him see how freaked out I am, but pride isn't what matters right now. It's getting out of this in one piece.

At least I know Ren is human, after all. That he's just as weak as I am, just for a different person. I wonder if Q really would freak out on him if he ever found out. Isn't that kind of old school, archaic? You might be my best friend, but I'll cut your hand off if you ever touch my sister. It seems silly.

Then again, I reason as I jump onto the elevator and hide in the corner until the doors close, nothing about these people makes any sense.

They all live by this code that seems completely outdated.

One thing is for sure. Whether or not Q will kill Ren if he finds out, Ren believes he will. It doesn't occur to me until I reach my room that this might mean I have a little something to hold over Ren's head.

Not that I would, but he doesn't know that.

I have to wonder if I could use this to my advantage. Not that I would ever blackmail him or anything, but he might use this as a reason to be a little nicer to me. Maybe if he knows who's behind my attack and the destruction of my room, he might call off whatever else they have in mind.

I can hope, can't I?

Right now, hope is all I have.

*M*y relationship with Lauren has always been the love-hate kind. Today I'm leaning more toward the latter. Why does she always have to be so right? It's infuriating.

"I feel like I hit a nerve," she points out the obvious.

"Why would you tell me that my actions were selfish hit a nerve? Isn't being selfish my thing?"

"It is, but this time you thought you were doing it for Aspen. You purposely keep Charlotte away from Aspen and tell yourself it's to protect her."

"I am."

"Are you? Or are you scared that Charlotte will tell Aspen about your past? Maybe Aspen and Charlotte will have no trouble building a strong, meaningful relationship in no time, leaving you out."

With each word coming from her mouth, my irritation grows. She is literally listing every one of my fears, and I've had enough. "Okay, I get it. You don't have to rub it all in my face."

"Sometimes, rubbing it in your face is what you need."

"Is that what they taught you in school?"

"No, I learned that from knowing you for years. Now, get your shit together and let Aspen meet her mother."

A part of me knows there is no way around this. I can't keep them apart, and the longer I take, the worse it will be. "Can you be there, maybe mediate a little?"

"Sure. I have time now." Lauren puts her notebook on the side table and runs her palms down the skirt like she is ready to go.

"Of course you do." I guess the sooner we get this over with, the better.

Lauren locks up her office, and we make our way to my place. I text Aspen and Charlotte quickly, asking them to come to my room. When Lauren and I walk around the corner of the hall, Charlotte is already waiting in front of my door.

"You must be Charlotte," Lauren greets her with her sing-song voice. "I'm Lauren. It's so nice to meet you."

"Hi." Charlotte gives her a nervous glance before giving me her full attention. "I thought Aspen was going to come."

"She is. Lauren is here to support. Why don't we go inside."

Charlotte nods and forces a smile, but I don't miss her fidgeting next to me while I unlock the door to my apartment. We all pile in, and I motion for them to sit on the couch.

To make matters even more awkward, I realize I'm in a room with two women I've slept with. At least Charlotte doesn't know that, though I highly doubt she would care. I think all she cares about is meeting our daughter.

Our daughter. I still can't wrap my mind around that.

"I can't imagine what you are feeling right now, but it's okay to be nervous and even scared," Lauren soothes, taking a seat next to Charlotte. "You being alive is going to be a shock to Aspen, but she is a very smart and loving person. So even if today doesn't go as you hope, I don't want you to be disappointed. This is only the first step."

"Thank you for saying that. How long have you known Aspen?"

"Since she got to Corium. I'm the head of the medical department. I take care of all the students. Both their physical and mental health."

"Oh, that makes sense… I mean, why Lucas asked you to come. He isn't great at this stuff."

"You don't say." Lauren frowns while giving me a dirty look.

"Listen, Charlotte. I think it might be better if you let me explain everything first. Let me talk to Aspen before I introduce you."

Before Charlotte can answer, a knock echoes through the room. "Coming," I yell on my way to the door.

My hand wraps around the doorknob, making me realize how sweaty my palms are. I turn it and pull the door open, finding Aspen and Quinton on the other side.

"Isn't it past your bedtime, old man?"

I ignore Quinton's joke. My eyes find Aspen's baby blues. This is it. My chest tightens, and for a moment, I think I might be having a fucking heart attack.

"What's wrong?" Aspen's concerned tone doesn't make it better. If anything, hearing how similar her voice is to Charlotte's only makes it worse.

"I asked you here to tell you..." The rest of the sentence gets stuck in my throat. Fuck me. When have I ever been at a loss for words? Never, that's the answer. I clear my throat and try again. "So... erm, there is someone here to see you."

"Lucas, please tell me what's going on. You are really freaking me out."

"Seriously, spill," Quinton interjects.

"It's me. I'm here to see you," Charlotte pipes up behind me.

Aspen pushes past me to walk into my apartment. Quinton follows closely behind. All I can do is close the door and helplessly watch the trainwreck that's about to happen in my living room.

"Who the hell are you?" Quinton questions Charlotte.

"I—I'm Aspen's mom. I mean... birth mom... mother. Birth mother," Charlotte stumbles over the words. She gets up from her seat and faces Aspen. "I'm sorry. I'm so nervous. I've been waiting, dreaming of this for so many years. I'm sorry, I just came here. I realize this must be a huge shock to you, but I couldn't wait any longer."

Aspen remains stoic, her eyes wide, her mouth hanging open in shock. Quinton grabs her hand, covering it with both of his. "Babe, you okay?"

It takes her another few moments before finding her voice. "Did you know?" She asks Q first. He immediately shakes his head.

"I had no idea."

Then Aspen's gaze is on me. "Did you?"

"Just for a few weeks—"

"Weeks?! You've known for weeks!" She is angry, but it's not the anger in her voice that's the worst. It's the hidden disappointment in her words that slices through me like a dull knife. "You had all this time to tell me. We spent all afternoon together yesterday..."

"I know. I just didn't know how to tell you."

Aspen shakes her head like she doesn't want to hear any of my excuses. "I can't believe you. I trusted you."

"You can trust me."

"All I can trust is that you keep things from me."

"Aspen, I..." The apology lodges in my throat.

"Aspen, why don't you sit down, and we all take a minute to breathe," Lauren suggests, but Aspen is already shaking her head.

She turns to Charlotte, her gaze filled with so many emotions as she sees her mother for the first time in her life. "I'm sorry," Aspen apologizes, although she is the one who has nothing to be sorry about. "I can't do this right now. This is too much."

"Come one, let's go back to our place for now." Quinton wraps his arm around her waist and pulls her toward the door. Aspen leans into Q for support and lets him lead her away.

The door closes behind them, and I can feel the fragile relationship between Aspen and me crumbling to the ground. She might be a forgiving person, but even her kindness has limits. How often can I disappoint her without her turning her back on me?

"Lucas?" Charlotte's timid voice pulls me out of my self-loathing thoughts.

"This is exactly what I wanted to avoid." I know this is not Charlotte's fault, but it's hard not to snap at her.

"I know, I'm sorry."

"You didn't do anything wrong," Lauren comforts Charlotte. "This isn't easy for any of you, and it would be a shock to Aspen no matter what. Give her time to process, and I'm sure she'll be happy to meet you."

"What if she won't?" Charlotte sobs, hanging her head low as she buries her face in her palms. "What if she never wants to see me again."

"That's not gonna happen. If anything, she is going to hate me for this." I take a seat on the couch next to Charlotte. There is a foot between us, but she still scoots an extra few inches away from me.

"Lucas is right," Lauren agrees, "and that's something I don't say often."

Charlotte is not convinced, her sobbing only intensifying. I don't know how to console someone or comfort them when they are hurting, but there is a strong urge to do so now. I owe her that much. After everything I've done to Charlotte, I owe it to her.

"Lauren, you can go now."

"Are you sure—"

I shut her up with a stern look that leaves no room for discussion. "Go."

She glances over at Charlotte with a rueful expression. "Fine, I'll go, but call if you need me. Both of you. Charlotte, feel free to come and see me in the medical wing."

Charlotte simply nods, not even looking up at Lauren, who gets up and leaves the room in a hurry. She closes the door softly, leaving Charlotte and me alone in our misery.

I let her cry in silence for a few more minutes, giving me time to figure out what I am going to say without sounding like the huge asshole I am.

"Lauren is right, you know," I break the silence. "Give Aspen time; she is going to want to meet you. I should have told her as soon as you called. I'm sorry."

At the last part, Charlotte finally looks up. Her bloodshot eyes scan me carefully. "Did you just apologize to me?"

"Yes, and I mean it. I am sorry. Sorry for today and back then."

"Wow... I imagined this day to go all kinds of ways. You apologizing wasn't one of them. You've really changed, and I can tell how much Aspen means to you."

"She does, and I'm not used to that."

"I always knew this part of you was just hiding, waiting to come out."

"No!" I jump up from my seat, knocking against the coffee table. My quick movement has Charlotte jolt, pulling up her arms like she is getting ready to protect herself. Her fear only drives my point home. "Just because there is a tiny part of me that's good doesn't make me a good person. The rest of me is still rotten."

"I don't believe that." She drops her hands into her lap, interlacing her fingers as if that would hide how they are trembling.

"Believe what you want. It won't change the truth. I'm a bad person and an even worse father. You were right to keep her away from me."

"The fact that you worry about not being a good father is the very thing that makes you a good parent. I think you are being too hard on yourself. Aspen clearly cares about you. She loves you."

I throw my hands up in frustration. "She almost died because of me. She was literally starving, bullied so badly she didn't want to leave her room, and what did I do? Nothing."

When will Charlotte stop trying to make me into a good person? Even now, she looks at me like she wants to help me. There is no hope. Why doesn't she see it?

"You know I was the one who dropped her off at her house. I drove her to her place and left her there, knowing it wasn't safe, I left her, and they took her. Did you know they drugged and raped her so badly that she lost the baby she was carrying?"

Charlotte's face crumbles, shock and sorrow written all over it. There is so much pain in her eyes it makes it hard to look at her. "Lucas, you couldn't have known."

"Aren't you listening?" I'm full-out yelling now. "I did know. I knew she was unprotected, and I knew people were after her. I still left her there."

"You know what. I was wrong. You haven't changed. You still try your best to make everyone see the worst in you. Every time someone gets close, you find a way to hurt them, to drive them away."

Her words hit me like a thousand-pound weight.

28

DELILAH

*E*verything is different now. It's only been a few days, but I hate the distance that seems to have formed between us. It's like there's an ocean, and I have no way to cross it. I can't shake the feeling that something is up, even if I can't put my finger on it. Against my better judgment, I follow my gut instinct and take the elevator to Lucas's apartment.

I should stay away, but I can't. I just can't. Maybe that makes me desperate or fucked up, but I know he feels the same way.

Lucas wants me like I want him. I know it. I felt it the other night.

As soon as I step off the elevator, I hide in the dark corner closest to his door. It's dark enough that no one will see me unless they run right into me. I hope to catch him as he comes out since the fear of me knocking and Xander possibly being there might give me a heart attack.

I can still see the way he looked at me with blatant disgust. It was enough shame to last me a lifetime. I'm not sure how long I wait, but now I worry he's not in his apartment at all. I guess I should have checked before I decided to stay here forever.

I'm starting to wonder if I should return to my dorm when the knob turns. I hold my breath, pressing myself into the corner as tightly as I can in case it is Xander who comes walking out. I know he's only a man, but I get the feeling he would somehow sense me being here. Just to spite me. He wouldn't want to miss a chance at hurling an insult.

It isn't Xander. It isn't even a man. It's a woman, blond and beautiful. She has a sweet, angelic face, and she's obviously older than me.

She turns and looks over her shoulder before stepping past the threshold. "Let me know if you change your mind." As if I needed the truth smashed upside my head. I would have guessed this was the mystery woman without hearing her voice, which is the same as the one I heard coming from inside Lucas's office.

So this is her. And she's here, staying at Corium. She must be. She's not wearing a coat or carrying a bag. Like she wandered over for a visit, the way our neighbors used to do back at the trailer.

She walks away from me rather than crossing my path, and that can only be a good thing since I'm not sure I'm strong enough to stay still, hidden, if she was that close. I don't know what I would do exactly. Say something? Ask who she is, why she's here, and who she is to Lucas. As if I have any right to know. I'm sure she would laugh at me. How could I ever think I meant anything to him when he already had someone in his life?

Instead of pressing myself into the corner, I'm leaning into it as the strength drains from my body, and a hot, sick feeling takes its place. How much more of this am I going to put myself through? I can't even blame Lucas for this. I know this woman exists—and I told him so, though we never did get around to discussing her after I threw her in his face. We sort of got distracted.

But I knew she existed the whole time and let myself forget about her. Why do I keep walking into situations I know will only hurt me? Stupid, Delilah. I've never been good enough for anybody, just as I am. Never smart enough, never pretty enough. Not enough to be part of my own family. Not enough to have any real friends. Always on the outside, wishing for a chance to show somebody how worthwhile I am... and never getting it.

The situation might look different on the surface, but it's the same underneath. This other woman is everything I'm not, obviously. I can give the man every part of me and offer him my understanding, patience, and even my heart, but it doesn't matter. Why do I even bother? I should know better by now. People like me don't get what they want.

And what am I supposed to do now? I want to see Lucas more than ever, but now it's because I'm pissed off and hurting worse than before. Whenever I want to talk about us, something always comes along to get in the way. We could have talked about this woman in the morning after we had sex, but Xander went and showed up. Now I'm too upset over this blond woman to remember why I thought it was so important to talk to him in the first place.

In the end, curiosity is what holds me in place. Is he going to come out and take the same route she did? Is he going to disappear into whatever room he stashed her in? Or maybe she upset him, so he's going to head to my room instead. Maybe she gets all the good parts of him, and I get all the ugliness.

I'm still seething and aching when his door opens again. There he is, and I wish my heart didn't hurt so much at the sight of him. He's angry, scowling. And alone.

He's also dressed like he's going somewhere, wearing a leather jacket and jeans. He looks dangerous, like he wants to get into trouble. Or maybe that's what I already know about him, coloring the way I see him.

He turns in my direction, and I hold my breath, staying completely still. Does he sense me here as he walks past? It's ridiculous to think he would, though I can't help how my heart pounds. I'm surprised he doesn't hear it.

No, he's too busy checking something on his phone. He marches past me like a man in a hurry. I should let him go. I know I should. It's none of my business, especially since he clearly wants nothing to do with me unless his little girlfriend is unavailable. Nothing should matter to me less than what this man does with his time.

And that's what I keep telling myself as I follow him at a distance. He's going to the elevator—I tuck myself into another dark corner when he comes to a stop. *Don't look over here. Please, don't look over here.*

I can finally breathe again when he steps into the car and the doors slide shut. I watch the numbers above the elevator doors light up as the car climbs. Where is he going?

All the way up to the castle level, it turns out, beyond the dorms and the classrooms and all that. Now, there's nothing that could stop me from following him. Where is he going? What kind of secret life is he living?

That's why I run down the hall to the next elevator and jam my finger against the button over and over until the doors open. I choose the main castle level the way he did and chew my lip, willing the damn thing to move faster.

I can't burst out of the car the way I want to, not up here. This is where outsiders stay, family, and important people. With my luck, I'll end up running straight into Xander or maybe Quinton's sister, Scarlet. I have to be careful.

I peer out from around the doorway in time to catch a glimpse of Lucas walking toward the castle entrance. So he's leaving, but is he leaving alone? I wish the question didn't eat at me. I wish it didn't force me to keep following him. I will never rest unless I know whether he's going somewhere by himself or with that woman.

As I jog behind him, it occurs to me that I'm turning into a stalker. I guess I'll have to worry about that later. It isn't my fault the man is impossible to understand.

It's cold outside, as expected, and I shiver when the air hits me. *No coat, genius.* Even though I should stay inside, I keep going until I watch from behind a tree as Lucas climbs aboard the waiting helicopter. There's no one else inside but the pilot. I wish it didn't come as such a relief.

Something holds me in place as the helicopter begins to lift. Where is he going? Why is he so secretive? Why doesn't he know I only want to help him? I just want to be with him. No matter what that makes me, no matter what it means, it's all I care about. But he would rather keep pushing me away, flying off on his own.

I'll bet he told his little girlfriend where he's going. Red-hot jealousy races through me and warms my chilled skin. I'm surprised there's no steam rising from me by the time I turn back, ready to hide in my room and lick my wounds.

"Thinking about heading into town?"

I'm barely able to bite back a scream at the sound of Ren's voice. He's practically on top of me, smirking, his eyes darting back and forth between the retreating helicopter and me. Like he knows something.

Well, I know something, too. And it's remembering how I sort of have leverage over him that keeps me from shrinking back under his snarkiness. "It would be a shame if I was since the helicopter just left. Why did you follow me out here?"

"I don't normally see you up here. It seemed worth learning more."

"I'm sorry you wasted your time."

"Did I?"

I can't get a read on him. One second, he's being cruel and threatening, and the next, he acts like this is all a big joke. "What do you really want? Because if it's to make fun of me, we can do it inside where I'm not going to freeze to death."

"If you would give me a chance, I would have already offered to get you another helicopter."

I roll my eyes, nudging him aside and starting back for the doors. "Ha, ha. Very funny."

"Who's joking? I mean it. I could arrange to have a helicopter here in no time. You could go to Takotna."

"And why would you do that?"

"Can't you take a nice gesture and accept it?"

"Coming from you? No." Now we're back inside, and I can talk without my teeth chattering.

"Come on. I'm trying to be friendly. Do you want the helicopter, or don't you? I don't really care either way."

On the one hand, it would mean being able to follow Lucas. It's eating me alive, not knowing where he went or why he left. As far as I know, he doesn't make a habit out of wandering off.

But this is not the sort of thing we're supposed to do. "I don't need to get into any trouble. I'm already high profile enough."

"You're not going to get into any trouble. What, do you honestly think nobody ever does this? Please. You'll be fine." He pulls out his phone. "I can make the request right now. You know, if you want to go back to your dorm, put on some warmer clothes. It'll be waiting by the time you get back up here."

I shouldn't trust this person, but it's too tempting. And somehow, he knows it. "Why do I feel like I'm making a deal with the devil?"

He chuckles. "I've been called many things, but that one's new. Like I said, it's up to you. I've already spent more time on you than I should." Because, of course, he can't let it go without getting one last dig in at me.

"Fine. I'll run down to my room and get changed. You promise this isn't a trick? For real?"

"For real. Now hurry." He's snickering as he types out a message on his phone. "I wouldn't want anybody to see us together and get the wrong idea." I have to remind myself he's doing me a favor to keep from telling him how I feel about being seen with him. It's not exactly complimentary.

I know Lucas will be angry once I find him, but right now, it doesn't matter. So long as I know he's okay and not doing anything to get himself hurt—or worse. I would never forgive myself if that happened, and I didn't at least do something to try to stop him.

29

LUCAS

This is what I needed. Cheap booze and plenty of it, and nobody telling me I'm fucking with my responsibilities by enjoying it. Nobody pretending to worry about me when what they're really doing is judging me.

And that's all it is. They can put any kind of spin on it they want. It's all judgment. Thinking they're better than me.

"Hey." I lift my empty glass, signaling for another. How many has it been now? Four, five whiskeys? What's the point of counting? "You might as well leave the bottle," I tell the bartender, but he pretends to laugh it off like I was joking. The man doesn't know me.

"Maybe you ought to slow down, buddy."

He definitely does not know me. "Maybe you ought to pour me another drink and enjoy that I'm a good tipper." He scoffs—then pours the damn drink. Because at the end of the day, we're all driven by very simple needs. Money is right up there at the top.

There are others, as it turns out. I thought I was beyond them. Stronger than that, better. I used to despise the weakness of needing others. What was the use of needing people when they'd only screw you over at the first chance they got? I still believe that for the most part.

But I went and started needing people. And it turns out I'm the one who did the screwing over. Aspen was my chance to get something right for the first time in my wasted life. To prove I could do the right thing. To set an example and all that shit.

What did I do? I made her hate me. No. She loathes me. The look in her eyes, the anger and disappointment. She had every right to be angry. The sound of her disappointment resonates in my skull even now, bouncing around like a rubber ball, ensuring I don't get a moment's peace. The only thing she can trust me to do is keep things from her. Fuck, she hit it on the head.

I down the full glass without tasting what's inside, relishing the burn. "Another." The bartender pretends to ignore me, turning his attention to a couple of flannel-wearing guys at the other end of the scarred bar. "Hey. I'm talking to you."

"Calm down." The larger of the two men snickers. "Nobody is timing you to see how fast you can empty a bottle." He then mutters something that sounds like *fucking lush*, and he and his friend have a snide laugh about it while looking my way.

Oh, this is good. This is better than I could've hoped for. I thought I'd have to do a little digging to find somebody willing to engage in a fight. That's what I need. To drink until sanity is completely blotted out and to fight. To spill blood.

To ache. Fuck me, I want to hurt. Because that I can deal with. That I've managed countless times before. I can focus on the physical pain, at least once the physical pain is intense enough to block out everything else. There's only so much self-recrimination a man can inflict when he can barely move for the damage.

It's what I need and deserve for hurting or fucking over everyone who's ever gotten close to me.

"You got something to say to me?" I swivel on the stool, smiling with my mouth alone. My eyes are a different story, I'm sure. I've watched men the size of the two of these assholes cringe when I don't bother masking the darkness inside. "Why don't you come over here and we can have a conversation? Or are you only man enough to make a snide remark when twenty feet of bar are between us?"

"He's not worth it," the smaller man insists, shaking his head at his friend before picking up his pint glass. "Everybody feels big and bad when they have enough liquor in them."

"I'm big and bad when I'm dead sober," I assure them both before slamming my glass against the bar to get the bartender's attention. "But I'm also smart enough to watch who I insult."

"Listen. We don't need any trouble here." The bartender holds up both hands in mock surrender. "Okay? But if you keep stirring up shit, I will have to ask you to leave."

"I'm not trying to stir up trouble," I lie smoothly, turning my smile in his direction. "I only want another drink, which, if I understand correctly, is something you serve here. I'm not sure why this song and dance bullshit has to be. Pour the whiskey."

"These fucking outsiders," the big guy grumbles, glaring at me. "Come into town thinking they can flash their cash around, act like assholes and get away with it. Sickening."

"What's sickening is hearing your fucking voice." I jerk my chin toward the smaller guy. "Why don't you shove your shriveled little dick in his mouth and shut him up? You'd be doing us all a favor."

They both shove away from their stools. So do I, practically bursting with anticipation.

"That's it. Out of here, all of you. I don't want any fighting in my bar." The bartender extends an arm, pointing at the door. "You wanna brawl like animals? Do it outside."

"With pleasure." I drop a stack of bills on the bar, more than enough to cover twice what I drank, then stroll outside and around the corner to a narrow alley between this building and the one beside it. The pavement is slick thanks to recent rain and the odor of garbage hanging heavy in the air.

Soon it will be the tang of blood filling the air. I intend to breathe deep.

"You made a big mistake, fuckface." One of the men laughs behind me as they follow my progress. Let them laugh. They have no idea the damage I'm about to cause. I strip off my jacket and leave it lying across a plastic crate before cracking my knuckles and turning to face them.

There's barely enough light to see, only a pair of bare bulbs mounted to the wall. It's enough to give me a glimpse of their smug, self-assured grins. They believe the odds are in their favor, two against one. Maybe if they were fighting an ordinary man, they'd be right.

"Let's see you back up that smart mouth of yours," the smaller of the men mutters with a sneer, elbowing his friend. "He can barely stand up straight."

Yet when the larger man strikes first, I block his swing easily before delivering a sharp jab to his ribs, leaving him bent over, gasping for air. "Broke my fucking ribs!" he groans. His buddy charges forward, and I give him a smooth uppercut. He recovers quickly after staggering backward but isn't as quick to charge me again.

"Aw, ladies," I mock, shaking my head slowly. "And I thought you wanted to fight. I didn't know you were in the mood for a make-out session in a dark alley."

"Fucking prick." The bigger guy stands up straight, and I brace myself for his attack. This time, I let him get a punch in, his knuckles kiss my jaw, and I swing my head to the side. He knows how to throw a punch and put all his weight behind it. I reward him in kind before his partner comes at me with a kick to the back of my knee that almost takes me down.

I manage to stay on my feet, but the distraction is all the big guy needs. He lands a blow to the side of my head that makes everything spin while stars sparkle in front of me.

I stagger, a little dazed, and the two of them laugh. The little guy takes advantage with a series of blows to my kidneys.

"Fucking dirty fighters," I grunt, throwing him off me hard enough that he hits the ground and sends muddy water splashing up.

"Maybe you should've watched who you were fucking with."

The big one lands another punch against the side of my face, and the impact makes my teeth cut into my cheek. The coppery taste of blood pools in my mouth. The pain affects me but in a different way than other people. It fuels me, heightens my senses, and makes me thirsty for more.

With a roar, I take him by the head and butt mine against his. He staggers against the wall, dazed, while I catch my breath and they climb to their feet. I get the sense they're beginning to regret this, and my heart sinks. I'm not finished with them. Not by a long shot. I won't be finished until I'm in the agony I deserve, dammit.

"Come on." I'm swaying slightly and have to spit out a mouthful of blood before adding, "More."

They exchange a look that I know is confusion even though they keep going in and out of focus. "This guy for real?" one of them mutters to the other.

"Fucked in the head," the other one agrees.

"That's right." I lift my fists and tuck in my chin. When they hesitate, I throw a couple of jabs that make them lean back to avoid being hit. The big guy cocks his fist, and I lower mine slightly to give him room.

The entire world falls on its side once he makes contact with my jaw. No, it's me dropping to my knees and then onto my side in a puddle of dank, muddy water.

The little light around me is beginning to drain away in favor of encroaching darkness. I welcome it, smiling a little as everything starts to fade away. No rage, no helplessness, no guilt. Just darkness.

"Lucas? Oh, my god!"

It's a faint sound coming from far away. I fight to open my eyes, staring down the length of the alley. Somebody is there. A girl.

"Lucas!" She's screaming, and her feet slap against the pavement. For someone reason, I could swear I see Delilah. But there's no way; it can't be Delilah. I must be seeing things because I know she's what I need deep inside. What I crave hardest. But it isn't her that's here.

Though damned if it doesn't look and sound like her running toward me. I push myself back onto my knees, prepared to tell her to stop and go away. There's nothing for her here.

Either I'm too slow, or she's too fast. No matter the reason, Delilah —it's her, it's really her even if I don't know how—tries to get between me and the man now preparing to deliver one final strike. He has time to pull his fist back but not enough time to avoid hitting her altogether.

His fist lands on the back of her head. Instantly, it's light out, her body dropping like a sack of potatoes. My heart's in my throat by the time she lands against me, unconscious but breathing. "Delilah," I whisper, ignoring the pain radiating through my body in favor of holding her for a moment before lowering her the rest of the way to the ground.

"Oh, shit," one of the men whispers. "Come on. We better get outta here."

Like hell.

Something snaps inside me, and I climb to my feet in a flash. I take the smaller of the two men by the back of his collar and pull hard enough to knock him on his back. He lands hard, stunned for a moment, which is all the time it takes for me to lean down, haul him up part way by his jacket, and start pounding on his face until I hear the satisfying crunching of bone. His buddy makes the mistake of trying to pull me off—my elbow connecting with his nose is enough to make him fall back, shouting in pain behind his hands.

I return my attention to my prey, his face unrecognizable now. He's gurgling blood, choking on it. The sound is music to my ears. I drop him, and his head bounces off the pavement. He lies still, the gurgling stopping all at once.

I turn my attention to his friend. I'm not finished.

"No... please..." The big guy's eyes bulge as he realizes I'm coming for him next, his feet slipping on the wet pavement when he tries to run. "No, don't, I won't tell anybody."

He's right. He won't.

I take hold of him and throw him against the brick wall face-first. It stuns him, and he tries to swing at me. I easily duck it before taking him by the back of the head and smashing his face against the brick once, twice, until there's nothing but a red smear on the wall that follows his progress as he slowly slides down its length, landing in a lifeless heap.

I want to roar in triumph as I look over what I've done. My blood's pumping, adrenaline coursing, blocking out everything but the pure rush of domination.

Until my gaze lands on an unconscious Delilah, and reality rushes back in.

I pull out my phone, my bloody fingers streaking the screen when I tap Nic's contact entry.

When he answers, I mutter four words. "I need cleanup services."

The announcement catches him off guard, judging by the way he pauses. "Location." There's heaviness in his voice. I know where it's coming from but can't bring myself to give a shit.

"Takotna. In the alley behind a bar called Ralph's."

"What are you—"

"Immediately. Two messes in need of cleanup."

"Two? Lucas, what the fuck are you doing? Why are you there? What—"

"Just get it done. I need to get out of here."

With that, I end the call, tucking the phone away before covering Delilah with my jacket and lifting her oh-so gently in my arms. She's still breathing evenly. Hopefully, there's nothing but a bump on the head to worry about. If he cracked her skull or caused internal hemorrhaging...

Well, I suppose I can't kill him again.

I'm a mess, but it's dark, and there aren't many people on the street. I passed a hotel on the way from the helipad and head in that direction, Delilah's limp body resting in my arms, tucked tight against my chest.

A glance in a darkened shop window tells me I'm bruised, but not badly enough that I'll raise too many red flags. I could always say we had a little accident and needed somewhere to stay the night. I look down at Delilah. Her eyes are closed, her face that of an angel that's merely asleep.

"Don't worry," I whisper, though I know she can't hear me. "We'll get you taken care of."

30

DELILAH

"*A*re you still with me? Delilah? Are you awake?"

I think I am, though I'm not sure I want to be. My head. It's like somebody drove a concrete truck through my skull. I don't want to open my eyes, knowing how much worse it will be once the light hits them.

"You're all right, and everything will be fine." I flinch at a cold sensation on the back of my head. It's just ice, I realize once I hear it moving, the cubes jangling around.

It takes me a moment to put everything together—my thoughts are moving so slowly. "Lucas?" I whisper, trying to pry my eyes open.

"You gave me a little bit of a scare," he murmurs, his voice warm and even gentle. I gave him a scare? When he's the one who ran off? I don't know how long I spent looking for him.

Only that it was dark by the time I found him getting beaten by two men.

"What happened?" I lift my hand, prepared to test the area that hurts the worst, but he keeps me from doing it.

"Leave the ice where it is for now. Believe me, you'll feel a lot better if you do." He shakes a pill bottle close to my face. "Something for the pain."

"Thank you," I whisper. So now I'm with the kind Lucas. The gentle, protective one. All it took was getting knocked out.

"What were you doing? Were you trying to get yourself killed?" I take a couple of pills, then sip the water as slowly as I can. My stomach's a little queasy, so I want to be careful.

He closes the curtains over the windows, but there's still enough light to catch sight of the damage done to his face. It's not too much, but enough that it's clear he's been fighting.

Is this what he does? Gets himself all worked up until there's no way to keep living unless he vents everything built up inside? Like a volcano.

"I could ask you the same question. What the hell are you doing here? Why did you leave school? How did you even manage this?"

I can't keep up with his questions, and trying to think only hurts my head. But I know better than to think he'll let this go unless I give him an answer. "I wanted to make sure you were okay. That's why I'm here. I saw you leaving, and I was worried."

"About me?"

"Who else?"

"Delilah. I'm the last person who needs somebody following them to make sure they don't get hurt."

"Are you sure about that?" I open my eyes just enough to shoot him a dirty look. "Because I found you lying in a dirty alley."

"That's my business." Then it's a pretty fucked-up business, but I keep my mouth shut. I like Kind Lucas and don't want him to go away.

"How did you know I was leaving? Did somebody tell you?" I hear the suspicion in his voice.

"No. It's nothing like that. I was following you."

"That makes me feel much better."

"You know what I mean. I checked on you, and you were headed out to the helipad."

"But why were you checking on me? That's what I'm trying to understand. Why would you do that?"

Maybe it's the irritation in his voice that stirs my own irritation. "Because you haven't been honest with me. I saw that woman."

"Which woman?" he mutters.

"Which one would I be talking about? The blond lady who came out of your apartment. I heard her in your office, too. That's who I was talking about when I went to see you the other day. I know she's around."

"Wait a minute." There's laughter in his voice, the jerk, like my feelings are all a big joke. "You think something is going on there? Is that what this is about?"

"Don't make a joke about it. It's not funny."

"No, it's not funny." That doesn't stop him from chuckling. "But in a way, it kind of is because you have no idea what the fuck you're talking about."

I wish my heart wouldn't swell the way it does at his reaction. "Yeah?"

"Yeah. That's not what it looked like. I know, people say that when they get caught and don't want to fess up. But it's really not like that at all."

He leans down, a grin touching the corners of his mouth as he parts my hair to get a better look at what I know has to be a bump on my head.

"If it interests you, I'll tell you the truth. You're the only woman I've been with since we... became involved. I don't exactly make it a habit of sleeping around. Women are a complication I can't really have in my line of work."

There goes my heart, swelling again. I hate to think he has this power over me, but I wouldn't change it even if I could. Because it feels too good being cared for now, with him being so gentle and tender. It doesn't mean I'm not annoyed with him for being so secretive, but the good feelings are muting all the negative ones right now.

He picks up a second ice pack lying on the nightstand and flops down beside me, and I stroke the side of his face. He lets out a long sigh. "Now. On to you. What are you doing sneaking away from school? This was a bad idea, and you know it. I can only defend so many bad decisions before you have to be punished."

"I understand. But like I said, I had to see you."

"Let's put that aside for a minute." Like somehow, the thought of it makes him unhappy. Is it that unthinkable, somebody caring about him? "How did you manage it? I know someone must've helped you."

I nibble on my bottom lip. "I don't want to get anybody into trouble."

Lucas lifts a brow. "Answer the question. Who did it?"

I shake my head. I don't want to tell him, but I can only hope I don't regret this. "It was Ren. He saw me follow you out to the helipad and offered to get a helicopter for me."

Lucas snorts, "How helpful of him."

"Please, don't get me in trouble with him. I already have enough—"

He holds a finger to his lips, shaking his head. "Relax. Getting yourself all worked up in the pain you're in will only make things worse. I hear what you're saying. That doesn't mean I'm happy about him helping you sneak around."

"He was only trying to help."

"Was he?" He blows out another sigh, his eyes narrowing. "Or was this something else entirely, a move on Xander's part? Maybe he was helping to get rid of you?"

How could I be so stupid?

"Oh. I didn't think of that."

"Obviously."

"Don't be mad at me. Please." There's only so much I can take right now.

"I can't help feeling a little irritated with you, but that's because you put yourself in danger. I'm not worth that. I wish you'd get that through your head."

"I wish you would get it through your head that I disagree."

He snickers. "Anyway, I hope you learned a lesson. Don't ever get in the way when men are fighting. You never know what's going to happen."

"Don't worry. I'll remember. So anyway, what happened? Did they run off?"

"Yeah, something like that. Don't worry about them."

I don't know if I like being brushed off like this. It sounds like he's hiding something. He's lucky I don't feel like arguing about it—or about anything. It's too nice being in bed, just the two of us, nobody getting between us.

I close my eyes, content to rest beside him. It doesn't seem like he's resting much. He's tense, in a strained kind of mood. After a little while, he gets up with a pained grunt and goes to the bathroom.

By the time he comes back, he's made up his mind. "I think it would be best if we hung around here today. Take it easy, lay low."

Nothing would make me happier. It's not until I hear him say it that I know I was hoping he would all along. "Where is here, anyway?"

"A hotel not far from where you found me. I told them we had an accident, just in case we ran into anybody."

I'm content to let him call the shots now. I'm so glad to be with him and know he's okay.

Also, to know that he's not sleeping with that blond woman. There's still a story there, one he obviously doesn't want to share with me. I don't mind. At least I know I'm the only woman in his life, sexually.

That has to mean something, right?

He turns on the TV, and for a while, I zone out while the meds I took start to take effect. After an hour or so, I'm feeling much better. I'm not even queasy anymore. It's easy to laugh at the brainless comedy Lucas turned on.

After a few seconds, I find I'm laughing alone. When I glance up at him, he's not even looking at the TV but staring at the wall above it.

His features are pensive and tense, and he has a permanent scowl.

"What can I do?" I whisper, sitting up. "I hate seeing you like this."

He looks pained. "I wish you didn't feel like it's your responsibility to take care of me. That's not fair."

"Who said anything about fair? Besides, it's my choice. Nobody is making me care about you. I can't help it."

I wish so much I could take away the pain that etches itself across his face. Not physical pain—something tells me he can handle that pretty well on his own. It's deeper than that, and I've always sensed it there. It's the worst sort of helpless feeling, watching someone suffer when there's nothing to be done about it.

Or maybe there is, at least for a little while. I can make him forget.

I look up and down the length of his body. He's stripped down to his boxer briefs, and I see a bruise along his ribs. I lean in and place a gentle kiss over it.

"What are you doing?"

"Nothing." I kiss him again, this time over his abs. The muscles go tense.

"Delilah. Come on."

"Come on, what?" I lift my gaze, looking him in the eye. "You expect to lie in bed like this and not have me wanting you?"

"Don't even pretend you're in the mood for this with that bump on your head."

"I hardly feel it anymore." I allow my fingers to dance along the ridges of his abs before slipping further down, playing along the edge of his waistband. When his breath changes, it stirs heat in my core.

He's crazy if he thinks this isn't a turn-on. I wasn't remotely horny before, but now, I'm getting wet at his reaction.

I have to remember this is about him, about getting his mind off things. I focus on his growing bulge, twitching under the cotton shorts.

I drag my nails gently over that bulge, and he hisses. "Oh, fuck..."

"Just relax," I whisper, caressing him again. He closes his eyes and lets his head fall back against the pillows while I continue playing with him. Pretty soon, a small wet spot grows, hinting at his arousal.

"Oh, yeah," he groans as I lower the waistband, taking it an inch at a time. I want him to think about me, only me. What am I going to do next? How am I going to tease him this time?

All I want is to please him and take his mind off everything for as long as I can. So I drag it out, by the time his dick springs free of its cage, he's rock hard, and his body is rigid with tension.

I lean down, extending my tongue and taking a slow, deliberate tour of the underside of his shaft. The way he gasps and moans the higher my tongue travels makes me bolder than ever, so I experiment with taking his head between my lips and sucking gently but giving him no more than that.

"That's right. Suck. Take all of me."

I don't give him what he wants right away, scraping my teeth gently around the ridge before replacing them with my tongue, swirling it around like I'm licking an ice cream cone.

"Are you trying to kill me?" he grunts, thrusting his hips upward like he wants to take control. When he does, though, I pull back.

He grits his teeth and groans helplessly. I can't pretend I don't love the sound. Knowing I can do this to him, for him.

Finally, once his precum leaks from the tip, and he's panting and helpless, I give him what he wants. I take him between my lips and lower my head slowly, taking him deep into my throat.

I don't stop until my nose is buried at his base.

"Fuck, yes. Yes, Delilah. Take all of me. Take me deep, just like that. Let me fuck your throat."

The naked need in his voice and the approval under it do something to me, making me even bolder than before. I cup his balls with one hand, tentative, experimenting a little. He seems to like it when I massage them, so I do while my head bobs up and down.

"You're so good at this," he moans, surging in my mouth. "You're so good to my cock. I love the way my cock looks in your mouth."

I murmur my agreement, then his hips lift, his head banging against the back of my throat. I fight off my gag reflex, and it passes quickly enough.

Soon he's running his fingers through my hair—gentle at first, but he becomes more forceful before long. *Demanding.* He cups the back of my head, and I gasp, freezing in place when he makes contact with the bump. He gets the message and moves his hand lower, to the back of my neck.

Then he holds me hard, growling. "You want more? You want my cock deep in your throat? Of course you do. I bet your pussy is dripping, all sloppy and wet, wishing my cock could fill it?"

Fuck. I'm getting more and more turned on by the second.

"Fuck. I'm going to fill that throat of yours with cum!" I moan around his length, lost in the moment, in the thrill. He begins lifting his hips, thrusting upward, and now all I can do is hold on until he's finished.

His hand tightens around my neck. "You're gonna swallow every drop and not waste any of it, or I'll make you lick it up off the floor."

I yelp a little when his fingers dig in tighter but that only eggs him on until I'm fighting not to choke on him as he pummels me with one sharp thrust after another. He loses his rhythm until all he's doing is frantically fucking my face, desperate to reach the end. When he does, he fills my mouth with the taste of him, coating my tongue and my throat. I gulp him down, catching every drop as instructed. Finally, it slows, then stops, with him sinking into the bed and withdrawing from between my lips.

"Holy shit," he pants before letting go of me. I can't help but feel proud, seeing him completely undone like this. And I did it. I'm so good that he doesn't need to sleep with any other woman. Only me.

Suddenly, his eyes open wide and he sits up, taking me by the arms. "Fuck. I didn't hurt you, did I?"

The honest concern in his voice and eyes touches me deeply, and I can't help but smile. "You didn't hurt me. I'm fine."

He lies back down, pulling me into his arms. There's nowhere else I'd rather be, even when everything around us is up in the air, totally unsettled. He's relaxed, finally. His heartbeat eventually slows into a nice, steady rhythm as he calms down and drifts off to sleep.

Right now, it's just the two of us. And it's enough as I close my eyes and let sleep take over.

31

LUCAS

There's nothing like the sense of hanging in limbo.

Waiting to see what will happen next.

Who's going to reach out to me first—my brother? Xander? Charlotte? Somebody else? Knowing we can't stay here forever, that I have to go back and bring her with me but dreading it like I can't describe.

She's asleep in my arms. We spent most of yesterday and overnight in and out of sleep, ordering food once we both realized we hadn't eaten.

The remnants of our takeout meal sit in a paper bag on the dresser, beside the TV that's still on with the volume turned down almost all the way. The bluish light it casts over the room gives Delilah a ghostly appearance.

I brush back a few errant locks of hair from her cheek and smile when she makes a happy little sound. She's dreaming of something nice, pleasant. Something not based too deeply in reality, obviously.

I can't give her anything good. She'll never know anything but darkness when she's with me. I don't know how to make somebody happy, and I've hardly tried to learn how.

Why does she want to be with me? Why does she take these risks? I'm not worth it. What's it going to take to make her see that?

Charlotte's words echo in my head. When she accused me of pushing people away. She's right. Is that what I'm trying to do with Delilah?

All the times I've tried to hurt her. When I've vented my darkness on her. She keeps coming back for more, for some reason. It isn't easy to believe she wants me, really wants me. Eventually, I will need to accept it or find a way to convince her for good that nothing will ever come of us.

The thing is, I don't believe that. I don't want to. I want this. I want her, need her, and no matter how I try to convince myself otherwise, there won't be a day of my life when she isn't on my mind.

How am I supposed to turn my back on that and pretend it isn't true?

My phone buzzes on the nightstand. I grab for it quickly before it can wake her. She stirs, then rolls onto her back, away from me. Dread blooms in my chest. Who is it going to be?

As it turns out, it's the person I dread hearing from the most, though she poses the least threat on the surface.

Aspen: Can we talk soon?

The fact that Aspen used so few words tells me this isn't going to be a happy reunion, but then I wouldn't expect it to be.

I'm not looking for her to spare my feelings. I deserve her anger and the sense of betrayal that I know she's struggling with.

Does she know I'm gone? I can only assume she does. By now, Xander would have made a comment about it. I'm sure he wouldn't miss the opportunity.

I type a quick reply.

Me: I'll be back asap, and I'll let you know when I land.

I see that she reads the message but doesn't respond to it.

I can't deny her any more than I can keep running away. I deserve whatever is coming, as much as I dread seeing the hatred on her face again.

I hate breaking into Delilah's peace, too, but it can't be helped.

"Hey. We need to get going. Back to Corium."

She groans, then buries her face in the pillow. Even now, I can't help but laugh a little since I understand the impulse. "I know. But we can't stay here forever. I have some shit I've got to take care of."

"I guess you won't bother telling me what it's all about." She lifts her head far enough to shoot me a doleful look.

"I will once things are settled. That's going to have to be enough for now." And then I get out of bed and get dressed because this is not the conversation I need to have now. There's too much on my mind as it is.

She doesn't seem bitter or angry as she dresses, at least. "It was nice to have a night when I didn't have to worry about anybody screwing with me," she admits before touching tentative fingers to the back of her head.

"How does it feel?"

She answers by popping another pill and washing it down with what's left of the melted ice in her takeout cup from dinner last night.

I have no doubt Nic cleaned things up efficiently, but I can't help wondering if word has gotten around about the men who went missing after visiting Ralph's. Something tells me I shouldn't make a habit of visiting in the future. With that in mind, it's a relief to board the helicopter.

I have no idea what I'm heading into, but at least Aspen wants to speak to me. I didn't think she'd reach out this soon.

Is that a good thing? Or maybe it only took her a couple of days to decide I'm not worth building a relationship with. That's just as possible.

"You look worried," Delilah observes as we take off.

"I'm not," I lie and take hold of her hand, wanting to reassure her, "stop worrying so much about me."

She frowns. "I wish it was that easy."

For her sake, I wish it was, as well. Once she finds out about Charlotte and Aspen, she'll understand what a waste of time I am.

Maybe that's why I don't want to tell her yet. I don't want to see the look in her eyes when she finds out I'm a complete coward.

Along the way, I text Aspen as promised.

Me: On my way.

Again, she reads the message but offers no response. Anger clouds my judgment. How it's going to be. I can only imagine what she has in store for me once I arrive.

As it turns out, she isn't my primary concern as the helicopter begins its descent. I should have known he'd be waiting. He is probably telling himself he's making sure I do the right thing. When Delilah spots Xander waiting near the helipad, my hackles rise.

"He's not going to do anything to me, is he?"

The anxiety written on her face when she turns to me, searching for reassurance, is enough to make me wish he was one of those men in the alley. He's hurt her much worse than a single punch to the head ever could.

"I won't let him do anything to you. You have my word on that, always." I reach for her hand and wrap my fingers around it, squeezing tight. "Don't let him intimidate you. Yes, he's powerful and dangerous, but I promise you, I won't let him do anything to you."

She offers a brave if shaky smile. "Easier said than done."

Yes, I can see how that would be true. And it's more of a reason than ever to hate him.

"So you saw fit to finally return." There's Xander in a nutshell.

Always stating the obvious. Ren stands a few steps behind him, his expression unreadable, his hands shoved deep into his pockets. I want more than anything to demand he tell me the truth about why he helped Delilah follow me, but I'll bide my time. I don't want to appear too eager.

Xander makes no effort to conceal his disdain for her, sneering when I help her descend from the helicopter. "And you. You would do better to return to your room, where you should have been all along."

I have to bite my tongue before I remind him I'm headmaster of Corium. I don't want her to see us argue like that. Besides, I'm sure every moment she spends in his presence is torture.

Ren steps up, and now I understand why he's here. "Ren will escort you back to your dorm," Xander tells her coldly.

"Wait a second." I hold out an arm, barring her from stepping forward. "She can find her own way back to the dorm."

"Forgive me if I don't trust her—but then you already knew about that, didn't you?"

Delilah places a hand on my arm, then lowers it. "I'm fine. I'll go." I shoot Ren the filthiest look I can manage—a slight dip of his chin tells me he gets the message, but he's still unreadable.

What's his play here? What's in it for him?

"Now that we're alone," Xander continues as we walk toward the castle. "I'm going to tell you straight out, man to man. It's time to get your shit together, or else you need to step down from your position. I know you're going through a lot, but Corium needs to be your main priority. If it can't be, then we need to consider hiring someone else."

We step through the front doors, and I turn to him, waiting for him to meet my gaze. "I'm going to tell you this straight out, too. You can fuck off. I love my job here, and I'll figure this shit out on my own. My main priorities at this moment are Corium and my daughter."

I didn't think that would hit him hard, and I was right. He only smiles wide like that was exactly what he expected.

"And Delilah? Is she one of your priorities?"

278

"She's none of your concern, and if it wasn't obvious before, I care about her greatly. I'm not asking for a handout from you. I'm not even asking that you don't show concern. I'm asking that you trust me and let me do what I need to do without interfering. If I thought Delilah was a risk to anyone, the first person to know would be you."

"But would it really? I get the feeling it wouldn't, and I don't know if I can trust your judgment anymore."

I shake my head. "Then why the fuck am I even here?"

Xander ignores my statement altogether and instead changes the subject. "Your daughter is waiting for you in the conference room."

His previous comment jars me, but not as much as us all meeting in a conference room. I thought we would meet up at my apartment, at least. Since this is a private matter and not school related.

What is this, mediation? Does she plan on bringing a lawyer with her, too? I have to fight to keep my irritation at bay—I don't want Xander to see how this rattles me as we walk side by side down the hall.

I want to ask exactly what the hell business this is of his, but again, I know better. He's looking for the first opportunity to strike me down. I'm not going to hand him the ammunition that easily.

Xander opens the door to the conference room. Aspen is waiting, as promised, sitting at a long table with Quinton standing behind her like a guard dog, waiting to attack at any given moment.

He's clearly no fan of mine right now. I can't take it personally when I know it's out of love for Aspen. At least he goes back to rubbing her shoulders after shooting me a death glare while she stares down at her folded hands.

I take a seat across from her, watching for any little reaction she gives off. I glance up at Xander, who lingers in the doorway. Does this mean he's leaving? He needs to leave. I'm not having this discussion in his presence.

As it turns out, we're waiting for another participant.

"Charlotte." I rise from my chair as she enters the room. She nods in acknowledgment, and I take a seat while she does the same, leaving a couple of chairs between us. She can't take her eyes off Aspen, who's begun tapping her foot in a quick rhythm.

"We'll leave you three alone," Xander exclaims.

It's obvious that's the last thing Quinton wants to do, and I'm sure Xander would rather stick around. When Q glances down at Aspen, his eyebrows raised, I know this is the way she wants it. She nods briefly, and he exits the room with his father behind him.

"Thank you for sitting down to talk." Aspen's voice is soft but firm. Like she's reciting something she's practiced in her head. "I've had a little more time to think things over. I'm sorry I reacted the way I did."

"You had every right to. You were reacting from your emotions. Anybody would."

Her gaze brushes against mine ever so briefly before landing on the table between us. "Anyway, I wasn't proud of myself."

"Do you have any questions you need to be answered?" Charlotte asks.

The way she wrings her hands together in her lap reveals her strain. What she wants more than anything is to leap across the table and wrap her daughter in a big, tight hug.

"I have a million questions," Aspen admits. "But the biggest one is where have you been the last few years, and why did people think you were dead?"

Charlotte explains everything she has told me before. Aspen is shocked about her adoptive parents' involvement, but she doesn't seem too surprised either.

"I traveled through Europe for a bit, trying to find my place in the world. I was lost for a long time, figuratively and sometimes actually. I ended up settling down in Italy, where I found someone."

"So you have a boyfriend?" Aspen asks curiously.

"Actually, I'm married, and... I also have two young boys."

"I have siblings?"

Charlotte nods, and her eyes light up, talking about her boys, the love for them so evident.

Aspen's gaze bleeds into Charlotte, and she smiles at her mother. "I can't wait to meet them. I mean, if that's something that's okay with you?"

"Of course! I would love that. You have no idea how much that would mean to me."

That's good. At least they have that.

"Are there any more burning questions?"

"So many, but I don't think they could all be answered right away. More like they'll come up with time."

"But you're willing to give me the time?"

Aspen's head bobs up and down, eyes shining as they fill with tears. "Willing? I want to. I want to get to know you. I'm sorry things started out the way they did."

"That was my fault. I should have—"

I hold up a hand, signaling her to stop while clearing my throat. It does nothing to dislodge the lump forming there. "It's my fault. I'm willing to take the blame because I deserve it. I let too much time pass when I knew how important it was to you that Aspen knows you're alive. I hope you can forgive me." It's Aspen who I direct that to, my gaze swinging her way.

She chews at her lip nervously while averting her eyes. Not a good sign and not something easy for me to sit through and witness without pushing her in any way. "I'm going to need time for that," she finally mumbles. "I don't know how long. But it's not happening right away. In fact, I... don't think I want to see you for a bit after this."

It isn't easy to hear. I know it's what I deserve, and I certainly didn't expect much better—in fact, I wouldn't have been surprised if it was much worse.

"I understand." But it's still disappointing, knowing she's hurting badly.

It's time for me to do what I know has to be done, so I offer Charlotte what I intend as a reassuring nod before standing. "I'll let the two of you talk. And for what it's worth, I'm glad you're finally together. That's how it should be."

Charlotte smiles in gratitude, eyes shining like our daughter's. Aspen merely glances my way before looking at the table again.

So that's as much as I'm going to get from her now. I'm not okay with it, but I have to at least pretend to be as I walk from the room with the sense of having destroyed the one good thing I had going for me. No matter if she forgives me, there'll never be any putting things back to the way they were before.

32

DELILAH

"*D*id you like your little trip?" There's amusement in Ren's question that makes my hackles rise, but I'm not going to play into it. I won't let him get under my skin anymore.

"Very much, thanks for asking. It was very relaxing."

"I bet." The elevator doors slide open, and he extends an arm, signaling me to take the lead. I wish he didn't make me feel so unsettled. I still can't figure out his place in all of this. What's in it for him?

When we reach my room, I hesitate in front of the door. What's next? Will he watch while I go inside so he can report back to Xander?

I lift my eyebrow, questioning him silently. "Here you are." He still waits for me to open the door. Now I wonder if some terrible surprise waits for me on the other side. I open it slowly, dreading what's about to happen. Except nothing does.

The room looks normal, just the way I left it. I turn to him, and his expression is blank. "Thanks?"

This is too bizarre. At least he doesn't try to follow me inside, strolling away as I swing the door closed. Leaving me with a million other questions revolving around Lucas.

What is going on up there? It seemed pretty serious and important. Why wouldn't Lucas tell me? Does it have to do with me? I can't sit still for all the nervous energy leaving me jumpy and skittish, so I pace helplessly. Who is he meeting with? Would he even tell me the truth if I asked?

I wish I didn't have to ask myself that question, but it's pretty obvious there are still a lot of things I'm not allowed to know. Okay, so he's not sleeping with this blond woman—but what's she doing here?

He didn't go that far into his explanation, did he? And what the hell does Xander have to do with any of this? It was obvious he savored that whole interaction on the helipad. He's getting off on this for some weird reason—not that I would put anything weird past him.

I'm not getting anywhere pacing my room, that's for sure. How can they expect me to hang around here when it feels like there's so much hanging in the balance? One thing about me nobody seems to understand: I don't sit around and wait for things to happen. I'm too impatient.

And that's how I talk myself into sneaking out of my room again. Not that I really need to sneak. It isn't like Ren was told to stand guard and make sure I didn't leave. And it's not like anybody told me I had to stay here or else. Hell, if Xander had, I would have already left. I'll be damned if I follow orders from him.

They're up in the castle, so I take the elevator again and wind up not far from where we just entered only minutes ago.

There are staff and guards up here, but I keep my head down and stay close to the wall as I walk the hallways. It only hits me now that I don't know where they were having their little meeting, if that's, in fact, what's going on. And I don't know enough about this place to know of an obvious choice.

So all I can do is go up and down one hall after another, listening for any familiar voices. I doubt Lucas would go out of his way to be quiet, anyway. But I don't hear anything. I'm sure the big, heavy doors play a part in that. This place must have been built centuries ago, and everything is monstrously oversized, right down to the thick stone walls.

A door opens ahead, and I duck inside the nearest doorway to wait and see who it is.

My heart clenches at the sight of her. The blonde whose name I'm still not allowed to know. She steps out of a room and smiles, even beaming. It doesn't seem right that I should hate her for her happiness, but that's what boils in my chest as I watch her walk away. Who the hell is she, and why is she such a big deal to Lucas? He can pretend all he wants, but if she meant nothing, he would have told me. Right? He wouldn't be keeping her identity a secret.

If I'm not going to get any answers from him, I'll need to get them from her. I almost can't believe I'm doing this, taking off after her at a light jog. Does she even know who I am? I doubt it—I'm not that important, am I? Just another student as far as she's concerned.

What am I going to do if she asks why I care? I don't know. I'll figure it out if the time comes. Nothing matters more than knowing who she is and why she's here. If that makes me obsessed, then I'm obsessed.

She rounds a corner, and I'm prepared to call out to stop her when suddenly, an arm clamps around my waist, followed by a hand over my mouth. Panic explodes inside my head. The woman retreats, disappearing from sight, unaware somebody's attacking me. Somebody who pulls me into a pitch-black room and shuts the door with his body.

Oh, my god, what's happening?

Who is this? It could be anybody, I realize. My attacker?

This is it. This is when he kills me. I claw at the hand over my mouth and swing my feet in a desperate attempt to get him off me, but he only holds on tighter before bending me over a table I can't see. I can't see anything—not a scrap of light anywhere, but I feel the wood under my body as he presses me against it with his own, holding me still while I fight and kick and strain to get free. I have to get free. I can't die like this.

Even if I could scream, I doubt anybody would hear me. And if they did, would they care? It all goes through my head at once, along with so many other things. My entire life is flashing before my eyes while my attacker holds me down. I reach up behind me and try to grab for his face, his hair, anything that might get me free. But no matter how I scramble and fight, he manages to avoid my taking hold of him.

Tears fill my eyes when he shoves a hand down the back of my pants. It's not enough to kill me. He wants to rape me first. My palms slap against his head and shoulders, but he only laughs before cupping my pussy, pressing his fingers against me hard enough to make me sob behind his hand.

He doesn't stop there, sliding a finger inside me while I scream in helpless rage.

"That's right," he growls in my ear. "That's how I want you to fight me. Just like that."

It takes a second for the voice to sink in past my fear. And when it does, that fear is swept aside in favor of fury.

He pulls back, withdrawing from me and letting me go so I can turn around and pummel his chest with both fists. "Dammit, Lucas! What the hell is wrong with you? I thought you were trying to kill me!"

I can't see him in the darkness, but his chuckle is unmistakable as he takes my jaw in his hand and pulls me close. "Since when do I let you question my motives?"

And then he's kissing me—hard, deep, invading my mouth with his tongue while he invades my body with his hands, touching me, groping and squeezing like it's the last thing he'll ever do.

And it's amazing how fear can so quickly turn to something else. My heart's racing not out of panic anymore but out of need. Hunger. I need him to remember us, this. That no matter what happens, he can come back to this. I'll always be waiting for him.

He works my pants down before lifting and setting me on the table. I lie back and spread my legs for him—then barely stifle a moan when his mouth is on me, his tongue plunging deep inside my pussy. His animal grunts fill the air, paired with my rapid breaths. It's all happening so fast I can barely make sense of it, but I don't have to. Nothing matters more than feeling; what I'm feeling right now is unbridled need burning me up from the inside out.

I cup the back of his head, pulling his hair while pushing his face closer, grinding my hips. He doesn't try to take control back, letting me be the aggressor for once. Letting me take from him while he greedily laps up what's gushing from me. Thanks to him, all thanks to him.

This time when he enters me with his fingers, I gratefully accept them, jerking my hips in time with his sharp, quickfire thrusts.

"So fucking wet," he growls before sucking on my clit until my eyes roll back and my body tenses, and I fall over the edge, biting my knuckles to hold back my screams.

It's a shock when he pulls my hand free. "Don't do that. I want to hear you come for me." He covers me again with his mouth, holding my clit between his teeth and flicking it furiously while massaging my G-spot and dragging out the most delicious agony imaginable. I scream because I can't help it. I scream into the darkness and almost—but not quite—drown out his dark chuckling. I'm giving him what he wants while he gives me what I need.

By the time he finally lets up on me, I'm drained, dizzy, but hungry, too. Hungry to give him the kind of pleasure he gave me. That's why I sit up, reach for him, find his waistband and unbutton his jeans so I can dip inside and take him in my mouth the moment he's free.

He sucks in a surprised breath that ends on a groan. "Greedy girl," he growls, stroking my hair. "Are you hungry for this cock?"

I moan in agreement, sucking hard, saliva flooding my mouth and rolling down the length of his shaft while I slurp eagerly.

"That's right. Make sure I'm nice and hard before I pound your pussy. Is that what you want me to do? Do you want me to fuck that sweet pussy?"

I moan again because, yes, that's what I want more than anything. To have him inside me, deep, locked with me. I want there to be nothing else in the whole world but us. I need him to forget everything and everyone. I want him to give me what only he can.

I'm panting in a frenzy when he pulls me off him, taking me by the hair and pulling my head back so he can crush his lips against mine. I taste myself on him, and that dirtiness only gets me hotter and wetter than ever.

He pulls his mouth away and grunts two words. "Lie back."

I stretch out across the table with my legs locked around his waist. He gives me no warning before shoving his entire length inside me, pushing me across the table a little before taking hold of my hips and drawing me back.

He shows no mercy, taking me hard from the beginning, so hard it hurts in the best possible way. I have to hold on to my boobs when they bounce, and he replaces my hands with his, working them under my shirt and pinching my nipples while I tighten my legs around his hips. I can't keep track of all the wild, intense sensations racing through me. I only know they're building into something huge, something racing toward me. I want it, and I welcome it, pulling him in with my legs, jerking my hips in time with his strokes.

"Mine," he grunts, again and again, punctuating each crash of our bodies together. "Say it."

"Yours!" I sob. "I'm yours!"

"Forever. Always."

"Always. Yes!" His rhythm dissolves, his pace picking up until all we're doing is rutting like animals, using each other's bodies.

"I'm going to come," I warn him. "Lucas, I'm going to come!"

"Come on my cock. I want to feel you dripping on my cock."

"Lucas... Lucas, I—" *Love you. I love you.* "I'm coming... oh, god...!"

And then it hits, my back arching, my pussy clenching around him. I hear his helpless groans over my ecstatic cries, and then he's crying out, too, hot cum splashing along the inside of my thighs while he leans against the table. A deep sense of satisfaction washes over me, which goes beyond physical pleasure. This is how helpless he is for me, just like I'm weak for him. He can't help but break all the rules regarding me, to this. For somebody who's never had an ounce of power in her life, it's almost too much to wrap my head around.

"I wish I could see my cum all over you right now," he pants. "Marked. Mine."

He drags a finger over my inner thigh, then probes my mouth. "Take it." I do happily, sucking his finger clean. I'd do anything for him. I wish he understood that.

"See how much fun we have when I sneak up on you?" He's still a little breathless as he laughs, and I laugh with him—softly, more cautious now that the rush of heat has passed and reality begins to seep back in. What if somebody had come in and found us? What if somebody is waiting outside right this very minute, prepared to pounce on us when we leave?

But somehow, though I know that's a real possibility, I can't bring myself to care. Because I was with the man I love. No matter what happens, that's not going to change.

I only wish he felt the same. I only wish it didn't seem like love was the last thing he wanted from me or anyone.

33

LUCAS

"At least this room finally got used for something." I fumble in the darkness before finding Delilah's underwear on the floor. I use it to wipe the rest of my cum off her thigh, then ball them up and tuck them into my back pocket. She finishes getting dressed while I do my best to straighten myself out.

That was exactly what I needed. It's almost enough to make me wonder how different my life might have been if I'd had someone like her in it from the beginning. A way of venting what always raged inside me.

Then again, that was how I used Charlotte, which didn't do any good. I was different then, somehow. Maybe it was always meant to be Delilah. It was just a matter of waiting for her to show up.

"Are you sure nobody could hear us in here?" I shouldn't laugh at the apprehension in her voice, but I can't help finding it funny. As if it matters. As if any of it matters.

"You might be surprised at what goes on under this roof some-times. What we just did isn't the half of it."

"You sound like you know what you're talking about," she points out, and I hear the disapproval in her voice loud and clear.

"No comment." I know it drives her crazy, which only makes me laugh again.

There's no choice but to leave now, as much as I wish we could stay. That's all I ever want to do, it seems. To be alone with her.

No such luck. The last thing I need is Xander sending out a search party if he can't find me. I take a deep breath and open the door, the light from the hall jarring compared to the darkness we're leaving.

And now that we're in the light, I run my hands through my hair and look down at my clothes, which are still rumpled. There's no question what we just finished doing—she's got sex hair if I ever saw it, which I gesture for her to try to smooth down with her hands as we walk down the hall side by side. Her cheeks flush, and she giggles, and I can't help but grin.

Until we round the corner, and I find myself face-to-face with Xander, Quinton standing beside him.

Shit. I manage to maintain a blank expression, but Delilah isn't as practiced as I am. She gasps, reaching for my hand and gripping it tight.

I hold Xander's gaze, lifting an eyebrow. "Yes?"

His lip curls in disgust, his gaze bouncing back and forth between us. "You've got to be kidding me. Are there no depths you won't sink to? This is absolutely unacceptable. Are you even thinking anymore? Or have you completely lost your senses?"

He points a finger, jabbing it in my direction. "I gave you this goddamn job, and it was one of the worst mistakes I've ever made. You haven't changed a bit. You're just as unreliable and out of control as you ever were."

Mindful of Delilah's tight grip on my hand and Quinton's presence, I modulate my response. "Everything is just fine, and I'm completely under control," I tell him with a smile that only makes his already flushed face turn a deeper shade of red. He wants me to react and lose my shit so he can prove to himself what a mess I've turned into. I refuse to give him the satisfaction.

"Is it?" he hisses, teeth clenched. "Of course, you would think that. Because you don't have the first clue what was happening around here while you were off in Takotna." He eyes Delilah in disgust. "Keeping yourself busy."

"What are you talking about? What happened?"

He looks toward his son, who lifts his chin in silent affirmation. When Xander turns to me again, his eyes are blazing. "Someone attacked your daughter."

My stomach drops sickeningly like I was just launched off the tallest hill of a roller coaster. Now I'm plunging straight down, unsure of what's below. Completely out of control, unable to stop it.

"She didn't want you to know about it until after she spoke with you," Quinton mutters. "So it wasn't a distraction."

"What happened? She didn't seem injured earlier."

"It could have been much worse," Xander informs me in his imperious tone. "They pushed her down the stairs, whoever they were, but she was able to catch herself in time. Nothing more than a few bruises, according to the doctor."

And here I am, sneaking in a quick fuck while my daughter suffers, knowing someone wants to hurt her—again. "But we're sure she's all right? Did Lauren—"

"It's a little late for that," Xander informs me. "It may surprise you to know it, but it's still possible for people to do their jobs even when you aren't here—a good thing, considering."

"She was thorough," Q assures me. "It's a good thing you were gone," Q tells Delilah, who flinches at the attention. "I would have blamed you for it."

She rolls her eyes. "Right, because I'm sure it couldn't be the same person who already attacked me. Rather than think that, you would have rather blamed me for it when you know very well somebody's after me, too."

Xander's thoughtful nod surprises me. "Yes, you're right. It might be the same person, though I can't imagine how the two of you are in any way connected." He can't help but let disdain leak into his voice. Why would he? He has no problem making sure she knows what he thinks of her.

"Any idea who it might have been? Did she see anyone? Was there anyone around?"

"That's not your problem anymore," he informs me, folding his arms. "As you are no longer in charge here."

Delilah gasps, but I merely stare at the man in front of me. Is he bluffing? Xander rarely bluffs. "You aren't serious," I insist anyway. "You can't—"

"Don't tell me what I can't do. You are no longer needed here, so it's best for you to go. Immediately." A glance at Q tells me nothing. I don't know why it matters. Maybe because he's the closest connection I have to Aspen right now, and I'm hoping to get some idea of what she might think about this. But he's unreadable.

I swing my attention back to his father. "Like hell. You think I'm going to leave here now, with Aspen in danger?"

"What difference does it make whether or not you're here? You haven't done a thing to protect her before now. What use is there in thinking you'd be effective all of a sudden? Let's face it, you weren't doing anyone any favors by being here."

I've never hated a man as much as I hate him. Not because he's wrong. Because he's right.

I've done nothing to help my daughter. I had to find out from someone else that she could have been killed while I was tying one on in Takotna.

"Well? Standing here staring at me isn't going to get your things packed. You better go do it, then remove yourself from the premises."

What can I do? I can tell him to get fucked, which is exactly what I want to do, but it won't change anything. He has the power to remove me from my position, and that's what he's done. With the mood I'm in now, it's better for me to go. I might have to kill him otherwise.

Rather than give him the satisfaction of smiling smugly at me for another minute, I drop Delilah's hand and turn around, marching for the elevator. She follows me because, of course, she would, but I don't acknowledge her. All I hear is the sound of her struggling to stifle her emotions, sniffling and choking back tears.

Most of the shit in the apartment was already there when I arrived. Very little of it is mine. I could always send for the nonessential items. I can't believe I'm doing this. I always knew the possibility was there, but to have it in front of me is another story.

It's not until we reach my apartment, and I head straight for the bedroom to pull out a suitcase that Delilah bursts into tears in the doorway. "You can't just give in like this!"

"What would you have me do?" I go to the dresser and start emptying drawers, shoving handfuls of underwear and socks into the bag before adding T-shirts and workout clothes. I'm not particularly interested in packing neatly. All that matters is getting the fuck out of here. My being here has only ever made things worse for Aspen.

"Fight back! What, you're just going to leave? Because that asshole wants you to?" I can barely breathe for the pressure in my chest, much less soothe her feelings right now. I settle for concentrating on getting my shit together so I can get out of here as soon as possible.

"Please, talk to me!" She starts following me back and forth, weeping, reaching for me though I avoid her again and again. She doesn't need me, either.

"Where are you going? Can you at least tell me that? What are you going to do now?"

It's a good question. "I'll go to Nic's, I guess," I groan. I have nowhere else to go.

"Please take me with you! Don't leave me here alone."

"You aren't alone."

"You know what I mean." She sits at the foot of the bed, wiping her eyes with her sleeves. "You're going to leave me here on my own, with nobody to defend me? With nobody who cares about me?"

"You know that's not true. Aspen cares about you." I almost choke on my own daughter's name. Does she know about this? She probably thinks it's for the best.

"It's you I want. It's you who's deserting me now. You can't expect me to stay here without you—you're the reason I'm here in the first place! This isn't fair."

"Fair? You want to talk about fair all of a sudden? I would think you, of all people, would understand how useless that is. There's no such thing." I continue cramming jeans into a second case. "This is how life goes sometimes. We don't always get a say."

"But you do have a say in this. You get to decide if you want me with you or not. Please. Take me with you. Don't leave me here. There's nothing for me here without you."

"That's not true. Stop telling yourself that."

"So that's it? All those things we just said upstairs didn't really mean anything?"

"What are you talking about?"

"All that stuff about me being yours. That doesn't mean anything? That's all just, what, an act to get you off? Because I meant it. I—I love you."

It's enough to make me fumble the shoes I grabbed from the closet. "What did you just say?"

She surprised herself. I wonder if she meant to say it, whether she really means it. Or if this is some insane last-ditch effort to keep me around because she feels safer when I'm here.

"I said I love you. Because I do. All I want is to be with you, wherever that is. I would even stay here if you were staying. All that matters is you. Please, I just want to be with you. Take me along. Don't leave me here without you."

There I was, thinking I was above this kind of thing. Emotion, sentiment.

It looks like I was wrong. I do feel something. I feel something for her, but love? Calling it love might be a stretch.

"You don't love me, Delilah. You just think you do because I'm the only person who ever gave a shit about you. I do care about you, and I hope that someday you know the difference."

"Call it what you want, Lucas. I still want to come with you."

I drop my shoes into another bag, my mind made up. "Okay. Go to your room. Pack your things." I zip up my luggage. "You're coming with me."

34

DELILAH

I don't know what I expected. A tearful kiss? For him to tell me he loves me, too? I guess I know better than to think anything like that would ever happen, but still, it would be nice if he at least would act like he's glad I'm with him as we sit in this jet and soar thousands of feet above the earth.

He's too busy brooding, seething, to pay me much attention. In fact, he's hardly said a word since he told me to get packed. I was too glad he agreed to think much of it at the time, but now we've been through leaving the building, climbing on the helicopter with our bags, then boarding the jet. He still hasn't done much more than grunt when I ask a question. Eventually, I stopped. There's nothing worse than somebody repeatedly giving you the cold shoulder no matter how hard you try. It's easier not to try to let them work it out independently.

No matter how much it hurts. What do I have to do to make him understand I'm in this with him? He's not alone. No matter how much he clearly wants to be. Somewhere along the line, somebody gave him the idea he's not worth caring about. I wish I couldn't relate to that, but I know all about it. And I don't want him to feel that way. He's worth so much more than that.

And there I was, thinking I wouldn't have to go through the discomfort of facing Nic again. It's not like he went out of his way before to make it seem like my being around was anything more than an inconvenience. I doubt his feelings have changed very much by the time the car he's sent for us pulls up in front of his home.

Once we're inside, with Nic arranging for our bags to be brought in—I'm not used to having people do things for me—Lucas finally sees fit to acknowledge me. "Go upstairs to the bedroom we were in before. Wait there until I come for you."

It comes as such a surprise that I freeze in place at first. He can't mean to send me away from him like this, can he? But no matter how long I stare up at him, his expression never changes—until it does, revealing irritation. "Didn't you hear me?"

Even though I don't want to, I drag my feet up the stairs before I even have the chance to say hello to Celia.

So here I am again. I kick off my shoes with a sigh, fatigue tugging at me now that the frenzy of packing and travel has passed.

Now there's nothing to do but acknowledge the fatigue, the fact that I feel drained from head to toe, inside and out. To think, I started out this morning in Takotna, back in that hotel room with Lucas. Now here I am, after having flown in a private jet once again, my bags being brought in by a stranger. Not that I had much to bring with me—so much of it was destroyed, after all.

I wish he would have told me what he has in mind for the endgame, but then I guess he doesn't know. Maybe that's what he's discussing with his brother now. Next steps. Where will he go, and what will he do with his life?

And how is he supposed to deal with the fact that his daughter is still up at Corium, and she didn't do anything to stop this?

I know that's got to be bothering him, and it hurts to imagine his pain. I find myself wanting to blame Aspen, but I'm not naïve. I'm sure that even if she fought like hell against her father-in-law, nothing would have changed. He was dead set on getting Lucas out of there.

Mostly because of me, I'm sure. Is that why he didn't want to talk to me on the plane? I'm sure it's our involvement that pushed Xander over the edge. It's not like I wanted this to happen. Neither of us planned on it.

God, I'm exhausted. And I remember how comfortable the bed is. Celia was kind enough to leave pajamas on the foot of the bed like she did before. I changed into them before crawling under the covers and curling into a ball. It would be better if Lucas was here with me, but he has a lot to handle now. Eventually, he'll get tired, I'm sure.

I just wish it didn't feel like he always wants to get me out of the way. That's what's on my mind as I close my eyes, and sleep doesn't take long to catch up with me.

It can't be more than a few moments before the bed shifts, and my eyes fly open in surprise. It's fully dark now, so dark I can only make out Lucas's outline as he climbs into bed with me. "There you are," I whisper in relief.

"Here I am." He strokes my cheek before pressing a tender kiss against my forehead. "Go back to sleep."

"I didn't think you would ever come up."

He pulls me into his arms, and I let my head drop onto his chest. "I had some things to take care of, but everything is going to be fine now."

I can believe that when it's like this, when we're together in the dark, and I'm enclosed in the safety of his arms, with the strong, steady beat of his heart beneath my ear. I can believe everything will be fine in the end. A sense of deep peace settles over me, and I welcome it, smiling.

Even if there's still the question in the back of my mind of what comes next. We aren't going to stay here forever, I'm sure of that. I know he has money, even if I don't know how much, but he was prepared to set me up in an apartment and everything, right?

Sure, when he had a job. Now that he's been fired, what does that mean? Will he have to find something else? What would a man like him even do?

I want to ask all of it if only for my own peace of mind. But I'm too tired and too happy to be held like this. Why ruin it? It can all wait until morning.

Besides, he said everything was going to be okay now.

I'M ALONE AGAIN.

I sit up, looking toward the bathroom. The door's open, and the light is off. Not the first time I've woken up wondering where Lucas ran off to. This time, I'm not coming out of a nightmare, and I won't be wandering the house in search of him. It feels like so much time has passed since then, but it's only been weeks. Still, I feel older as I get out of bed and go to the bathroom to wash up, then get dressed in last night's clothes.

With all the excitement yesterday, I didn't really eat anything, so it's no surprise my stomach is roaring in displeasure by the time I creep out of the bedroom and head downstairs. It's still awkward walking around in a house that doesn't belong to me, one where it's obvious my presence isn't exactly welcome. I remind myself I'm with Lucas, and it was his choice to bring me. That means I belong, right?

That way of thinking lasts approximately as long as it takes me to reach the kitchen, where Lucas and Nic are seated at the table by the window. They're nursing cups of coffee, and neither of them looks thrilled to look up and find me staring at them.

This doesn't bode well. Right away, I try to figure out what I've done wrong, and why they're looking at me that way. All I did was sleep. I haven't even been here long enough to cause trouble.

Finally, it's Nic who speaks. "We need to talk with you."

"Okay..." I shoot a desperate glance Lucas's way, but he's unreadable.

"You must be hungry. Please come and help yourself." There's a plate of bagels and muffins on the table, cream cheese and butter, and other things I barely take a look at.

I'm much more interested in the men sitting there and whatever it is they are going to tell me, even though I'm starved. I force myself to grab a bagel while Nic pours me a cup of coffee. I murmur my thanks, then busy myself spreading cream cheese on both halves. It's easier than looking at Lucas, whose pained expression is enough to tear my heart out.

"We have good news for you." Nic offers a tight smile before looking at his brother like this was his cue to jump in. Only Lucas hasn't said a word. He's too busy staring into his coffee cup. How good can the news be when he looks so damn miserable?

"I could use some good news," I offer with a smile I don't feel.

Lucas clears his throat, and I sit up a little straighter now that I know he's the one delivering this news. "Over the past few months, Nic and Xander have taken it upon themselves to divvy up the Valentine businesses."

Oh. This is the last thing I expected to hear about. "That makes sense. There's nobody to run them otherwise."

"And anything they didn't want, they sold off."

I nod, picking at my bagel. What does any of this have to do with me?

"In the end, there's a substantial amount of money due to the sale of those businesses." When I lift an eyebrow, he raises a shoulder. "Millions of dollars."

"Wow."

"And it's yours."

His timing couldn't have been worse. A piece of bagel lodges in my throat, and I struggle with it for a second, coughing hard. Lucas pushes a bottle of water my way, and I drink deeply while my brain spins.

Millions. He said millions, didn't he? And it's mine.

"I don't understand," I choke out. "Why is it mine? Where do I fall in any of this?"

"You're the last living Valentine. As such, the estate is yours. The money from the businesses, along with the family home."

My head snaps back. Millions of dollars? That's theoretical, something so huge I can't wrap my head around it. But the family home? I've been there and walked through the rooms. It's a real place.

And it's mine?

"Have you known about this all along?" It's a question for Lucas, who might be speaking to me but is still holding himself back. Like he's reading from a prepared speech or something like that.

"I've been working on it," Nic explains. "Lucas knew it had to be done—someone needed to take control of Valentine's interests. But the behind-the-scenes work was handled without him."

There's something heavy in Nic's voice. I always get the feeling there's hidden subtext between them, which is unnerving.

Lucas rises from the table, and I follow his progress as he goes to the counter and picks up a manila envelope which he brings back and places in front of me. "There you go. Everything you need to get you started."

I stare at the envelope before touching it with shaking hands while my brain practically does backflips, trying to process all of this. How many bombshells can a girl take? The envelope is heavy, and I soon find out why once I manage to make my trembling fingers work.

There's a stack of cash inside, for one thing. I don't know how much, but I thumb through and see the twenties and fifties. Along with that is a bank card which I pull out. My name is imprinted on it.

One more item sits at the bottom. A key. "That's the master key to the house," Nic explains. "As for the bank card, you can set the PIN and login information through the bank's website. The cash in the envelope is yours and should be enough to cover your expenses for a while."

"Everything in the house is yours to do with as you wish," Lucas adds. "You can always sell it or remodel it. Whatever you want."

I should be overjoyed, right? I know I should. I just had the whole world handed to me. I should be screaming and crying and laughing. All my troubles are gone all at once.

"This is all so much," I whisper, looking at the money. So much of it, but only a fraction of what I'm supposedly worth. It doesn't feel real.

"You'll get used to it. It'll take time, but eventually, you won't be able to remember a time when all of it wasn't yours." Nic sounds pretty sure of himself.

I have my doubts. It's not like I could ever forget the trailer. My mom. Those awful visits to what is now my house. How awful my family treated me.

Now everything that used to be theirs is mine. I can sell all their furniture and everything else if I feel like it. It's a satisfying thought, but what's the point if they aren't here to know I'm erasing them from the world?

"I don't know if I want any of this." I look up from the money to find Lucas watching me. "I mean, it's amazing, and I'm grateful, but I didn't ask for it, and I don't want it. I don't want to live in that house."

"Sell it," Nic suggests. "More money for you. More security."

"For now, there's a car waiting for you." Lucas holds my gaze, unflinching. Is he really saying this? I stare at him, waiting for the punchline, but there isn't one.

"Lucas. Is this what you want?"

He avoids the question, pushing his chair back from the table. "You never unpacked, so you can take your bag at the door. The car will take you home." With that, he walks away. He just straight-up walks away without another word. He threw me out of his life with a bunch of money and a big house, and that's supposed to make me happy. I'm supposed to be grateful for that.

Nic stands but hovers, waiting for me. "Like Lucas said, the car is outside whenever you're ready." What he means is, move your ass. Go explore your new home I made sure you'd inherit.

"Thank you for everything." I barely hear the words over my pounding heart. This can't be happening. I'm alone again. Me, by myself, in that huge house. Where do I even start putting a life together?

How do I do it without Lucas? What's any of it worth without him?

As promised, my bag is waiting. I pick it up and walk through the front door—sure enough, there's a sleek, black car parked there, the driver standing beside it. Waiting for me.

This is it. The beginning of the rest of my lonely life.

And he never even kissed me goodbye.

35

LUCAS

I watch her through the window as she gets into the back of the car, and the driver shuts the door and walks around to get behind the wheel.

This is for the best.

At least that's what I keep telling myself.

Stepping away from the window, I head to my room. Sending her away was hard enough. I don't want to see the car drive off just to hollow out the open wound in my chest further.

My phone buzzes in my pocket, and I get it out, intending to decline the call and shut my phone off. I change my mind when I see Aspen's name flashing across the screen.

I hit the green button and bring the device to my ear.

"Aspen," I greet, failing to hide the now ever-present guilt in my voice.

"Lucas, I didn't know Xander was going to send you away. I'm sorry."

Despite everything, I can't help but chuckle. "Why in the world would you feel like you are the one who has to apologize? I'm the one who fucked up. I'm supposed to keep you safe."

"Did you and Q rehearse that line together?" I can almost hear her eye roll through the phone. "You can't be everywhere all the time. I'm responsible for keeping myself safe, and I did. Thanks to your training, I had the reflexes to catch myself and the strength to pull myself up in time. Nothing really happened. I have two tiny bruises on my leg, and that's it."

I know she is downplaying it, so her words only make me feel slightly better.

"I'm glad you're okay, and I'm sorry I left without saying goodbye. To be honest, I didn't know if you wanted to see me."

"Of course I do. You're still my…"

"Father," I finish for her, realizing that she might feel obligated to have a relationship with me. Is that all it is? An obligation?

"It's still weird to say it out loud."

"Yeah." I couldn't agree more.

"How is Delilah?" Aspen changes the subject.

"You don't have to pretend to care about her."

"I do care about her. She and I had a lot in common."

Another reminder of why Delilah and I will never work.

"She is safe and well taken care of." Just not with me. "I'm going to give Xander some time to cool off. Hopefully, he'll let me come back to Corium soon, and if not, I want you to know I'm always just a phone call away."

"I know." She sighs. "I better get back to Q before he sends out a search party. Talk soon?"

"Of course. Bye."

"Bye."

The line goes dead, and I'm left to wallow in my misery again. Making my way up the stairs, I wonder what Delilah is thinking now. Is she crying, hurt, angry? Probably all of the above.

She's hurting right now, but it's for the best.

That's my mantra as I get undressed while the image of Delilah's wounded eyes burns in my memory. I know how this looks to her. Like I'm getting rid of her, throwing a stack of cash her way, and turning my back. If it means she'll harden her heart and forget me that much sooner, it's for the best.

She'll be fine. She's overwhelmed. That's all. Anybody would be overwhelmed in her place. Once she gets over the shock and settles into her new reality, she'll be fine. Better than fine.

After all, she won't have me fucking up her life anymore.

But she said she loved you. Yeah, well, people say a lot of things. She's too young to know what she wants, anyway. I'm sure she thought she loved Nash, that piece of shit. She probably would have done anything he asked because he was nice to her. When compared to how poorly she was treated by everyone else in her life, the slightest nugget of kindness meant everything. She didn't know what love looked like, so she latched onto the closest thing.

That's what she's doing now. She doesn't love me. She feels connected to me. She needs me, and she's mistaking that for love.

She'll figure it out with time and a little more experience. Now that she's got more money than she'll ever need, life is wide open to her. She'll never have to beg for crumbs of affection again.

This is the right thing. Getting her away from me. What could I do for her? Hurt her, push her away, ruin her. She's too good for that. She's too good for me.

By now, she's in the car, on her way to her new home. I hope she guts the place. I truly do. I hope she removes every last reminder of who once lived there. She should make it her own. I can almost imagine her walking through now empty rooms, imagining everything she can do. No doubt it'll take her a while to settle in since some habits are harder to break than others. Growing up like she did, not having any money at all, she'll be hesitant or even reluctant to spend it. That's not true of everyone—plenty of people let a little money go to their heads and blow it almost as soon as they have it. She's not one of those people. She's too practical. Too smart.

Though I do wish I could be by her side for this. I'm sure she'll need to be talked through it, probably more than once. Reminded she has control over her life. That she doesn't need to ask anyone's permission to do exactly what she wants. I hope she finds someone who can give her that permission. It's not going to be me. It's never going to be me.

The water in the shower is hot enough to make my skin sting, but I welcome that. Maybe it will wash me clean of my guilt. The guilt over Aspen, most of all. Just another of the casualties in my life. People unfortunate enough to be close to me.

I needed this reminder. Needed to have the facts of my existence thrown in my face. This is why I can't be close to anyone. I have nothing to offer but pain. Once she figures out life doesn't have to be miserable, Delilah will thank me for cutting her loose the way I'm sure my daughter is glad to be rid of me.

I'm far past the point of being finished washing up. But instead of getting out, I prop my forearms against the wall and rest my forehead on them while the water runs down my back and across my shoulders. Nothing will ease the tightness in my chest. It feels like there's a ton of bricks sitting on me, making every breath I take a conscious effort.

You know you can never see her again. Nic's voice echoes in my head hours after his admonishment. I knew what was coming, what he was arranging, but having him remind me what it all means—and what's best for her—came as a blow. A small part of me still wanted to believe we could make this work together. There I was, thinking I freed myself of that kind of thinking a long time ago. After all, what good does it ever do anyone to hope for things beyond their reach? All hope does is break a person's heart.

But I must have hoped because having it thrown in my face that she can't have a future with me stung like hell.

It will take time. Just like it will take time to get over my craving for a drink. What I wouldn't give to escape this. Crack open a fresh bottle and drown my sorrows to dull the pain of knowing I can't set eyes on her again. There's no such thing as weaning myself off her. Cold turkey it is.

I'd stay in here forever if the water held up, but it doesn't, going cold after I have no idea how long. There's no hiding. I need to face what comes next, even if I'm not sure what that is yet.

Finally, the water is unbearably cold, so I turn off the tap and grab a towel outside the stall. We spent the night talking about what to do with Delilah, but soon it will be my turn in front of the firing squad. What's my next move? He'll want to know, though he must already know I won't have an answer. When have I ever?

And I have nothing to soothe the stress. No outlet. No Delilah. I can't believe I let her get that close to me. I can't believe I talked myself into thinking this situation was under my control.

I open the bathroom door, cursing my weakness as I step into the bedroom, where I come face-to-face with the one person I'm supposed to forget.

The sight of her is the closest I've ever come to witnessing a miracle. I can't help the way joy immediately flares to life in my chest even as my brain throws up red flags. "What are you still doing here?" I can't believe the way my heart's racing at the sight of her sitting on the foot of the bed with her bag at her feet.

She shrugs. "I told you I didn't want to go. Did you think it would be that easy to get rid of me?"

"I wasn't trying to get rid of you. I was letting you go. You have a life in front of you now." This is for her own good. I need to remember this is all for her. I should've known there'd be one final challenge, one last temptation.

"But that's not the life I want. I already told you before we left Corium. You're what I want."

"That's just what you think. That's not necessarily what you need. You'll find out if you only give yourself a chance."

"I don't want to. Why does everybody keep telling me what I need? I know what I need. And it's you. Like I said, it doesn't matter where I am or what I'm doing. All that matters is you." Her eyes shine with unshed tears, and her chin quivers as she shrugs. "I can't help it. I love you. All the money in the world doesn't make a damn bit of difference if I have to live the rest of my life without you. It might be wrong, and I probably sound stupid, but I don't care. I finally found what I really want. Stop trying to give me a bunch of other things that never once crossed my mind."

"They never crossed your mind because you didn't know it was possible. Now it is. Why me? Out of every other man in the world, why am I the one you can't let go of? Don't you know I'm no good for you?"

"Maybe that's how you see it, but it's not the truth I know."

"And what's that truth?"

"The truth I know is you're the only person I've ever met who makes me feel like I belong somewhere."

It might hurt, but she needs to hear it. "You've thought that before."

She winces, but the moment passes quickly. "That's fair. You're right. I did think that. But I was naïve. And desperate for some-body to care about me. This isn't the same situation. I would have done anything for Nash as long as it meant no longer being alone. Maybe having a future. The idea that somebody could actually care about me. But that's just it—he was only an idea. He never once showed me that he actually cared—if anything, I kept telling myself I needed to make him care. If I would just make him happy, things would be different. I never actually enjoyed our time together—I spent the whole time trying to make him like me, doing things I didn't want to do because I was afraid to say no. But that's not how it is with you. When we're together, even when it hurts a little or when I don't know what you're thinking or what's coming next, I don't feel forced, like I have to endure it—or else. Do you hear what I'm saying?"

"I hear what you think you're saying."

"Stop it." It comes out sharp, and any softness in her eyes hardens all at once. "I don't know where you got this idea that you need to save me from you, but I don't buy it, and I'm tired of it. Stop acting like I don't know what I'm talking about. For whatever fucked-up reason, something about you works well with something about me. Like we belong together. And you're not going to convince me otherwise out of some misguided need to, like, save me." She makes air quotes around the words, sneering. "I don't need that."

"Then what do you need?"

"You. Just you. And you need me, too, whether or not you want to admit it. Because I love you. I see the good in you even if you don't want to admit it. You would rather send me away than be with me because you think you're doing me a favor. You're that convinced you're no good. But bad people don't care what they're doing to somebody. Don't you get that? If you were really so bad, you wouldn't care. You wouldn't even think about it."

"I've done that in the past. Many times." As she sputters, looking for a way to argue, I remember there's something she doesn't know yet. What better time to drive the point home? "That blond woman. The one you were so interested in. Her name is Charlotte. She's Aspen's birth mother."

Her eyes fly open wide.

"I hurt her badly. I'm not proud of it. I was such a fucked-up piece of shit that she couldn't even tell me she was pregnant. She knew how I would react. Then she disappeared from my life, and I didn't care enough to find out what had happened. She was supposed to be dead, but it turns out she isn't. And I can barely face her when I remember my cruelty. That's what I would do to you. I would only keep hurting you."

"You don't know that. If anything, you prove my point."

"How, for fuck's sake?" My anger is brewing, bubbling, threatening to boil. This is why she doesn't need me. How can I make her see?

"Because you're capable of remorse. When are you going to get it through your head? You're not evil. You're not a lost cause. And I know you're only pushing me away because you think it's for the best. Not because you don't actually care about me."

"Are you sure about that?"

"Are you? Tell me you don't love me."

"I don't love you," I lie.

She accepts this without blinking. "Now tell me the truth."

She's tearing me apart. She couldn't do a better job of it if she used a fucking chainsaw and cut me into pieces. "Don't do this."

"Don't do what? Ask for the truth? Because that's all I want. Look me in the eyes and tell me you don't love me—if that is true. Because I don't think it is."

"You just don't want it to be."

"Or maybe you don't want it to be. But if you were the selfish, heartless son of a bitch you keep trying to make yourself out to be, you wouldn't be so dead set on protecting me from you. That's the truth. I know it. I feel it in my heart. What are you so afraid of?"

"I'm not afraid."

"Then say it. Say what's true."

Fuck this. I throw my hands into the air, dropping the towel I've been holding all this time. "Fine. You want to hear it? As if it changes anything? I love you."

She lets out a long sigh, and a look of peace comes over her. "Now that wasn't so hard, was it?"

"It doesn't change anything," I insist even as she scoffs. "I can't give you everything you deserve, and don't give me any shit about only you knowing what you deserve. You need a good man at your side. I am not that man, no matter what you think of me. I've done things you have no idea about. You don't need that kind of darkness. Nobody does."

"But you said it yourself. I see the light in you. And maybe that's why I'm here, to remind you it exists, so you don't get lost in it. And if that's all I'm ever good for—reminding you that you're a decent person? That's all I need. Because as much as you say I deserve good things, so do you."

"That doesn't mean we belong together. Love alone isn't enough."

"Why not? Why can't you at least give us a chance? That's all I'm asking for. Instead of being so sure this can only be a bad thing, why not actually find out? Because that's all I want. A chance to make it work."

There's no use in asking if she means it. I know she does. For some reason, she's got it into her head that I'm worth saving. And dammit, she makes me want to prove her right. Besides, I'm tired of fighting what I need most.

"Okay. Let's give us a chance." I hold out my arms, and she walks into them, tears coursing down her cheeks. She wraps her arms around me and squeezes tight, putting all of herself into it the way she does with everything. Leaving no room for doubt.

I hope she doesn't regret it in the end.

36

DELILAH

"How is everything with the new place?" Celia is all warmth and sunshine over dinner, the first meal where I don't feel like a completely unwelcome outsider. This time, we're not staying here. Just visiting. I'm sure that has something to do with it.

Once we found our apartment, Celia insisted we come over for dinner once a week—at least. "You're so close. It would be a shame not to see more of you." I have a feeling there's more to it than that. Maybe Nic wants to keep an eye on his brother, and setting eyes on him at least once a week is part of that. To make sure he stays on the straight and narrow.

"It's great." And it is, though, for some reason, I feel like I have to play it up even more while I'm in front of them. "The last of the furniture finally came in, so we're not eating all of our meals on the sofa anymore." Though I didn't mind when we were. It was an excuse to sit down together, watch a movie, and sort of relax. Relaxing is something Lucas isn't very good at.

"I can't wait to see it."

"You'll have to come by soon." I smile at Lucas, who nods since his mouth is full.

"I would like to see it, too." As usual, I get the feeling Nic's words have a double meaning. He wants to see the apartment to check in and make sure Lucas is doing okay. I get that he wants to do what's best for his brother, but there are times when he sets my teeth on edge. There's a line between being a caring brother and acting like a giant know-it-all. I'm sure Nic has done things in his life that he's not exactly proud of now, no matter how he acts now that he's married and civilized.

"You're more than welcome. I'd offer to make a nice dinner, but we might be better off having something delivered."

Lucas snickers. "She's trying."

"Excuse me if I never had many opportunities to learn to cook when the stove only had one working burner, and you could only use the oven at your own risk."

"That reminds me of the first time this one tried to cook for me." Nic offers his wife a genuine grin, and she rewards him by swatting at him with her napkin.

"This one? Who were you talking about, a cat or your wife?"

"It was pretty grim." He laughs.

"I was never exactly given the opportunity to cook for myself," Celia explains after rolling her eyes at her husband.

"Anyway," Nic continues, turning toward me, "you could afford to have somebody come in and handle that for you."

I know he means well, and of course, he is right. I have more than enough money for an entire staff if I want one. But that isn't the kind of life I want to live. I would always feel like a faker, a poser, somebody trying to fit in where they simply don't.

"I don't know. I kind of like the idea of being domestic."

Celia nods enthusiastically. "That's the thing about having choices. You can decide for yourself. You have that freedom now. I'm so glad for you." From the corner of my eye, I notice Lucas giving her a grateful look.

This is nice, almost like being part of a family. That's sort of what we are, even if Lucas and I aren't married. I don't know if that will ever happen, even if I know he's the only man I want to be with. And now that he's stopped trying to push me away, I know he only wants to be with me. I have every intention of this lasting forever.

I just wish I knew how to help him. I want so much to ask Nic what he thinks I can do, but I know it would kill Lucas if his brother knew how he's struggling. And he is, no matter how much he tries to pretend otherwise for my sake.

Like when I wake up sometimes and find him pacing the living room in the middle of the night. Or the way he spends so much time working out, like a man on a mission. When I innocently asked after the first few days in the apartment why he spends so much time practically beating himself to a pulp with his workouts, he shrugged. "I have to do something." At the time, I thought he meant he was bored, but after thinking about it for a while, I understood he meant he needed a way to vent all those dark things inside him that didn't involve drinking, fighting, or hurting anybody.

I'm proud of him for trying so hard to improve, but it hurts to see how he beats himself up. A part of me thinks he's punishing himself, still, over the situation with Aspen. It's driving him crazy, not being able to check in on her all the time. He's not a man who likes sitting back and letting other people handle things while he has no input. He needs to be part of things.

I know how much he wanted to make things work. He just didn't know how. He probably still doesn't.

So it's like living two different lives, sharing an apartment with him. On the one hand, I'm happier than I've ever been. It feels natural, us being together. There's nobody around to threaten me, and we don't have to sneak around. We're free to be together, as simple as that. And it's amazing.

On the other hand, there's still a wall between us. He tries. I know he does, but there's no getting over it. We can't be really happy as long as he isn't. There's still a part of him missing, though he's trying so hard to pretend otherwise for my sake.

It makes me wonder if I'll ever be enough for him. That's all I want to be. I want to take everything else away—all his pain and guilt. It isn't easy, but I keep reminding myself it's not my fault. He has to deal with some things on his own, just like I have things I need to deal with on my own.

Like the nightmares that still sometimes visit, I can go a week or two without one, then, all of a sudden, I'll spend a whole night afraid to close my eyes because every time I do, I see Nathaniel in front of me.

But at least when I wake up from a nightmare, Lucas is there to hold me and comfort me. I can't do that for him. He won't let me. Aside from our usual rough and sometimes kinky sex, I can't offer him solace.

He reaches into his back pocket when his phone rings. A glance at the screen makes his face go slack for a moment. "Xander." I can't stifle a soft gasp. Nobody from Corium has reached out to Lucas since the day we left, Xander included. A sneaking sense of dread creeps up my spine and makes me shiver.

Rather than excuse himself, he answers while sitting at the table. "Xander. What can I do for you?" I glance at Celia. She's grimacing, her gaze darting back and forth between Lucas and a curious Nic.

"What? What happened? Is he all right?"

Nic leans in. "What is it?"

"Yes, I'm here at Nic's." He takes the phone away from his ear and touches the speaker button. "You're on speaker now, Xander. What were you saying?"

I hate the sound of his voice, but there's an obvious difference right away. He doesn't sound as full of himself now. "Quinton was attacked earlier today. He's fine, for the most part."

Q? Who would risk going after him?

"How was he attacked?" Nic asks.

"As with Aspen, he was pushed down the stairs from behind. Someone must have been waiting for him. He wasn't as fortunate as Aspen, though. I suppose his reflexes aren't quite as quick. Lauren diagnosed him with a concussion, a sprained ankle, and a strained rotator cuff. Plenty of bumps and bruises, as well, but that's the worst of it."

"I'm sorry to hear that," Lucas murmurs. "How is Aspen?" It breaks my heart to hear the strain in his voice when he says her name, almost like he's afraid to.

"Badly shaken up, which I suppose is understandable." He sighs loudly. "Which leads to the reason for this call. She wants you to come back."

Lucas looks at me, his eyes lighting up. This is all he's wanted. "She said that?"

"Very clearly. She wants you here."

Some of the happiness drains from his face. "I no longer have a job there."

"This has nothing to do with that. I suppose she wants her father here with her."

His eyebrows draw together for a second, and I see the pain, relief, and hope wash over his face all at once. He doesn't want to admit out loud how desperate he is to be with her and to know she doesn't hate him. Now, he has proof there's still a chance at building something real.

And because I love him, I'm happy for him. I want whatever he wants.

But does he really need to be part of that world again? I know he misses it, but how will he move on if he keeps getting pulled back into Corium?

And is it selfish to wonder where I fit into all of this?

"Will you come?" Xander prompts when Lucas doesn't answer right away. I realize I'm holding my breath, waiting to see his decision. It doesn't seem like there's much to think about—of course, he'd want to be with Aspen at a time like this. So why is he hesitating? Is he still afraid he's going to ruin her or something?

"I'll come," he decides in a firm voice. "And I'm bringing Delilah with me." Now I wish we were alone because I want to kiss him. Hard.

Another sigh from Xander. "Is that necessary?"

"It is. Non-negotiable, too."

"Very well. If that will get you here so you can comfort your daughter, so be it. You'll find your apartment as you left it."

"I didn't say I planned to stay forever."

"I didn't plan to stay forever when I visited weeks ago, either, but it seems fate has stepped in and had its way. As long as someone within these walls attacks students with impunity, I'm not going anywhere." Gee, he's such a hero. Maybe he wouldn't have to sound so frazzled and worn out right now if he hadn't kicked Lucas out of there. They could've been handling this together all this time.

"I can get the jet ready," Nic offers, already pulling out his phone.

Lucas nods. "We'll be there as soon as we can. I'll keep you posted on our progress." He ends the call before sinking back in his chair and exhaling. I reach for his hand, and he accepts the gesture. So long as he knows I'm with him. That he doesn't have to face this alone.

"Who would attack Quinton Rossi, of all people?" Celia muses. "Whoever this is, they're ballsy."

"Or flat-out stupid." Lucas wipes his mouth with his napkin, which he drops to his plate before pushing his chair back from the table. "We'd better head home and grab a few things before driving to the hangar."

"The jet will be ready when you arrive." Nic's frowning, though, as he and Celia follow us out of the room. Good thing we were pretty much finished eating. Nothing will stop Lucas from rushing back to Aspen now that he knows she wants him there.

"Thank you for everything," I offer. Celia gives me a warm, if awkward, hug. "Hopefully, we'll be back soon and can show you the apartment."

"I'm looking forward to it." She leans in close and murmurs in my ear. "You have to be able to roll with the punches in this world. But you're doing great."

She has no idea how much that means. "Thank you," I whisper before following Lucas to the car. I'm already making a list in my head of everything I want to bring with me. It would be nice if I had an idea how long this would last. But like Celia said, it's all rolling with the punches. The way she did when Lucas first brought me to the house after I killed Nathaniel.

It isn't until we're halfway to the apartment that Lucas groans. "I just realized I didn't ask whether you're okay with coming along."

And he thinks he's unredeemable. The Lucas I first met wouldn't have even given that a thought. "I want to be wherever you are."

"But it could be dangerous for you."

"I'll be safe with you. I'm not going to take any risks. I promise."

"Please don't. I've already come too close to losing you."

And the love in his eyes and voice makes me pack quickly once we get home and put on a happy face for his sake. I want to be with him, and it's such a relief knowing he wants me there.

It's just that I was hoping to never set eyes on the place again. I don't exactly have a lot of happy memories that don't directly involve him. Like Celia said, it's all about rolling with the punches.

If this helps him find closure, then it's worth it.

37

LUCAS

*H*ere we are again. In some ways, it feels like I never left.

Of course, it wouldn't be Corium if we weren't in the apartment ten minutes before an email came through on my phone.

It's Brittney, and I'm not the only recipient. I leave Delilah, who's unpacking, and read the message away from her. I can't escape the sense of needing to protect her, though I'm sure she'd interpret it as trying to keep secrets.

Brittney: I need to see you all. Privately. As soon as possible.

The email went to Aspen, Xander, and Quinton, too. I had planned to reach out to Aspen anyway despite the late hour, if only to let her know I'm here. No sense in waiting until morning if everyone's still awake.

I hit the reply all button and type out a quick reply.

Me: We've arrived and are settling in. Feel free to join us whenever you can.

I send it off before returning to the bedroom.

"We're going to have company."

"So soon?" Delilah questions, surprise written in her features.

There's no good reason that should make my chest swell with pride, but not much of how I react to her has a logical explanation.

"Brittney has something important to talk about. She wouldn't say what it is over email."

"I can hang out in here if you want. You can tell them I'm tired after the flight—"

I silence her with a kiss that ends with her wrapped in my arms. Until now, until her, I was never much for the concept of people being meant for each other. Finding the perfect partner, all that happy horseshit. And that was what I thought of it, too. It was a joke made up to sell cards and candy in February.

I know better now. Not many women could handle the ups and downs, the sudden changes. At the end of the day, all she wants is whatever works best for me. She would hide in here if I asked her to, thinking that might make things easier.

"You will absolutely not stay in here unless you want to," I murmur, pressing my lips to her forehead. "I would rather have you with me, but do what makes you feel comfortable. I know Xander can be difficult."

As if she wasn't already perfect. She screws up her mouth, narrowing her eyes. "Please. Like I'm going to hide from that jerk. That's what he'd want me to do." Fuck, her stubbornness turns me on.

She rests against my chest, her eyes moving over the room. "This is where it all started."

"It feels like a long time ago."

"Like a lifetime ago. I was a different person when I came here."

"So was I, when you get down to it. So much has changed. I can't look at this room the same anymore, and it's only been what? Three weeks since we left?"

"Don't act like you haven't been counting the days. I know it's been eating at you."

"I didn't know I was that obvious."

"I probably wouldn't have said anything, but somehow, it's easier while we're here." I know what she means.

This is familiar. This is where we built what we have now. Our new apartment, though comfortable and everything, is new. We're learning to live together as two regular people—something neither of us has ever had much experience with.

Here, I know who I am. I might have gone off the rails for a while, but I have someone worth pulling my shit together for.

Two someones, in fact. My heart leaps at the knock on the door. I have to remind myself it could just as easily be Brittney or Xander visiting alone. Better to get my expectations in check.

But it is Aspen, accompanied by Quinton.

"Dad's on his way down," he explains. He's limping and wearing a sling to support his right arm.

"How are you holding up?"

"Like a guy who got his ass pushed down the stairs. I can't believe I didn't see it coming. I let my guard down for one second and now look at me."

"Don't be too hard on yourself. Nobody would expect that." Meanwhile, Aspen stands beside him, her head lowered a little.

What is she thinking?

I open my mouth, prepared to ask how she is, but she's too quick for me. "Here. You should really sit down." He grumbles and rolls his eyes but doesn't fight too hard against her leading him to the sofa. She grabs a few throw pillows and makes him prop his sprained ankle on them. Though I know I had nothing to do with the person she grew up to be, I can't help the flash of fatherly pride that stirs at the sight of her taking care of him.

But there's only so much she can do, only so long she can avoid me. She turns my way, her eyes pointed at the floor.

"Hi," she murmurs.

"Hi. How are you holding up?"

"I'm okay. I'm a little worried."

"We're going to find out who's behind this," I assure her.

I don't know what to do. How to be.

I'm willing to let her lead the way; that much I know for sure. I won't ruin this by forcing something she doesn't want.

I see her chin quiver an instant before she throws herself at me, arms around my waist, her face pressed against my chest.

"I'm sorry. I'm so sorry for everything I said."

"You don't have to be." Can this be happening? I can't let go of the idea that I don't deserve this.

"But I am. It wasn't fair."

"I wasn't fair, either. I'm sorry, too."

She's sniffling when she lifts her head, but she's smiling through it. "And by the way, I love you. I really do."

I take her face in my hands, fighting back the emotion threatening to choke me. "I love you, too." It's becoming easier to use those words. I can thank Delilah for that, along with so many other things.

Aspen grins, disentangling herself from me and crossing the room to where Delilah's lingering in the doorway to the bedroom.

"Hey, you." She gets the same tight hug I did, which I can tell means the world by the way her face lights up. I know how it feels. "I heard you're pretty rich now, huh?"

Delilah shakes her head, but her lips have a teasing smile. "Yeah, I can actually go shopping in real stores. It's kind of fun. I can show you pictures of the new apartment if you want."

Aspen nods enthusiastically.

It comes as no surprise when Xander barges in without knocking.

"It didn't take you long at all to get here." I notice how his attention drifts over to where Delilah and Aspen are standing before snapping back to me. Smart man. He wants to play nice for the sake of keeping everyone safe? He needs to learn to speak carefully.

"Your call lit a fire under me." And I'm glad we wasted no time getting here. Aspen's forgiveness is a gift I never expected.

He looks around the room. "Where's Brittney?"

"I expected her to be here by now. Whatever it is seems serious."

Xander looks to his son, then Aspen. "Do either of you have any idea what this is about?"

Aspen's head swings back and forth. "She didn't say anything to me."

We don't have to wait long, as it turns out. Everyone else is settling into chairs, with Aspen replacing Q's pillows with her lap over on the sofa, when Brittney raps briskly against the door before easing it open.

"Can I come in?"

I wave her in. "You're the one who got us all together."

She offers a tight smile. "Good to see you. I'd say it's been quieter around here without you, but by now, you know that's not true."

"What's wrong?" Aspen, as always, is the first to address what's obvious. "You look upset."

Brittney rubs her hands together, her lips pressed in a tight line. "I have something to tell you all. I don't quite know how to say it."

"Here." Delilah pulls up one of the remaining chairs from the kitchen. "Do you need something to drink?"

Brittney accepts the chair but shakes her head at the drink. "No, I'm fine."

She's anything but. "Out with it. Whatever it is, it can't be—" I cut myself off because, of course, it could be bad. Right now, anything is possible.

Only now do I notice how she keeps glancing at Q before her gaze darts away. Again and again. This has to do with him, but she wishes it didn't.

"Well? What is it?" Xander prompts. "Have we been hacked? What's going on?"

"In a sense, yes, but not the way you think." She presses her hands between her knees and nearly rocks back and forth. "I just want to say first that I did it because I wanted to ensure everyone was safe. After Aspen got that hit on the head, it seemed important to keep track of everyone."

Delilah is openly confused, but then she would be. She's not as familiar with Brittney's special skills as the rest of us. I, on the other hand, fold my arms.

"What did you do?"

"I installed tracking software to run behind the scenes." She gulps. "On everyone's phones."

"You tracked our phones?" Quinton blurts out.

"To keep a lookout on where people were at certain times of the day. In case something like Aspen's attack happened again, there would be a way of tracing who was near the victim at the time it took place." She shrugs helplessly. "I wanted to keep her and everyone safe."

"And you know who attacked Quinton?" The mixed excitement and fear in Aspen's voice ring out. "Who was it?"

"Let me just say I wouldn't be coming to you if the proof wasn't right there in front of me."

"For God's sake, who was it?" Xander demands, his voice thin.

She winces before looking at Q. "It was Ren."

Delilah gasps, as does Aspen. Xander is out of his chair, eyes wide, the color draining from his face. I don't know how to react. Ren? Of all people?

I look at Quinton, the only person who hasn't reacted yet. He hasn't moved. I'm not sure if he's blinked yet. Aspen reaches for his hand but pulls it away, distracted, still staring at Brittney. "No way. You're wrong."

"I wish I was. Believe me, I'm not telling you this lightly. I checked, and then I double-checked. The ID number associated with his phone was the only one in that stairwell at that time other than yours. And it was close to yours, too. I set up checkpoints throughout the school and the castle that ping me at scheduled intervals. Those two phones pinged from that location at the same time. Only those two."

"But he wouldn't. He would never." Quinton looks around the room at his father, Aspen, and even me. "Not Ren. Why would he do that to me?"

I exchange a look with Xander. "There's only one way to find out for sure. We bring him here, now." Xander nods, taking out his phone and turning away for a muttered conversation.

Q's still not having it. "This is ridiculous. He would never betray us —you realize that means he would have been the one who hurt Aspen, too, right?"

And Delilah, though I don't think he could be faulted for forgetting about her right now. But I haven't. I go to her, sliding an arm around her waist.

"Are you okay?"

"But why would he? He would have been doing it on his own, right? I don't understand. He was almost acting nice to me for a while." Delilah bites her lip, frowning. "Then again, he was also being kind of weird."

"Weird how?" Q prompts. I recognize the energy in his voice, almost frantic. His whole world has been turned upside down, and all he wants is to find out this was all a misunderstanding.

"I don't know. Don't listen to me." She waves a hand, shaking her head. "He was just being sort of weird, but then a lot of people treat me weird around here. I was probably being paranoid."

Xander ends his call. "The guards are going to his room now. I told them to bring him here." Every time he looks at his son, his jaw tightens. "We're going to get to the bottom of this."

Q only shakes his head. "No offense, Brittney, but you're wrong about this one. There's no way."

"I hope you're right. I'd love nothing more than to be wrong about this."

Yet she doesn't believe she is. She looks and sounds like someone stuck watching a train wreck unfold in slow motion, aware of what's coming and unable to do anything about it.

Xander's phone rings. "Yes?" His head snaps in the direction of Quinton's, his eyes burning into them. "Fine. If he's not in his room, he's somewhere else. Go by my room, and check on my wife and daughter. Then find Ren. I want the entire premises searched!"

"We can look, too," Delilah offers.

I shut her down immediately. "Absolutely not. Not until we know for sure what's happening here. Because if he is behind this, and he knows he's being searched for—"

"Don't talk that way," Quinton snaps.

"Until we know the facts," I insist. "Unless you'd like both girls to go together in search of him. Maybe they'll find him. Who knows?" When his face falls, and his eyes lower, I know he gets the message. He's not willing to risk his wife, which tells me he knows there's a possibility of this being true. None of us have to understand it for it to be true.

It's a tense five minutes that unspool into fifteen. The temperature in the apartment feels as though it's dropped since we arrived. Brittney apologizes more than once, though we all assure her there's nothing to apologize for. I don't particularly enjoy being tracked without my knowing about it, but if it means putting an end to these attacks, it seems like a worthwhile sacrifice.

"Wait a minute," Aspen whispers, snapping her fingers. "If they can't find him, maybe you can. Can you track him, see where he is?"

"I can try, but it would only work if his phone is on—and if he's on the premises. Outside of Corium, there's not much I can do."

After a half dozen calls with various security team members, Xander slides his phone into his pocket. I know what he's going to say before he opens his mouth, and it leaves me wanting more than ever to protect what's mine. There was a predator in our midst, and we overlooked him.

"You don't have to bother trying to track him," Xander murmurs. "The entire security team has searched every inch of the premises. Castle, dorms, all classrooms, and even outside the walls." He offers his son an apologetic shrug. "Ren's not here. He's gone."

EPILOGUE
DELILAH

I could get used to living like this.

The last of the light from the setting sun washes our bedroom in amber, and a sweet, cool breeze stirs the gauzy curtains at the doors leading out to the balcony of the villa Lucas rented for our vacation. I can't believe I'm in Italy—me, who grew up in the most depressing trailer park imaginable.

Not only in Italy, which would be incredible enough, no matter where we ended up staying. But it's like paradise, all lush rolling hills beyond the balcony and a sparkling lake that stretches out as far as the eye can see. When I sit up and look toward the balcony, I can spot a few boats dotting the water. We were out there earlier on a rented yacht, swimming and eating the freshest seafood I've ever tasted.

Me. On a yacht. Is this my actual life?

Is this my actual man? Lucas sits up and plants a lingering kiss on my shoulder. "We'd better hurry if we're going to avoid all the knowing looks and whispers when we get there."

"We were taking a nap," I remind him with a happy grin. "After swimming all day, we were tired." Nobody needs to know about what happened once we got back here and took a shower together... and then again once we got into bed for what was only supposed to be an hour's rest.

He chuckles before sliding a hand under the sheet covering me. "Nobody could look at me while I'm looking at you and believe I'd only be interested in taking a nap."

As always, my body reacts to his slightest touch. All I want is to close my eyes, lie back and let him do whatever he wants. No matter what it is, I'll end up liking it.

Instead, I groan softly before swinging my legs over the side of the bed and forcing myself up. "Food first. Besides, Xander will send out a search party if we don't show up on time." If anybody told me only a few months ago that I'd someday be vacationing along with the Rossi family, I would've recommended they get professional help. At least we're staying in our own villa to give us a little privacy, but we've spent a lot of time together. Like this afternoon, on the yacht. We generally have dinner together, too. Tonight, it's going to be a big feast at Charlotte's home, across the lake.

Dusk has fallen by the time we've washed up again and gotten dressed. We climb aboard a small boat and zip across the lake. The wind in my face and hair is delicious. I close my eyes and bask in it while leaning against Lucas, who wraps an arm around my shoulders and holds me close.

"Are you enjoying your vacation?" he asks before kissing the top of my head.

"What do you think? Though I might need a second vacation after we get home." Not that I'm complaining. I love always having something fun to do, something exciting to see. Like when we took the train to Rome and spent a few days exploring or our upcoming visit to Venice. I can hardly wait to float along on a gondola.

I'm tired, but it's a good tired.

We reach the dock below Charlotte's home and climb the stairs to her courtyard. Voices float down from there, laughter. Lucas takes my hand as we approach. It's the most natural thing in the world.

"There you are." Charlotte shakes her head, wearing a teasing smile. "We thought we'd have to hold the meal."

"You know I'm not the young man I used to be. All this activity is exhausting." Lucas accepts a glass of wine, winking when Charlotte gives him a knowing look. I've never seen him so relaxed and happy. He's like a different man right now.

Aspen strolls over to hug him, though we were just together a few hours ago. It's like they're making up for lost time. "Hope you brought your appetite. Charlotte has enough food to feed an army." Like me, she's tanned and glowing after days spent in the sun.

Quinton snorts before glancing at his sister, who's sitting next to their mom and staring out over the lake. "If there's so much extra food, we should invite those two greaseballs who kept trying to flirt with Scarlet at the market this morning." Light, teasing laughter fills the air, but Scarlet doesn't react. She's more interested in watching the boats and the twinkling lights across the lake.

"Scarlet." Q waves his hand in front of his sister's face. "Earth to Scarlet. Come in, Scarlet."

Her head snaps up, and her cheeks go as red as her name. "What? Jeez, can't I sit here and enjoy the view without you waving your hand and ruining it?"

He tries to do it again, chuckling, and she slaps his hand away, wearing a smirk. I always wondered what it would be like to have a brother to pester me. My brothers never cared enough about me to bother. Now I've seen it for myself throughout this trip. It's almost kind of sweet watching how protective he is of her.

But he doesn't understand why she's so distant and thoughtful. Why she sometimes sits by herself for hours while everybody else is busy swimming, relaxing out on the yacht, or shopping.

I can't count the times her mom has invited her to shop, with Aspen and me encouraging her to come along. Even the few times she has, she's been low-energy, listless. Not interested in much of anything.

I know why, and I think I'm the only person who does. The memory of her and Ren sneaking a few moments together in the hallway at Corium is still as fresh as if it happened yesterday. I'm sure it is for her, too. As upset and confused as everyone is about Ren, it's even worse for her.

I've been betrayed. I've been left looking back on every moment I had with someone I thought cared about me, wondering what I missed and if anything about it was ever true. It's enough to drive a girl out of her head. Enough to make her question everything she believes—about herself, about her worth.

I don't know Scarlet very well, but I feel sorry for her.

It's obvious she isn't interested in my sympathy. The few times I've tried to let her know—quietly, secretly—that I'm here if she ever wants to vent, she's shut me down by pretending to have no idea what I'm talking about. Either she doesn't want to go through it, or she would rather pretend it didn't happen. I understand how she feels but also know it's not that easy. She can't pretend her way out of it.

"It is beautiful, isn't it?" Aspen joins them, sliding an arm around Q's waist and putting herself between him and Scarlet at the same time. I doubt she knows about Scarlet and Ren, but she's the kind of person who's super in tune with everybody around her, sensing trouble and always wanting to jump in and help. "I could stand here and look at the lights forever, I swear."

"It's probably not as interesting when you live here all the time," Q points out. "You'd get used to it."

Charlotte hears him as she finishes the final touches on the long table where we'll eat our dinner. "Not even a little bit," she says with a light laugh. "There are still days when I have to pinch myself, even after all these years."

"You have such a beautiful home." I can't help but gush a little. The woman's living a dream life, at least as far as a girl like me is concerned. Living in an Italian villa off Lake Como, which even I knew before now is an exclusive area only the wealthy and connected can call home. And here I was, thinking she was a threat to Lucas and me while she had a husband and two little boys.

Two little boys who are now running around, trying to sneak bits of food off the table no matter how often their mother tells them to knock it off. "That's for everybody!" she reminds them before hustling them away from the table again. They run over to Aspen like their big sister will protect them. It's only been a couple of weeks since we arrived, but they're totally enamored with her.

And she adores them. "I don't know what you want me to do about it," she offers with a shrug. "You heard her. And if you don't behave, we won't be able to go swimming tomorrow like we planned." That seems to change their tune, even if they don't look happy about it.

Quinton's mom laughs indulgently from her chair beside Scarlet. "I remember when Quinton was that age. Always getting into little boy trouble."

"I was a perfect angel," he deadpans. Even Xander has to laugh at that, and he hardly laughs at anything. Especially lately. I know it has to still be under his skin, the way he completely missed the threat Ren posed.

As far as I know, the guy disappeared. Nobody knows where he ran off to, only that there's no trace of him. I'm sure Xander hasn't left a stone unturned. It's personal for him. He needs to know how somebody could get that close to his family, then betray them— and evidently get away with it.

"Let's eat." Charlotte claps her hands briskly, and we all make our way to the table where a feast has been laid out. I'm surprised the table can stay in one piece under all that weight. I sit between Lucas and Aspen, beneath strings of lights swaying gently in the breeze.

It's bizarre, considering these people part of my extended family, but it's the truth. Thanks to Lucas, I now have the big, boisterous family I always dreamed of. And unlike those awful visits to my father's house, I feel like I'm part of things. I'm wanted here. Even Xander has calmed his attitude toward me. We're not exactly friends, but I feel more welcome around him than I ever did around my father and brothers. It's a step up.

Lucas leans in and brushes his lips over my earlobe. "Eat fast. I need to get you back in bed as soon as possible." A little shiver runs through me before our eyes meet, and I see the hunger flickering in his. But he's not fooling me. He's happy to have an excuse to spend time with Aspen and repair things with Charlotte. It's almost funny now when I remember how jealous I was of her.

I guess in our world, questions will always be unanswered and vague, shadowy threats lurking in the background. Like Ren, wherever he is.

But right now, things are pretty much perfect. And if there's one thing I've learned, it's how to grab onto the perfect moments when they come along because there's no way of knowing what happens tomorrow. That's what's on my mind as I raise a glass with everybody else and toast to being together. To being a family. And to being loved.

Thank you for reading the Corium University Series. This chapter of the storyline might be over, but don't worry, we are not completely done yet. Ren's book is coming early 2023!

Betrayal cuts the deepest.
I knew when I left I could never return.
I'd sealed my fate, but I couldn't leave her behind.
She was always meant to be mine, enemies or not...
Preorder Touch of Hate, NOW!

ABOUT THE AUTHORS

J.L. BECK AND C. HALLMAN ARE
USA TODAY AND INTERNATIONAL
BESTSELLING AUTHOR DUO WHO
WRITE CONTEMPORARY AND
DARK ROMANCE.

FIND US ON FACEBOOK AND
CHECK OUT OUR WEBSITE FOR
SALES AND FREEBIES!

WWW.BLEEDINGHEARTROMANCE.COM

Printed in Great Britain
by Amazon